The Eagle
and
The Butterfly

The Eagle
and
The Butterfly

by

Maggie Shaw

eregendal.com

First published in the United Kingdom in 2020 by
Eregendal.com, Rosehill Road, Crewe, Cheshire, CW2 8AR.
Printed in the United Kingdom by Lulu.com.

ISBN 978-1-9996071-6-6 (paperback)

Contents

Introduction
and Acknowledgements

The Eagle and The Butterfly tells the story of a person who passes through a thin place into the mythical world of Berren and becomes the butterfly Eregéndal. To atone for the past, Eregendal must face hell and death in a quest to save Berren from Zoust and the forces of evil at the Last Battle. Eregendal's sacrifice helps the child-goddess Zana ascend to her throne.

I wrote the novel in in two weeks during the long hot summer of 1976, when I was twenty-one. The story was pieced together from a series of poems I had written over several years. It is steeped in folklore and includes many symbols drawn from North European myths and legends. Two versions of the story are published in this volume: the original novel, and a children's version which follows the same story but with most of the violence and reflection removed.

The novel's working title was *Eregendal*, named after the leading character. I created the name using syllables relating to the key of light, ritual frenzy, and God, as described in *The Lost Language of Symbolism* by Harold Bayley (1912). *Eregendal* also became the name of our publishing company as it is unique.

The story is an allegory about my struggles as a young adult writer to find acceptance and recognition beyond West Cumberland, where I lived then. In returning to the book decades later, I can also see how prophetic it was. Just as the butterfly, Eregendal, had to die to become the powerful eagle Ladnegere, I too had to die to my old self and be reborn through recovery to establish myself and find success.

As always, I would like to thank those who helped with the book in any way, including Rev. Edward Robertson and the artist Heather Bolton. Any faults in the work are my own alone.

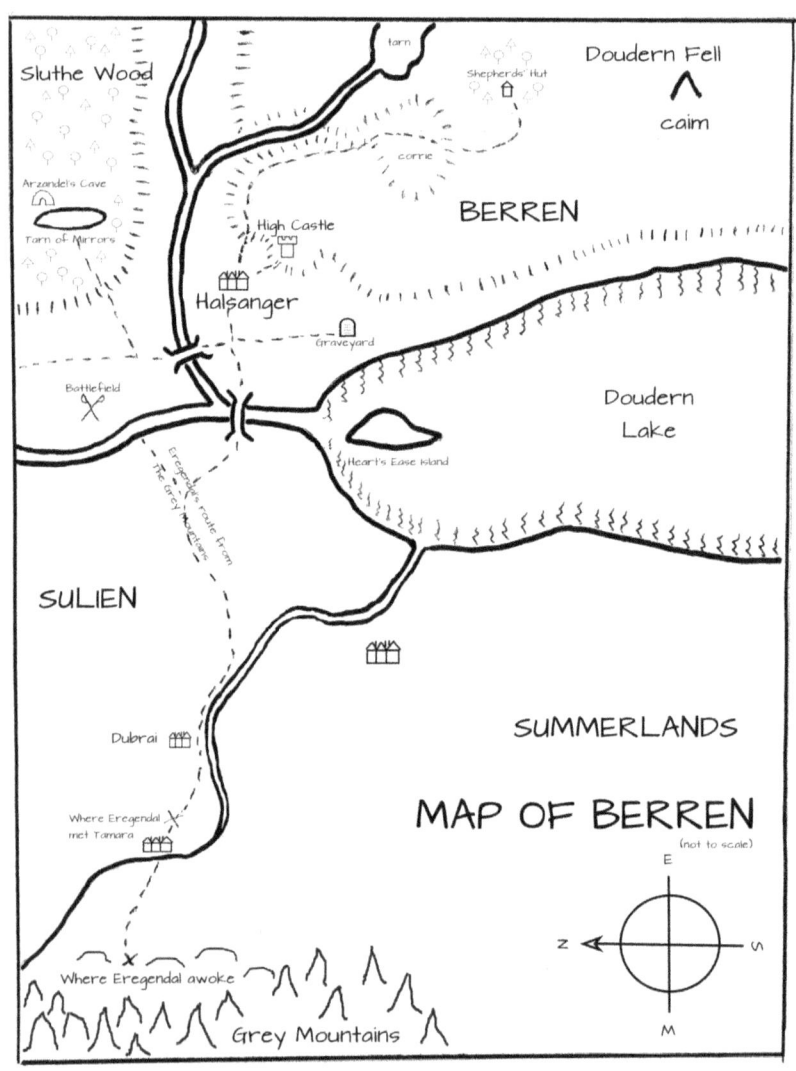

Prologue
The Calling

The night felt charged with promise. Three bright stars had appeared in the sky towards the north, their points breaking the circle of the constellation of the Northern Crown. The sign had come at last.

The aged magus, Arzandel, left his cave to bank his hearth with ashes so that the eternal fire of fate would shed no light. He had a long, dark, ancient face and an untrimmed white beard, and his flowing purple robes were trimmed with scarlet and gold.

He descended the few yards to the Tarn of Mirrors on the edge of Sluthe Wood. This was a thin place, where dreamworlds crossed and touched. The landscape looked eerie in the moonlight. Along the edge of the tarn, the blades of the rushes rattled softly in a chill night breeze.

Arzandel raised his arms, holding his wand in his left hand. The rustling wind died down. In its place wove a strange melody, a haunting tune which echoed past, present and future as if all were one. The outlines of the trees, the tarn and distant Doudern Fell, shimmered in a dance to the illusion of reality.

The ancient turned, his right arm outstretched. He held a silver locket in his right hand. He raised the lid to reveal the image of a small tortoiseshell butterfly. It was so frail a creature, yet upon its feeble body depended the fate of the three spheres: heaven, earth and hell.

Into the haze that drifted across the tarn, Arzandel whispered the call which would bring the traveller home.

Chapter 1
The Arrival of the Night Rider

Night had fallen. I was riding along a grassy lane through a ghostly wood below a long-backed fell. Gaunt branches crowded above my head and gnarled trees stood to left and right, reaching sinister fingers to catch me. A chill breeze whispered with the voice of the rustling leaves, 'Go back!'

I had ridden that road since noon and was loath to retrace my steps. As I had not yet found the inn at the heart of the eerie wood, I faced the prospect of sleeping in the bracken that night. Still hopeful of chancing upon the inn, I rode on by the light of my lantern, awaiting the rising of the moon, which never came.

My mind was troubled. For many years I had ridden to repay my past. I had set out with The Four: for a brief time as their guide, all my life as their friend. They had seemed committed to the quest, until these last few months when, one by one, they had left despite nearing our goal. Why had one dropped by the wayside? Why had one become so greedy? Why had one become so complaining? And why had one never returned after going back to look for the others?

At about midnight I rounded a bend and entered an ancient region of the forest, where stunted oak and sycamore mingled with the rowan, the hawthorn and the gorse. Across an overgrown clearing, the night sky revealed three strange glinting points of light. I dismounted to rest my horse and stared at them, dousing my lantern. My surroundings shimmered in the eerie half-light of marsh gas Will-o'-the-wisps.

I stood on the bank of a deep peaty mere. The lights that had attracted me were the reflections of three stars. They faded as a dark cloud edged over them. When the last light left sky and mere in darkness, a shining green figure rose from the water, her blue-edged robes completely dry. Overawed, I knelt on the bank and bowed so low, my forehead touched the water.

'Greetings, traveller. Arise and welcome,' said the strange spectre: 'Do you not know where you now kneel?'

I stumbled to my feet and backed away fearfully, shaking my head in speechless bewilderment.

'This is the Tarn of Mirrors. You fled from here six years ago to ride as an exile in the dreamlands. Do you not recognise this pool?'

A veil lifted from my eyes. Suddenly everything looked familiar. I could not understand why I had not recognised the clearing and the tarn before.

'The gate to Berren. At last!' I whispered, stepping forward.

'Welcome back,' the Green Lady said warmly. She took my hand in her cold fingers. 'The land has not forgotten you, though you chose to lose yourself in your dreamland wanderings far away.'

We walked across the water, and descended its warm, dark depths to leave the dreamlands and rise upon a different shore. When I reached the water's edge, the spectre returned to her depths, her work done.

I stood on the bank of the Tarn of Mirrors, clothes and hair quite dry. The clearing looked like a mirror image of the one I had left, except for a fire burning in the centre of the glade and a cave instead of the whin bank which stood behind it.

An ancient man stood before the fire with his back to me. He had a long white beard and wore flowing purple robes trimmed with scarlet and gold. He raised his arms, holding a wand in his left hand. The fingers of the clouds released the moon and the haunting song of all pervaded the glade. The ancient turned, his right arm outstretched.

'Time gave me three stars, which I held in this hand; but the stars reached out and destroyed the rising sun, leaving me with nothing.'

His tired voice echoed about the shimmering glade until his words mocked me in a challenge to explain the riddle. Would I also fail like those before me who had tried? I walked to the ancient's side to answer.

'Your three stars shine still: on men. They are the past, the present and the future. If you have nothing, how came I here?'

The ancient stared at me and slowly smiled. He sat me down beside him on a fireside stone. I looked up into his dark, sincere face and saw a veiled sadness in his happy eyes.

'Friend, you have been away a long time. I have waited on you. Welcome to Berren. I trust this time you will stay.'

I had to shake my head, to be true.

'My friend, whose hospitality I once knew so well; you know I reach higher than the sky. I cannot promise you, Arzandel.'

'Aye, you are honest at least, Eregendal. Well I know the patterns by which you must live life, my little butterfly.'

Arzandel lifted his wand and waved it across the shimmering vision, which was but one of the many places gathered around the Tarn of Mirrors. As the wand completed its circle, the haunting tune evolved into that bewitching aria which once had taken me over oceans, mountains and desert sands in search of the one who sang what all people feel. And the vision became real; and the song became a dawn chorus with bells ringing, bowed string vielles humming, reed pipes buzzing and lutes strumming, while a million silent voices seemed to sing:

'Eregendal, welcome home.'

Chapter 2
The Carnival and the Letter

The music swelled with children's cries and women's laugher as the morning wore on. I longed to be with the revellers, but Arzandel would not let me visit the carnival town until the smell of the dreamlands had worn off me. Instead, I stood on the bank of the Tarn of Mirrors, staring at the reflection of my brightly coloured robe over my human body and my gaudy patterned wings. These had just shed their pupal case. I flexed them, impatient for them to expand and dry.

'Come, Eregendal; sit yourself down and eat. At noon you may safely go,' Arzandel said, smiling.

I sat near him by the ashes of the fire and picked up a wooden bowl of fish and oatcakes.

'You have grown much younger since this dawn, Arzandel. You are almost as you were before,' I said lightly. My thoughts were more on the chiming clock in the nearby town than on my host.

'Your return will bring many changes,' he gravely replied. He added in a kinder tone: 'Now eat, or your wings will never have the strength to reach Halsanger.'

But I gave little thought to the food in my bowl for admiring my changed appearance. My silk robe was patterned with reddish-orange merging into yellow, spangled with white stars and blue crescents and trimmed with dark brown bars. My wings repeated the same glorious pattern. In my vanity, I caught every reflection of myself in the tarn. Such a change had come over me while travelling through the Tarn of Mirrors, that it seemed what I had been in the dreamlands was but the drab underside of myself, less than half my potential. The magic of the dawn had given me the power to open my wings and, leaving my dark camouflage behind, become my true self.

At last, Arzandel said, 'The clock is chiming the noon hour. Fly, Eregendal!'

I rose up on my new wings into the air above the treetops. After a brief farewell wave, I turned and soared abreast the music-filled breeze to the carnival town.

Halsanger was an old town which had grown up with little planning. Half-timbered cottages with thatched roofs, stood by stone shops and a clock tower with slate roofs. Among these stood a few red brick buildings with tiled roofs. High on the hill nearby stood a stone castle with a moat around its curtain walls. Inside stood a turreted keep.

People from all parts of Berren had gathered in the cobbled market square in the centre of the town. Earlier in the day, livestock and farm produce had been sold there. Now the cattle pens had gone and a colourful procession passed through. I watched and laughed with the crowds as I wandered in their midst. Here, a young woman bedecked with ribbons smiled in a way that coaxed me to buy from her tray of fruit. There, outside the tavern sat three gruff farmers supping ale and wondering whether they should have paid quite such high prices that morning. In the procession, a small mermaid with sparking eyes offered me her net into which I cast a coin; while around me, the laughing children sang and played with the dancing clowns, and another bystander explained how he too had been drawn to Halsanger by the wind-blown music.

'So you too are a stranger in a strange land,' I shouted to him above the noise of the cheerful crowd.

'Aye, I come from far beyond Sulien. I have been travelling this twelvemonth.'

'Pardon? I cannot hear you for the crowd.'

The stranger repeated his words but saw I could not understand.

'Let us enter this inn,' he suggested: 'I cannot hear you either.'

I followed him out of the bright warm sunshine into the quiet, dimly lit welcome of the cool tavern. We took the window seat, not wishing to miss anything of the carnival, and ordered some food and ale.

'My name is Tuzos, a dedicated traveller. And you also are a traveller, I would judge from your accent and your attire.'

I nodded amiably and studied him. He was little taller than me, corpulent, and with a kind face lined by years of laughing. His unusual clothes looked to be from the dreamworld in fashion, in blends of smoky greys and fiery orange. The index finger of his right hand bore a large signet ring with the seal of a three-pointed star over a broken circle. Something about him fascinated me, though I knew not what. My eyes kept being drawn to him.

'I am Eregendal, a sojourner in these parts,' I said.

'You are THE Eregendal? I am lucky indeed to be supping with you! What brings you back to this region?'

'Little enough. I had been travelling with the Four, but they dropped away and I continued alone. By chance I entered Sluthe Wood and took the lonning below Doudern Fell. By chance too I came by the Tarn of Mirrors, and from thence arrived here.'

'What a remarkable chain of events! Will you stay here long? Or must you hurry back before your friends seek you?'

'No, I can stay here as long as it pleases me. Time here does not relate to time in the land they ride. Like a person who reads two books, I am unaffected by dress and place and time, and can pass freely from one to the other. Tell me about yourself. Tuzos. What did you leave behind to make the road your home and the sky your roof?'

He laughed. 'Ah, travel! It gives me that variety I crave for beyond the stultifying dullness of the daily round. The many miles behind me have made me love this way of life all the more, and still my thirst for the new is not quenched. Was not your philosophy, Eregendal, when you first stayed in Halsanger and studied at the High Castle, also one of change, an insistence to take the untrodden road?'

'Aye, and such still holds true for me, though now I know it is not for all people to follow. Each to our own allotted way.'

'A philosopher still! But surely you cannot think so highly of those who, like these carnival folk, ever stay the same, never risk all for nothing, cannot gamble the mundane life to search for the eternal?'

'Ah, but I can: indeed, I envy these people. They have a peace of mind which will ever be alien to me. In their courage and their fortitude, they far surpass me. Philosophy is a poor substitute for the heroic qualities they have. And to be able to place the weight of their burdens unquestioningly on the shoulders of their leaders, that is a faith I long for, but could never attain. Without these people, the world would be far less stable. Sadly, their trust encourages duplicity and wrongdoing in their leaders. What a false god is security.'

'Were you to become the Teacher in the High Castle, that would not be the case.'

'You think too highly of me, Tuzos. That is not the place for me. Nor would I want to gain such a high place, for that would require a revolution, which I could not espouse.'

'You underestimate yourself, Eregendal. Have you not noticed the decay in this land?'

'No: I have not been here long enough.'

'Then take my word, this Berren has grown strange and corrupt. Its people forget their loyalty. Their teacher is old and feeble-minded: there is no-one to lead them bar the Judges Council, which is rotten to the core. The people seek a new leader. You could serve them well and with compassion. From your last stay here, they know you to be a novel thinker, and they treasure your words far more than you realise. Should you raise your flag, you would have a much larger following than your present modesty lets you expect.'

'I was brought back here to learn, not to lead a revolution. Nor does modesty make me shake my head. However Berren may have altered, I know a violent change in its government would be unsupported by its people and impossible to sustain in the years following its disruption.'

'But think of the power, the prestige, the honour, the wealth.'

'What bauble is wealth to a true philosopher? Like you, I am a stranger in a strange land. Though allowed to stay a while, somehow I am ever forced to return again to the land of my birth. What use has Berren for a leader who comes and goes like spring sunshine? Born on the road, I am unalterably bound to follow it to its end or mine.'

'But you said that time here does not relate to time in the land where you travel with the Four?'

'True, but the time there is reflected here. And these are not the only lands in which I wander.'

'Then the dreamlands hold little for you?'

I looked sharply at Tuzos, wondering how he had known where I came from. His banter was taking a sinister turn.

'Yes,' I admitted guardedly: 'I have little hope of purging my homeland of all the corruption and the evil which have so dismayed me. The peoples' faint hearts, their hypocrisy, their selfishness, grate on my conscience and weigh down my soul. I know I too am weak, hypocritical, corrupt; but these things I have fought within as well as without all my life: I was born with them. How can I ever hope to see my ambition furthered by even one small step?'

'There is a place for you here if you tire of the road. Or is yours a back that will ever carry a burden? Wait! I have an idea, a message you could take back to the dreamlands. Tell them you have been through the vale of death and stayed in the world beyond. The dreamlanders doubt everything in their ignorance. But you know! The conviction of your word would convince them too that there is an afterlife! Then they would listen. They would receive your philosophies on truth, honesty and peace with honour and awe. You could travel from kingdom to kingdom preaching salvation.'

'Stop, Tuzos! I have no desire to take the place of God. There are enough false prophets without my adding to their numbers.'

Tuzos scowled and nodded. The kindliness in his face had vanished. Instead, I saw only contempt.

'So be it! Relax here a while; enjoy yourself while you can find some peace. On your return home you will find little chance of rest.'

He put on his hat and stood to finish the last of his ale.

'Remember our conversation, Eregendal, when you sit alone in your dismal garret, looking out on a world which is deaf to your entreaties, blind to your proofs, and has closed its mind to your words.

THE EAGLE AND THE BUTTERFLY

For today you could have held that world or this in the palm of your hand, but you let the chance pass you by.'

Tuzos left. My eyes stared at the closed door long after he had gone. In airing my convictions, I had bared my soul, and felt his final doubt a hard knock to withstand.

'The Carnival Queen is going by!' the landlord cried, throwing open the doors of the tavern.

I hurried out with him into the crowded street. The Carnival Queen's float slowly passed us, pulled by two dappled grey percheron horses. The emerald clad Queen waved gracefully to the crowds through their banners and confetti and streamers. Her long chestnut hair lifted in the gentle breeze. The happiness of the cheering people lifted my own heart. I joined in the dancing, forgetful of the three stars above.

Later, while I paused from the boisterous activities to rest, a lady turned the white mare she rode through the crowd toward me. She was a woman of bitter beauty, richly dressed as were all philosophers in Berren had their thoughts travelled far enough. Yet despite her white robes, she wore a crown of purple orchids in her blonde hair. She reined in her horse before me and took a gold-sealed letter from her breast, holding it out to me with a reverent air.

'I knew thee by thy costume, visitor,' she declared: 'This letter was sent thee by thine elder who lives yonder in the High Castle. Come, spread thy wings and dally here no more. For thee was I sent by my dear father who said, "I must speak with Eregendal".'

I took the mare's bridle and led the lady in white through the crowded streets of Halsanger. As we mounted the hill out of town to the High Castle, I kept the lady's side while breaking the gold seal on the letter.

'What is the meaning of this letter?' I asked at length.

'As it is writ,' she replied.

I handed her the paper. Not a mark was on it.

Chapter 3
The Man in the High Castle

The High Castle stood on an outcrop of Doudern Fell and looked down upon the town. The lady led me over the drawbridge and through the gatehouse. High stone walls surrounded the main courtyard. In the centre stood a tall stone keep.

The lady bade me enter the keep and go to the sanctuary. Then she led her horse away to the stables, which stood against the high stone curtain wall. I crossed the cobbled yard with dragging feet. I had been that way many times, the last none too auspiciously. Something also warned me that the carnival had been an omen, as in my dreams, with the joyous occasion presaging the sad.

The distant festive music mocked my sinking heart as I entered the tower keep and climbed softly up the stone staircase. It coldly echoed my cautious footsteps. I opened the door of the turret room like a fearful child expecting a deserved reprimand, but heard nothing. That silence was more chilling than words.

By the window sat the man who had summoned me: a tired old man whose dark green robes were too large for his bent and shrunken frame. He acknowledged my presence with only a nod, but his expression conveyed a strained, distant air as though he preferred his loneliness and had not wanted me to come. When I walked across to him, he stared through me as though I was not there. Yet on his ancient bureau piled high with dusty ephemerides and grimoires, I saw a note which read, *I must speak with Eregendal.* So, I sat down and looked with sadness at my former tutor, whose presence spoke of a deep yet distant sorrow. His soul seemed to travel afar, struggling with his silent voice to call the one he had once known, his Eregendal.

THE EAGLE AND THE BUTTERFLY

'Your pupil sits here holding your letter,' I whispered; 'But the student cannot read the master's words.'

'And I, I too look but cannot see,' he replied from afar, 'For though Eregendal sits here, the butterfly is not with me. I sit alone, waiting for my old friend. That Eregendal left Berren six years ago, and in that departure I saw no promised return. The student presumed to have learnt all that a youth needs to know, not realising that one never ceases to learn. You before me are naught but shadow, a wraithen image of my dear Eregendal.'

'Great Ashleigh, what laid ghost do you seek? Six years have passed. The world has changed me from that foolish child into this lost adult. Surely that is why Fate has brought me back to this memory, to find myself again with you. So leave your searching, silence your hopeless call. Here sits your scholar Eregendal.'

The old man looked into my eyes, saying nothing for his heart spoke more plainly than a library of words. I waited patiently the while, sensing that his pride alone kept him from ending the impasse. And the sun set over Halsanger while he studied his changed student.

His daughter, the lady clad in white, came to us and summoned us to the dining hall below to eat. She now spoke in her natural northern dialect while serving us the traditional meal of fish and oatcakes, which was supplemented that day with bread, meat and other delicacies from the carnival town. After saying grace, she ate a morsel but then pushed her plate away. She turned to me with a sad smile.

'I maun thank thee for coming at least, Eregendal, though I was not certain that we could still trust thee in Halsanger.'

I looked at her father who sat alone, oblivious to his surroundings and the food before him. He was lost in that maze which surrounds the Tarn of Mirrors when the Song of Time is sung. His daughter studied my look.

'Aye, that is your great Ashleigh,' she sighed at length. 'My father lives in the past. He has seen no present since thou didst climb Doudern

Fell to the shepherds' hut six year back. He perhaps was lucky not to see thy return frae the fell... I had hoped that thy six years in the dreamlands had mended thee; but th'art not the Eregendal he seeks, and thus this dark spell canna be broke. I am sorry to have wasted thy time here. It had been better hadst thou not come at all.'

'My lady, please forgive me my faults. Had I but known.'

My hazarded apology brought forth an unexpectedly bitter reproach from her.

'Aye, well shouldst thou wear the mask of shame. For the day that thou didst leave, thou didst renounce the world thou'dst seen – the land that had taught thee, guided thee, protected thee – walked away, destroying all with thy words, saying "Ashleigh the deceiver has run away and Berren is no more", when 'twas thou that wert the deceiver who ran away, and thy vision alone which was no more.'

Ashleigh stirred and raised his hand to chide his daughter with a gentle rebuke.

'Tamara, butterflies must ever flutter on: they seek those flowers where happiness still blooms. They cannot help the times they leave behind them such damage, such despair.'

'Aye, Eregendal,' Tamara continued, warming to her argument, 'I saw thee flitting here and there once free. I watched thee discard thy riches, choosing to be poor, renouncing our lands, and condemning my father to that same dread black night from which he'd saved thee once.' She turned away in anger.

'My lady,' I whispered, 'is there nothing that I can do to save Ashleigh from that fearful night?' For I had not realised I had possessed such power when I committed those fateful deeds; though had I known then, I now realised, the knowledge would not have stopped me.

'Nay, do no more, Eregendal,' Tamara replied. 'Again thou'lt flutter away, so proud of thy gaudy wings that thou'lt see no colours less bright.'

'Hush, Tamara,' Ashleigh bade in a peaceful voice. 'Eregendal, it is no fault of yours, that you must follow your fate.'

And so saying, he slowly closed his eyes and leaned back in his chair. His head dropped back with eyes and mouth open, and did not move again. I saw his spirit leave his body and dissolve into the air.

'Father!' Tamara cried, 'Father, where art thou!'

Her chair fell back as she leapt to his side to take him up in her arms. I reached across and touched his cold and lifeless hand.

'He has travelled on to the next land in the circle. Even now he passes through the Tarn of Mirrors, my lady.'

Tamara wept, clasping her father to her breast as though to hold back that which had already gone. I too wept, though my tears were not so great for the loss of one as for the burning wound of guilt in my heart.

'Please go,' she ordered me at length, adding more gently, 'Thou didst all thou couldst, Eregendal: I'll give thee that. Alas, I canna hope to make people as I want them, nor can I change the past, but only its memory.'

She fell to weeping again. I watched her with compassion.

'My hand may be stained in your eyes, my lady, but it is at your service should you find cause enough to overlook the marks.'

She nodded and turned away in what I decided was grief, though I thought it to be shame at first. For suddenly I perceived she had used me as the scapegoat for her public wrath and indignation at the past malice which some people had held for her father. However, as I had been a figurehead of that force at one time, being thus used by her could not absolve me from my guilt. I hurried from the High Castle keep and flew in deep reflection back to Arzandel's cave.

The ancient sage sat as always after dusk beside his smouldering fire, listening to the evening's drowsy hum and dreaming in the twilight warmth, while the first moonbeam tiptoed over the fell to the clearing. As I walked softly to his side, I heard him sigh, which puzzled me.

'Some wine?' he asked, pouring out some golden dandelion wine from an earthenware jug into a goblet-shaped cup.

I nodded my thanks and sat beside him to sip the sweet wine.

'The land is fine, is it not?' he asked softly, gazing down on Halsanger and the plain with eyes that could see through the covering trees.

I followed his gaze, but could only see the long back of sombre Doudern Fell in the distance above the treetops, silvered by the moon.

'Aye, it is still fair,' I agreed, which made him sigh again. I waited for him to speak his mind.

'Eregendal,' he said at length, 'I, Arzandel, did call you to return to your long-forgotten home. All has changed. Nothing is the same as it was when you were here last, because nothing now is as it appears to be. You have always held the keys to release the true vision, but you must open your eyes to see the locks which must be turned. Yet all you would do is dart hither and thither as the fancy takes you.'

He sighed again. I considered his criticism, which I deemed not valid for the day but had to accept for the years.

'Aye. The Four left their quest in the dreamlands. Why? Because of me, my desire to roam lost and aimless. Today my former tutor, the great Ashleigh died. Why? Because of me, my desire to rebel. Berren has changed for the worse. Why? Because of me, my desire to sow the seeds of question everywhere, that weed question from which blooms the seeds of discontent. For what reason do I choose to do these things? Why must I ever destroy all else to fly?'

Arzandel gave a wistful smile and stirred the embers of the fire.

'Eregendal, take the wind again this coming dawn, for work awaits you in Berren which was the reason for your birth. But this time, open out your heart and stop pretending you are blind. Look into the people's shadowed eyes: see their true blindness. Then realise you have a light to help them see, you have the keys to unlock their prisons. So take up your keys and use them.'

I looked down and saw about my waist a dull gold belt from which hung five silver keys. When I held the keys in my hand, they radiated a dim light akin to that of the moon.

'What are they for? And why five?' I asked.

'Stop asking yourself the question, why. For why can never be wholly answered. Nor plague yourself with other questions, for a question asked can only bring forth more.'

'But as a philosopher?'

'Eregendal, you have riches, aye; but not to squander on yourself. They are given you in trust. Use your riches to help those that are poor.'

At last I began to understand. That understanding brought a new fire to my heart where the ashes of six years had lain.

'I will go at dawn,' I promised myself. 'Rest assured that from now on, I will try.'

And Arzandel smiled, for much of the conversation I had been holding with myself.

Chapter 4
The Winged Man and the Cloaked Woman

The dawn breeze bade me travel south. At length I came to a river mouth on Doudern Lake, where stood a solitary figure. On landing, I saw that the stranger was a winged man with his long white wings taped to his sides. He was tall and slim, dark-skinned and wearing a cream tunic drawn in with a thick leather belt. I watched him, cautiously keeping my distance with respect for his greater years. The stranger smiled at me in greeting, however, and walked up to me with hands outstretched in a gesture of request.

'Friend, a lift please over this deep wide river. On yonder green island lies Heart's Ease.'

I stepped back in puzzlement and replied, 'I have no need to. If you untaped your wings, you could fly yourself over the river.'

'What wings?'

I plucked out one of his long white feathers, which he felt.

'If you really want to get there, you will fly there, yourself. Who taped your wings to your sides?'

'I'm not deformed! It is your eyes that cannot see!' He turned angrily upon me, but saw the feather in my fingers. Full of shame, he admitted, 'Others don't have wings. It was the way I was born.'

'Sir, you have a gift. Has it not been that to you?'

He turned and gazed across the water to Heart's Ease Island as if he had not heard me.

'Others don't fly,' he said.

'Therefore you don't?'

'How could I? They taped down my wings because they were jealous. They told me it was better for me, because I should live the life they led.'

He dropped his arms sadly to his side.

'Sir, gifts are to use, no matter what others say or do.' I untaped his wings and raised the tips to the sky. 'Now fly, my winged man!'

He could not disobey and tried to flutter his wings. They were pitifully weak with misuse. I opened out my own bright wings and took his hand. His wings began to take his weight.

Upwards we rose, hand in hand, bathed by the sun's bright golden light and bathed in silver by one of the keys on my belt. Together we flew on the breeze to Heart's Ease Island. He landed with a happy cry. I released his hand and hovered low.

'Eregendal! I did not recognise you before,' he said, his eyes opening in joy. He tried to catch my hand. 'Come, join me here awhile, tell me your mysteries. Some say you have wandered long in darkness. Here on this island you would find light.'

I could see into his heart and knew he would misunderstand my staying.

'My friend, it is not the journey's end but how men travel to this island which gave it the name of Heart's Ease. I do not desire heart's ease, so nothing would I gain by landing here.'

He turned about, distraught, and turned back to entreat me.

'Can you not see how much I love you, Eregendal? Please don't leave me now: this island would be nothing without you.'

'Then your eyes are opening, for you see this island of escape cannot bring content. Only those who blind themselves would want to stay.'

'But I do love you.'

'Only because my love for all people made me free you.'

I stirred my wings against the wind. He turned away sadly, but called after me as I soared upwards.

'Farewell, dear one. You may leave me now, but I will always be there when you need help. Just call my name, Arken.'

His tears grieved my heart because I sought to heal rather than to hurt, but in that grief I understood that sometimes people must be hard to be kind. My own eyes began to open, and I saw my dull gold belt glint faintly in the sunrise.

The whispering breeze bade me follow its voice. Because my own wings were also but newly freed and soon tired, I followed slowly and took many rests. The wind took me towards Doudern Fell, where I had often walked when I first came to Berren. About midday the breeze dropped. I came upon a familiar pathway leading across the fell. It was the route to an old shepherds' hut set in the fellside, a refuge where I had once hidden one long winter.

I landed where the path traversed a bleak corrie bottom. The horseshoe ridge of the fell foreshortened the horizon there. It felt right to wait there a while. I sat on one of the many boulders scattered about and ate some bilberries which abounded in the corrie. About two hours later, a rattling stone made me look up.

There approached from below, a cloaked figure with a hooded face, hiding away from the world in woollen winter garb far too heavy for such a warm sunny day. The figure walked past me without comment, as if I were not there. An inner voice prompted me to catch up with the lonely figure and offer some peace.

'Greetings, friend. Whither are you bound?' I asked but received no answer. I repeated my question.

'Go, gaudy stranger. You are no friend. Alone must I travel, for I am the outcast of the pack,' declared the stranger. She sounded like a friend I once knew, but bitter instead of kind.

'Then you too travel to the shepherds' hut?'

'Aye. Do you also wish to stay there?'

Despite her tone of disappointment, I sensed she did not want to be alone. I walked by her side, looking at her shrouded appearance. The slender wrist which held her cheap coarse cloak was ringed with three gold bangles, and four aquamarines glinted on her fingers.

'No, I will not stay at the hut this night,' I said at length; 'But once I did stay there, one long winter before the time of Ashleigh's fall. Memory called me back there today by the voice of the wind.'

'Then you also know the pain of life, for all your gaudy silks.'

'Aye. Riches bring only sadness when they are ill used. While poverty may bring contentment in little when little is enough.'

She turned sharply and looked into my face, her own face in shadow within the hood of her cloak.

'I know your voice, gaudy one, and your features raise a distant memory. But if you are the adult from that youth, time has greatly changed you.'

'Draw back your hood, hermit, and show your face to me. For I think I know your voice also.'

'Nay, not yet. The time is not right.'

We walked on in silence, following the steep path around the lip of the corrie. The path dropped into a sparsely wooded gully where stood the shepherds' hut. How grateful I had been to stay in that hidden valley six years before. Its position had enabled me be completely alone with myself. Though high on the fell, the steep gully sides and the trees had prevented any views of Halsanger from persuading me to return.

A late afternoon breeze tugged at my clothes and chilled me back to the present.

'You light a fire with fuel from the woodpile behind the hut, while I gather sticks to replenish the store,' I suggested.

'Aye,' she agreed, and busied herself with the task.

Before darkness had enveloped the gully, we were sitting snugly in the old stone hut, lit by a blazing wood fire. My eyes looked again at the hooded stranger who, I realised, was also staring at me.

'Are you – the one who is known as the butterfly?' she asked.

'Aye, I am Eregendal. And are you not – Anya?'

She nodded and pushed back her hood. I held out my hands to her.

'Oh, joy of joys! My old friend Annie, with whom I walked and talked so much six years back and more. How often have I written about you since! What brings you here?'

'It will seem little to you, but to me it is much.'

She undid the pin and draped the cloak about her shoulders. Her graceful manner and her sky-blue dress had altered little in the time I had been away. Only in her face did I see the marks of change. Her once laughing eyes spoke of being lost. Distraught reflection now lined her pretty mouth, which had always been ready to smile before. She pushed her long black hair away from her face.

'It was little which brough me here that winter, Anya, yet it was enough to make me stay through the snows,' I admitted. 'I found my lessons in this land hard to learn, though I believe now my tutor had been kind to me. It was the lesson of patience in long-suffering which I could not master, so I left to recover alone. It felt like my last winter, but it was not. I have seen many and longer since then and have now learned to accept them. Without the storms of winter, how can I feel the promise of spring or appreciate the beauties of summer?'

'And after your stay here that winter, what brought you back down to Halsanger?'

'It shames me to admit it, but it was my bitterness of heart. After the winter's meditations, I wanted only to ruin my tutor Ashleigh and destroy Berren. Then I fled through the Tarn of Mirrors, back into the dreamlands.'

Anya stared into the fire, deep in thought for some time.

'Aye, then perhaps you would understand my reasons, for you also see much in small things. Perhaps you, like myself, see only the part and never the whole. I once mocked a very rich man for his conformism. Since then I have been a target for the jackdaws, though not their prey. Their assaults were so many that I went to the Judges Council to put my case. The Judges laughed: I was not in their charmed circle. They ruled that my existence was nothing, that the jackdaws were only teasing: the birds had no need for me except to practise upon, with so much better prey around. In the Judges' eyes, my riches were naught. Thus I donned the poor man's cloak and have come here to stay while I think about beginning a new life. First, I plan to bury my wealth and become one of the townsfolk.'

'No, Anya: were riches thoughts, you could not do that. I burnt my wealth in this fire, but metal cannot burn. Too soon I regretted the ashes of my clothing and the molten gold of my jewellery. For I found I had to begin again. So this black-clad night rider rode through the dreamlands, seeking but never finding, conscious of what I had destroyed, but so blind as I sought the means to replace that property. Then Arzandel summoned me back.'

'What are your travelling regrets to me?'

'You would bury your wealth to begin a new life. I know how that buried treasure would haunt your conscience until you had to dig it up again. There it would be still, decaying by your neglect, but still real enough to give you hope. Then the jackdaws would return to snatch it away before you could use it again. You would fight with its rusted sword, strive to your death to keep your trove from them. And all for

THE EAGLE AND THE BUTTERFLY

what? You too are only passing through the winter season. It is bleak and may well last for some time. But seasons always change, and in the coming spring you will regret throwing away last autumn's seeds in this wintertime.'

'What can you know of my winter when you live in summer? The seasons and their times are so different for us.'

'Little, perhaps, but one thing I do know. The world turns, and the tides follow their cycle, and the butterfly lives its circle. And within us too are circles where invisible planets orbit their own minute suns. All circles travel through different planes, but all are completed. As the egg becomes the larva, which in turn becomes the pupa, out of which flies Eregendal.'

'All this is to do with Eregendal. Naught about Anya!'

'Nay? Have you not seen winter before? That I know is not true. We talked of that season's afflictions often when I was last here. You told me once, shortly before I left, that you had walked through the sands of time, your heart set to observe the sunlit night of humanity. There you found the Tree of Knowledge, and by it a man shadowed for a moment in the limelight as he kicked at the strewn rocks of hate. Together by the Tree you observed the past, learning of the rock-strewn paths of those before you, to help you choose the way you should each take yourself.'

'Aye, winter came then, with so little summer before its return. Petros walked back into the limelight of a well-trodden road. He did not have the courage to follow my rugged and disused path. A short while later, soon after you left, the jackdaws began their attack. Somewhere still that great Tree stands, surrounded by grey boulders, lit by its own pure silver shadow. I would so love to return there. Perhaps by retracing my steps and choosing a different path, I could succeed at last; where, as Petros had warned me, I failed before.'

'You cannot retrace your steps, Anya. There is no map and your memory will not be that clear. Recent events will have distorted the past into a picture you desire rather than know. But it might be possible to return there by a different route, if you are willing to search.'

'I have spent all my life searching, and I am so tired.'

'Then come with me to Arzandel's cave. Perhaps he knows a signpost for the way, or someone else who blindly seeks what you already know. You could help that person find the way. And because you would not be alone, you would need fear no pompous Judges or mobbing jackdaws.'

Anya reached out and clasped my hand. Her eyes glistened in the firelight, pricking with tears at the suggestion of future hope.

'It is not yet spring, but the winter storm abates a little. Alas though, I am too weary to travel further this night.'

'Then take off your cloak, and I will carry you to Arzandel.'

Anya stood up against the firelight and let the cloak fall. It seemed to me as if daylight had entered the eve-darkened room. Her sky-blue gown shone in brilliant splendour, against which her long black hair gleamed like the star-spangled sky outside.

I doused the fire and tidied the hut for the next traveller, while she waited at the door. When all was done, we stepped out into the silent gully. I gathered her up in my arms and began the long flight back to the Tarn of Mirrors.

Though Anya was light, I had to rest many times through the journey, while she slept peacefully in my arms. I became so tired, I lost hope of ever reaching our destination. But a silver light surrounded me as I flew, and the twinkling belt around my waist supplied a small reserve of energy which did not wane, though perhaps this energy was born of the warmth of fellowship.

It was midnight when we arrived at Arzandel's cave. He awaited us, seated by his blazing fire. As I landed, Anya woke in my arms.

'The wind told me of your coming,' he said to her. 'Come, sit and eat. You both have much to do in the morning,'

Anya sat dazedly by the fire and ate with me. Then we slept in the comfortable bracken-strewn cave, while Arzandel sat outside like an eternal sentry, as one who never sleeps.

In the morning a youth arrived at the tarn. He wore the tunic of a burgher and spoke very fast. He wanted to arrange an expedition to the Tree of Knowledge and the Land at the Top of the World. Arzandel sent Anya off with the youth, suggesting she might like to be his guide. When I tried to go adventuring with them, Arzandel held me back.

'Not yet, Eregendal. Just trust that all things will eventually come to pass. Alas, today we have more pressing matters to attend to in Halsanger.'

Chapter 5
The Funeral

Halsanger was decked in mourning. People dressed in dark clothes lined the streets. Behind the draped bier formed a column of those who had loved and respected Ashleigh. Many in the town would miss him now that he had travelled on to the next world.

Tamara rode beside Ashleigh. A long dark blue shawl covered her white dress and blonde hair. A mantle of dark blue silk draped her white mare. The bereaved daughter saw little of what surrounded her. Her eyes looked only on the peaceful smile of her sleeping father.

Arzandel and I headed the column, leading the procession barefoot through the town to the burial ground. We were both clad entirely in black, and I kept my wings folded to hide their brilliant patterns. Arzandel wore on his silver head a crown of black roses.

The burial ground lay in the shadow of the great side of Doudern Fell. It was some distance from Halsanger. As we neared, a mournful song struck up from those people who had already gathered by the Castle Tomb. Vielles, lutes and reed pipes sang in canon, a round of sorrow which became heavier with the people's tears with every step we took.

The Castle Tomb was an ancient sepulchre with a doorway sealed by a granite slab which ten strong men dragged open as we approached. The column of people encircled the tomb. Arzandel took his place in front of the dark opening and raised his hands to the grey skies. All eyes were on him except mine. As I followed his gaze upwards, two jackdaws glided across the edge of my vision and perched on a nearby monument of stone.

Arzandel sang prayers for Ashleigh in a strange tongue I did not know but still understood. At the end of each prayer, the mourners bowed their heads to say "God hear us", and another pair of jackdaws lazily joined the edge of the gathering. Soon the birds surrounded the mourners, which worried me. I could see the birds waited expectantly but could not understand why they were there. Recalling Anya's fear of them, I wanted to alert Arzandel, to warn Tamara, to cover up the bier. But my guilt stopped me from halting the service. I also feared such an incident would give the jackdaws the opportunity they awaited.

The escort placed the bier in the doorway to the sepulchre. Arzandel stood on Ashleigh's left to deliver his eulogy in the local tongue. He said that Ashleigh's dedication as a teacher had been to develop children into adults who could use their gifts and fulfil their potential. Few of Ashleigh's students had failed, many fought still for truth, and some had soared in triumph to the skies. Arzandel justified Ashleigh's harsher moments by their results: his crueller actions were the only way he could teach his students some of their lessons.

Then Arzandel looked me in the eye. He described my youthful struggle against Ashleigh's teachings and my departure from Berren with the destruction that had caused. He said I had realised after my return that I could not renounce Ashleigh's teachings, but my change of thought had come too late to save my master. He finished with a sigh, gripped his staff and slowly descended to his knees.

THE EAGLE AND THE BUTTERFLY

A young boy with a tear-stained face stepped forward, stumbling on his long black robes. He sang a song of sorrow which I had written in my night, his trembling voice accompanied only by the hushed wind soughing in the treetops. The wind accused me of destroying a saint and would not hear my protests that the saint had been as much a devil; for the wind comes from Nature's cruel kingdom and does not heed the philanthropic thoughts of humankind. I turned aside, trying to block the incriminating power of the scene from my senses.

The boy sobbed over the last verse of his dirge and could not finish. As his father led him away, my guilt crowded my mind so mercilessly that my conscience forced me to offer reparation to seek peace. I threw myself on the ground at the foot of Ashleigh's bier to abase myself in the tradition of Berren, and then stood up to face the people.

'In the legends of Berren, Llyrin hero of Halsanger by chance slew his father. When he understood what he had done, he threw himself on the mercy of the Judges' Council, offering himself as the black rose wreath from the people of the country.'

As I paused, a distant horn piped portentously in the chill silence.

'My conscience curses me for my wrongdoing. I would repay my debt so that I might find peace, whether it be here or beyond the Tarn of Mirrors, its timeless way. Therefore, as Llyrin before me, I offer myself as the black rose wreath from Ashleigh's guided people to their beloved mentor whom my deeds have slain.'

I heard the crowd's shocked intake of breath as they realised what I had committed myself to become. At that same moment, the jackdaws sprang up in flight, a grey cloud against the sun, casting an ominous shadow over the tomb.

'My lady Tamara!' I cried out in warning, too late.

The jackdaws fell from the sky. As the mourners dived to the ground under the attack, the largest jackdaws grasped Tamara in their claws and lifted her off her horse with exultant cries. I launched skywards after them. At once two dozen birds beat me down with their

35

wings.

The horn piped again. The flock of jackdaws soared back into the sky with their prize. A squadron of them circled the graveyard thrice widdershins. Then they all flew off to the west. We watched, confused, defiant, hopeless, struggling slowly to our feet.

'Arzandel?' I asked, hoping for his guidance as I helped him stand. He smiled sadly at me.

'You wove the spell, Eregendal. Only you have the key.'

He took the crown of black roses from his brow and stared at its barbs.

'You have offered yourself as the black rose wreath. You cannot go back on that.'

'Nor do I intend to. This hell within would make me accept any fate.'

'But Eregendal, by tradition, the black rose wreath is burnt over the Castle Tomb when it is resealed, by the nearest to the deceased. Ashleigh's daughter Tamara will have to choose now, between this wreath in my hand, and you.'

All the tense, puzzled mourners were listening to us. I made sure they would all hear my reply.

'I am not afraid of death, Arzandel. Death is but a journey through the Tarn of Mirrors, a border between one land and the next. I brought Ashleigh and Berren to this, and it is my fault Tamara was taken by the jackdaws – I saw the signs but failed to warn you. So I will go rescue my lady Tamara from her captors, that she may complete the ceremony. Then Ashleigh will travel to the next world unhampered.'

'Are you a fool?' demanded a shepherd: 'Better for you to burn alive on this tomb than be found in the jackdaws' stronghold.'

'Better for my conscience to suffer true hell and pay for my wrongs than to walk the coward's path of ease.'

'Eregendal!' Arzandel called sharply to stop me before I could say more. 'Return to the Tarn of Mirrors. You can do no more here. I will talk with you on my return.'

I threw off my black robes and flew away, leaving behind a crowd of people blinded by the gleaming light of my belt and the third key.

Chapter 6
Within the Enchanted Circle

I did as Arzandel had commanded, and waited for him near his cave by the Tarn of Mirrors. My thoughts brooded on the abduction of Tamara, and the riddle of the jackdaws' presence in a land where once the only evil had been in the people. I wondered about the people already held captive by the jackdaws, but doubted than many lived because I began to recognise the jackdaws for what they really were.

Arzandel returned at dusk and lit a fire with a wave of his wand. He did not speak with me for a while, being taken up with his own thoughts. When I walked over to speak with him, I found an invisible wall protected him from everything around. Needing something to do, I set out some food and wine, ready for his return to that reality.

His face had changed again, and the black rose crown had marked his forehead, drawing blood. When he eventually lifted his wand, his hand shook with exhaustion. The clearing shimmered around us under his spell. He took me back through the Tarn of Mirrors to where the Song of Time sings without end.

'Do not leave the fireside circle,' he warned: 'We are in an enchantment. If you leave the circle, you will either return to your lost wanderings in the dreamlands or travel on with Ashleigh in your maze of circles which surround death.'

'I shall not move. Now, let us eat.'

Arzandel sipped the wine, but looked into the distance as if he were watching or listening for something.

'This is the safest place I can take you to, though even here is not safe from them. All time meets at once here, and each second is all time. So those from the past and the future can do the work of those from whom we hide in the present.'

Two large birds disturbed Time's trembling music with an awkward landing on a nearby tree stump.

'Ignore them: they cannot harm you, though we will hear them. Through today's events you have secured yourself a place of death in the annals of Berren, Eregendal. If you go now, you will be spared much pain, but you will never be able to return.'

'Why should I go? I have a task before me: to undo the wrong I committed in my past.'

'If you stay, you must rescue Tamara. That will not be easy.'

'As I swore over Ashleigh's grave, I would rather suffer Hell than walk the coward's path.'

'Is there no discretion in you? For to rescue Tamara, you will suffer Hell!'

A clamour of voices struck up outside the circle, screaming in agony to be saved. Below their distressing cries, other voices plotted with low sniggers to win our souls and destroy us. The noises unnerved me. I sat still and concentrated on eating my meal, taking strength from Arzandel's presence.

'Eregendal, you are weak. Butterflies can weather no storms.'

'Talk like that never won battles, Arzandel. Better you said nothing than try to weaken my resolve with your arguments.'

'Then your heart is set to go?'

The clamouring outside the circle died down. In its place called the Four from the paths of the dreamlands. I leapt to my feet to answer their cries because they were desperate to find me. Arzandel grasped my hand and held me back.

'Don't die for shadows. They are not real.'

'But they need me, the Four who follow after me in the

dreamlands. We have found each other again.'

He pulled me down beside him.

'Friend, if they were the Four, you would see them. That would be your greatest temptation to leave the circle. Past, present and future are one here. If Zoust did not summon images of the Four and could only imitate their voices, it means that the Four who follow after you never came, are not coming, and never will come this way.'

The news shocked me. I stared emptily into the fire, mourning the dead companionship of the Four.

'Then I have all the more reason to rescue Tamara.'

The voices stopped. The Song of Time alone filled the clearing until the rippling of the tarn water disturbed it. We turned and watched the Green Lady of the Tarn of Mirrors rising quite dry from the water.

'Come, my friends,' she whispered peacefully, reassuringly: 'It is time for you to return to the land of your birth. Your work here is done, and you have seen what needs to be seen. Come back with me to those who await you near the end of the road.'

I looked at Arzandel, who shook his head.

'She herself is wraith. You cannot trust her words,' he whispered.

The Green Lady multiplied until the black pool was completely hidden by green images rising out of the water to whisper their muddled entreaties. When I did not obey their calls, they each slowly sank back into the depths of the tarn, still whispering softly until the dark waters silenced them. Arzandel and I turned back to stare into the fire.

'Zoust is interested in you, Eregendal. Tell me, during your stay here, has anything happened to tempt you away from Berren?'

I thought deeply before replying.

'No, except perhaps the traveller I met at Halsanger Carnival. He helped me understand myself and my cause more by showing me all the possibilities within my reach. The route to each would have betrayed my beliefs too much for me to consider it. But as he left, he said a strange thing which sowed some doubt in my mind. *Remember our conversation when you sit alone in your dismal garret, looking out on a world which is deaf to your entreaties, blind to your proofs, and has closed its mind to your words. For today you could have held that world or this in the palm of your hand, but you let the chance pass you by.'*

'Why did you not tell me this before? Had I but known? But no, the wheels are in motion and may not stop. This traveller, what was he like?'

'A friendly fellow, well fed and dressed like one from the dreamlands, in grey and orange. He wore a signet ring marked with a star breaking a circle, and he called himself Tuzos.'

'So Zoust saw some easy prey. It is well you did not fall to the silver tongue of his minion Tuzos. What he offered was not his to give, and he would have taken far more in return. Use faith to overcome the doubt he sowed. And take heed: you may meet up with others – Stouz and the rest.'

'Then you think he fears my attack?'

'Your attack? Nay: should Tamara be freed, he needs only to destroy this black rose wreath for revenge. No, it is your destiny he concerns himself with. Do not think that he would fear.'

'My destiny? If it is bound with Berren, that is good. I have a mind to stay here when I am through with quests. Tomorrow I go to the jackdaws' stronghold. Can you direct me?'

The air filled with a fearful screeching, and a hundred jackdaws dived towards us from the skies. Deafened and shying from their violent mobbing, I cowered by the fire even though I knew they could not break through the charmed circle.

'As you are, you do not have the fortitude to face them on their own territory,' Arzandel shouted. 'It is better we return.'

He waved his wand. The clearing shimmered, the screeching stopped, and we were back in the peace of a tranquil night we had left for safety.

Arzandel brought out his heavy silver locket and opened it. He chanted an ancient incantation to the mirror inside. The reflection clouded over with a writhing mist in fire-lit darkness. For a moment I thought the mist twisted into the shape of a woman's face, but nothing came of the image and Arzandel closed the locket.

'They do not wish us to find Tamara, or at least they wish to give you that impression, to spur you on so that you assail their stronghold before you are strong enough to fight them.'

'Then what should I do tomorrow?'

'Go to the Judges' Council. Seek their advice. If they will give it.'

Chapter 7
The Judges' Counsel

I arrived at Halsanger marketplace shortly after dawn next morning and secured a seat by the plinth where the Judges Council sat on certain appointed days. Several people had arrived before me, and many more joined us as the morning progressed.

The Judges arrived at noon to a fanfare of trumpets. They sat with much ceremony at the three stone tables set up for them. Like me, four of them were a curious mixture of human and beast. The Chairman, Micheldor the Bulldog, sat at the middle of the centre table. His ugly canine face looked fierce and threatening. Kanum the Sheep sat to his right, with a fleece for hair. Hapis the Bull sat to his left, human-faced with front hooves planted firmly on the table. At the table next to Kanum, sat an old woman knitting industriously and two youths who proceeded to play cards all afternoon. At the table by Hapis sat Sekma the Siamese Cat, human in form but cat-like in movement. Next to her sat Maredudd The Wise, described by gossip as an honourable man of thirty-six, and lastly, Torpeth the ancient Sage who used an ear horn to counter his deafness.

41

MAGGIE SHAW

The order in which Micheldor selected the plaintiffs' cases was random, though this was not immediately apparent because the first case he called was that of the first person to have arrived there that morning. This woman's case was simple but raised several questions about the past which I would have dwelt upon. Instead, Sekma raised questions about the woman's own doubtful past and reason for being there. The Council laughed scornfully at the woman's protests and swiftly dismissed her case without judgement.

Micheldor called the next plaintiff by name. This arrogant fellow had little to say and was poor in putting his case. However, the old woman put down her knitting and commented in favour of a minor point. Hapis agreed with her; the Council approved, and they discussed the entire case at length. They granted the man his case in full.

As the afternoon passed, I realised there was a secret inner ring of people with whom the Judges found favour. They heard cases from the inner ring with promptness and compassion, and although not all the privileged plaintiffs won their cases in full, they all left the Council well-satisfied. Those people not in the inner ring were heard with impatience, contempt and scorn; and they awarded only one a favourable judgement. I could see little difference between those within the clique and those without. Vice or virtue, opulence or poverty, town accent or country, ingratiating manner or offhand, immaculate dress or shabby, alone did not decide. Just one thing was evident: all the inner ring knew several of the Judges very well, and many had shared their hearths and homes with them.

I sat on and said nothing, though it discouraged me that the least worthy were the best heard. As dusk set in, I found myself one of only four people still waiting to be heard. Many people had left before they had pleaded their cases, frightened off by the treatment given to others.

The man who spoke before me was not poor. His rich attire made his boyish face look more innocent than he sounded when he spoke. He pleaded the cause of his sister, a woman who had lost her inheritance through a marriage of convenience. As he eloquently made his case, the Judges covered their faces with their hands, barely able to suppress their amusement. Before he had finished, Kanum roared with laughter. When he knelt to hear their final verdict, all the other judges bar one joined Kanum. They laughed and laughed and laughed until the man leapt up in embarrassed outrage. He mounted his horse and galloped back to his home in the Summerlands, scorning the once respected Berren Judges Council.

The Judges heard my case last. I stood before the centre table of this world-famed council. Once, people had travelled from the farthest reaches of the world to hear the Council's jewels of wisdom, suffering the greatest hardships in their journeys, yet counting these as naught for the worth of the rulings of the nine Judges. Now, having seen their contempt for others, I felt apprehensive about their treatment of me.

Their faces were expressionless as they observed me before I spoke. They seemed neither for me nor against.

'Your Honours, I am bound upon a quest to rescue Tamara, daughter of the late Ashleigh and Lady of the High Castle. The jackdaws abducted her yesterday during the burial ceremony for her lamented father,' I said. 'I need to find out where the jackdaws have taken her, and I need to know quickly, for there is little time to lose if I would bring her back unharmed.'

The Judges conferred in doubtful whispers, pointing to my appearance and shaking their heads. Micheldor hushed his colleagues and sneered a smile at me.

'So you would fight jackdaws alone?'

The other eight laughed and some applauded his words. They quickly hushed when he continued.

'Go, little insect. The Council has no love of riddles, nor will it be tested by some worthless butterfly.'

I opened my mouth to speak, but before I had uttered a word, the nine Judges stood up, turned their backs on me and walked off into the night. Alone, I stood in the marketplace seething with indignation and affront. I flew back to the Tarn of Mirrors, furious.

Arzandel was sitting by the fire outside his cave. His long white beard and hair contrasted strongly with his black face in the firelight. He had set out a meal for my return. I sat down beside him. He looked at my sad face and touched my arm in a gesture of compassion.

'Be brave, Eregendal. Though the Council of Judges mocked you, still you must not tire. This is only the first setback in a quest which will be beset with disappointments. But once you come through them, the Council will recognise your worth and acknowledge your work.'

'I am not certain I want their approval. That would be censure to me, for they are unfair and unjust. They have ears for their own circle alone, and their choice of favourites is most arbitrary.'

'You do not understand the full picture. There are many different types of people in many different walks of life. Though it may not be clear, those within the circle will have had better reason to secure the Council's favourable judgements, than those who did not.'

'And what of me?'

'You are learning, Eregendal, but you have not yet learnt.'

'Then I AM just a little insect, a worthless butterfly, and all my being IS only vain riddles, and my words ARE just so much wind.'

'No, Eregendal. You have much ability. But you need a cause completed, you need something worth saying. Then you will break through into the inner circle.'

'What is worth saying if "help me save my Lady" is not? Oh, how I regret the wasting of this day!'

'Impetuous child! It was not wasted. Now you have seen for yourself how much Berren has changed. And while you were there, I made enquiries on your behalf, in case the Judges would not consider your case. Your friend Anya will arrive shortly to speak with you.'

Arzandel said no more despite my questions. He sat beside me, absorbed by his thoughts as he stared into his misty locket mirror. I ate and then slept, lying curled up on the ground by the fire with my head resting on a stone.

Anya arrived at midnight. She wrapped me in a warm embrace. Then she sat beside me and took the cup of wine which Arzandel offered her. Her depression of the day before had gone, and her heart-shaped face radiated energy and joy. She tucked her long black hair behind her ears and spoke.

'How can I thank you for your help, Eregendal? Yet here I come asking you for more help, without even having repaid you.'

'Forget repayment, Anya. Whatever your request, if it is in my power, I will do it.'

'Better hear my request first before you commit yourself. I am bound upon a new expedition to find the Tree of Knowledge. The youth Kohtel who came here yesterday: he has found three others who also want to go. They have made many preparations and they were ready to start, only they do not know where to head for first. As I kept diaries of my own journey to the Tree of Knowledge, they have appointed me their guide because I can give them the directions they need. We set off tomorrow, at dawn.'

'This all sounds grand. But what you would have me do.'

'It is no small thing I ask of you, I confess. The first direction we must follow is to fly to the top of the world. But none of us have wings.'

'How did you start out on your journey there before?'

'By chance. I had been walking on Doudern Fell near the cairn when a mist came down. In the mist floated a flying ship, carrying sail but unmanned. I thought it might take me safely down the fell and stepped aboard. Instead, it took me high above the world on an ocean of cloud. Whether I travelled north, south, east or west, I do not know; nor do I know how far it took me, for I sailed many days. For sure, such an enchantment could only happen once in a person's life, so I know the boat will not come for me again. So I come to ask your help. We invite you to come with us on our expedition because we need your skill to take us the first part of the way.'

I looked with regret into my cup of wine.

'I would have gone with you, had I been able, for I too would love to find the Tree of Knowledge. But I have a quest which I must not delay, to rescue Tamara, daughter of the late Ashleigh, from the jackdaws which abducted her yesterday. Already I have wasted a day, and I still do not know where their stronghold is yet.'

'Then there is your reason for coming with us. At the Tree of Knowledge, you can look down on the world in your mind and see everything – whatever you desire to know. Nor fret about time, for time there is separate from time here.'

I looked to Arzandel for advice, but he said nothing. The decision was mine to make alone, and in this matter he was not free to advise. Then I recalled that it was on my behalf he had invited Anya there to see me.

'I shall be ready at dawn,' I agreed.

Chapter 8
The Departure of the Expedition to the Land at the Top of the World

The six people on the expedition met outside the inn in Halsanger marketplace as the cocks crowed in the dawn next day. The youth and his three friends seemed delighted that Anya had persuaded me to join their party. There was much excited, hopeful talk as we set off out of the town to climb Doudern Fell.

The youth Kohtel led the expedition. He was an excitable lad of twenty, lean and nervous, with ginger hair and a hooked nose. He wore a purple jacket over his bronze silk tunic. Whenever the conversation flagged between the rest of us, he talked rapidly about nothing which made me ponder about his fear of silence. His ambition was to change the system of the Judges Council. He wished to view the world from the Tree of Knowledge so that he could see the best way to effect this change.

Kohtel's right-hand man was Astor, a soldier by trade and about forty years old, who would protect the expedition from enemies and other dangers. He was a muscular man who wore chain mail and burnished leather over his rough wool tunic. His face was swarthy and clean-shaven, and his black hair was cropped. He longed to end war and bloodshed, an ideal which the Judges Council had found hilarious. He believed only the Tree of Knowledge could give him the insight to pursue such an ideal with any hope of success.

Our cook and keeper of that baggage common to us all, was a grizzled old shepherd called Yammas. He wore a linen smock and woollen leggings, and a copper-coloured coat. His wise old eyes missed very little. He wanted to find a way by which animals and humans could live together in peace and trust in the world. Anya was our guide, returning to the Tree to choose again from the choices she had seen before. My tasks were to secure transport and find places to camp.

The sixth member of our expedition, Zana, was not the sort of person I had expected to walk beside, although I should have learnt by then not to expect but only to accept. I drew Anya to the back of the party to ask her about the girl.

'Tell me, why does a nine-year-old child travel with us on the expedition?'

'It was not our intention,' Anya replied. 'Kohtel saw a vision and insisted she came with us. Why such an innocent chooses to make so dangerous a journey, we know not. She has no quest, but says she comes to fulfil her destiny.'

We climbed to the summit of Doudern Fell in blazing sunshine. Below us, a dense murky cloud covered the Berren lowlands. On

Anya's advice, though against the judgement of Yammas and myself, we encamped about the boulder cairn marking the highest point on the fell's long ridge back. After eating, my curiosity rose again about Zana. I took Kohtel to one side.

'Tell me, Kohtel: what made you bring Zana on our expedition?'

'Why, don't you like children, Eregendal? Or does Zana's innocence frighten you? I must admit, she makes me feel foolish and disillusioned.'

He laughed and stroked his long, hooked nose and his thin moustache. His hands never kept still. He was wound tight with nervous energy. I realised how shy he was, and how frightened of the responsibility he had assumed.

'I am far more disillusioned than you, Kohtel. It is true that Zana's plain leaf greens make my many-coloured patterns seem showy. But that is not why I ask, if I can trust my thoughts to walk with my heart. Rather, I fear for Zana's safety. Surely such an innocent does not need to face the dangers of the journey to a place where only the blind and disillusioned need to go, to learn.'

Kohtel smiled and played with the cuff of his bright mauve jacket.

'Why did you not ask straight out to be told my vision?' he asked. 'We keep no secrets here, for we are all grey within despite our bright facades. All except Zana, of course.'

I apologised and sat down beside him at the campfire, where Yammas was playing his haunting reed pipe while the others rested.

'My vision was strange. It came to me while I walked by the shores of Doudern Lake.'

Yammas stopped playing his pipe. The others moved closer to hear the tale again.

'I was considering what to take on the expedition – I wanted to take far too much – when suddenly, I found myself not on the lake's gentle shore, but clinging to the edge of a precipice. Demons and other evil creatures mobbed me. I cried out to God to save me. I had to call thrice, for I have called to Him in doubt many times and rightly got no reply. This time I knew only He could save me, and I knew that He would if only I kept calling. On my third cry, a misty light appeared to my right. It got brighter and brighter until it blinded me and it chased the terrified creatures of darkness away. Out of the light walked a silver angel which stood before me and took my hand. Then I awoke. I was lying on the bank of the lake with Zana smiling down at me. She said, "I am coming with you." So she came.'

'Then what are you, Zana?' I asked in awe: 'Some angel? A good magician in a changed form? A beneficent spirit to guide us on our way?'

Zana smiled with eyes full of mischief, shattering my feelings of awe. She turned away to ask Yammas if she could play his pipe.

'No,' Kohtel answered me: 'Zana is well known in Halsanger. She wandered into the marketplace about five years ago and chose to live with the good judge, Maredudd the Wise. No-one knows where she comes from. They called her Zana because she wears the colours of the little herb flower. Maredudd says a sweeter child never walked.'

'How could Maredudd let her go on a journey like this?'

'He said she should leave the way she came, a benign and charmed wanderer, having sojourned like the sun whose arrival and departure are both marked by the same twilight colours.'

Anya called for us to settle for the night and rest to prepare for the coming day. I spent my last few moments before sleep, reading Anya's diaries to learn which direction I should fly off in the morning.

When Yammas roused the camp for breakfast next day, the sky was still dark. Yet we all felt we had slept far longer than usual and had expected the sun to be high. As we broke camp, I listened for the wind's guidance because I still felt unsure which direction to take. Strangely, nothing but our deadened voices stirred the cool fell air.

'I like this not,' said Astor: 'It seems as if something already tries to block our way.' He unsheathed his sword Shartere and sliced an arc of air with the blade. At the highest point, it gleamed like quicksilver.

'Shartere speaks,' he said gravely and sheathed the sword. 'This night is the enchantment of one who tries to stop us. I cannot fight it, because I do not know who is against us, or at which of us the evil is directed.'

'Perhaps my torch will show the way,' Kohtel said.

He produced a conical object of glazed and patterned china and lit a resin inside. As he held the torch aloft, the cloud became translucent. Our advantage was of little help. We saw only the long ridge of Doudern Fell and the distant haze-masked horizon, with the sun high above, showing that much of the morning had passed.

'I will fly up and see if we can travel through the cloud,' I offered, stirring the air with my wings.

At first it was easy to fly upwards, but the higher I ascended, the harder it became to rise further. The sulphurous cloud felt like thick mud, choking my lungs and holding back my wings with sticky fingers. Still I pressed on, determined to break through after the effort I had made to get that far. At last through the smoky darkness shone a dull yellow-grey disc which could only be the sun. I put all my strength into a last surge upwards. The cloud arced and a shaft of lightning struck me down. I fell to the earth, unconscious.

Anya revived me with the bitter scent from a small bottle she waved about my face. When I jerked into life, she pressed me down.

'Careful. Are you hurt?'

I felt my arms, my legs and my wings, and found I was still whole.

'Just bruised and dazed.'

'What happened?' Kohtel demanded. 'We saw you fly upwards for near an hour before you vanished. Then you fell out of the sky.'

'The cloud is a polluted mire. It got thicker the higher I rose. Just before I fell, I saw the sun through the fog. Then lightning struck me.'

'How deep is the cloud? What is its substance?'

'Hold, Kohtel: let Eregendal rest a while,' Anya chided: 'We are lucky the fall did no harm.'

'Nay, we have no time for rest,' Astor warned. 'I fear that when night comes, the enchantment will strengthen and the cloud stifle us.'

Zana wandered over to us, holding a zana flower in her hand. It was a small, secretive plant, hard to find at that height, and not that common in the valley, though used locally as a herb for flavouring stews. The flower's many spiky petals were a bright emerald green with a silvery sheen which made them look as if some craftsman had fashioned them out of metal. No craftsman ever had the skill to form so small a rosette, nor had any artist ever truly painted its delicate symmetry. Zana offered me the bloom with childish pride.

'See, I have found one of my flowers. They are magic flowers. They grow in magic places. There are some around the cairn.'

I took the flower from her. My mind cleared and my bruises eased.

'It is indeed magic. If I flew with this in my hand, I would break through the enchantment.'

'And you could fly from the cairn. That will bless your flight,' Zana said.

I limped to the cairn. About it grew four zana flowers. The boulder cairn was steep and high. I used my wings to help me climb to its unsteady top. There I balanced, hovering awhile. Then I put my hope in the frail flower amulet and flew upwards once again.

The sulphurous cloud pressed in on me like thick mud, but when I put the flower to my lips, it no longer stifled me. Higher and higher I laboured until I could see the yellow-grey disc of the sun through the darkness. Again the sky arced, but I held the flower close and the shaft of lighting flashed past, exploding into a rain of fire. My surroundings flared with sheet and streak lightning; fireballs dazzled my eyes; but I flew through all unharmed and abruptly came out into bright sunshine. The midday sun warmed my flagging heart and gleamed on a distant object gliding towards me. I hovered, waiting for the object to draw close enough for me to make out what it was.

At last my eyes perceived some detail. On a puff of cloud rested a pastel blue boat, its gauze sails unfurled, gliding gracefully across the sky. Anya's ferry was coming for us. With a cry of joy, I plunged back into the yellow-grey hemispherical cloud, only to find now that it would not let me travel downwards. I clasped the flower to me and fought again to fly through the false night. A shower of hailstones marked my breakthrough out of the cloud. I landed to find myself about half a mile from the cairn. My companions' distant voices answered my calls, telling me they would find me. Zana ran up to me ahead of the others.

'What happened?' she asked.

'I broke through, but only because of your flower.'

'The zana is dead.'

I looked at the crushed flower in my hand. Its stalk had withered and its petals were crisp and brown.

Astor and the others caught up with Zana. They saw the dead flower in my hand.

'This is truly grave and awesome power which is raised against us,' Astor said.

'Perhaps, but I have won through. On the other side of this fog I saw the cloud ferry boat which took Anya before.'

She embraced me with tears in her eyes.

'Surely you are an encouragement to us all.'

'No. It is Zana and her flower that you must thank.'

'If the ferry is waiting for us, we should not dally here,' Kohtel warned. 'Eregendal, can you take us on your back?'

'One at a time, and with the help of the flower, yes,' I said, not as confident as I sounded.

'Then let us arrange an order for departure,' Kohtel said. 'First, you go, Astor: I fear the ship may need defending. You go second, Yammas. Then the heaviest of us have gone, and Eregendal's task becomes easier as tiredness increases.'

'Which means that you go third, Kohtel, I go fourth, and Zana goes last,' Anya said.

'No. I should go last as leader of the expedition.'

'You do not know how to pick the flowers,' Zana said, with a child's simplicity. 'I shall go last. The flowers only come out when I call them.'

Something in Zana's voice compelled us to agree. We accepted her decision without debate.

'What about the baggage?' Yammas asked.

'There would be no time for Eregendal to collect it in an extra journey,' Kohtel said.

'Nor would I have the strength. I cannot take anything apart from the person and anything vital to the success of the expedition. It was hard enough for me to fly alone.'

'But we must have our baggage. The tents, our food!' Yammas protested.

'My books, our papers,' Kohtel added.

'Would you risk all for a few worthless objects?' Astor demanded. 'When we came into this world, we had no baggage, nor will we take any with us when we leave. Let us now take only that which is vital and can be carried with ease. Leave the rest to Fate.'

Kohtel and Yammas continued to complain. Astor and I left their protests behind to climb the cairn. After the soldier had settled securely on my shoulders, Zana handed me a second flower. I launched into the air with a shout, struggling a little under his weight.

Once we were winging through the darkness, I soon forgot Astor. Again I pushed through thick, choking mud, holding the flower to my lips so that I could breathe.

'What is the matter,' asked Astor when my labouring became too obvious for him to ignore.

'The cloud… is trying to… choke me,' I gasped.

'But I feel nothing.'

He thought a while, and said gravely, 'Then this enchantment is for you alone, Eregendal.'

'Zoust!' I spat: 'He is the one against me – Zoust!'

The skies arced and rumbled with the name. Astor exclaimed in understanding.

'So it is that with whom we pit our wits, and for the sake of you. That devil's picked a good one! Take heart, Eregendal. I think I see the sun ahead.'

Lightning saluted our departure from the cloud into the sunlight and the azure vault of the sky. The pastel-blue ferry floated across to us on its couch of silver mist. Astor climbed aboard in wonder. He wanted me to join him there for a rest. With the zana wilting in my hand, I refused.

'Then I have but one thing to say,' he warned: 'Do not mention your enemy's name, for wherever that is said or writ, there will he be. When you go down the last time to fetch Zana, I will tell the others as best I can. It is better the child does not know.'

I saluted him with a wave and plunged back into the cloud to struggle down to the fell for my next passenger. Yammas I took up with relative ease despite the cauldron he insisted on carrying and wore on his head. Kohtel caused a problem, though. When we had risen halfway through the cloud, I found I was no longer moving upwards.

'Kohtel, what have you… with you that is… useless?' I demanded.

'Nothing. All very essential,' he replied.

'What books?'

'Some theosophical discussions, a couple of discourses on politics, and a review of various religions.'

'Throw them away!'

'What?'

'If you… want to… get there…'

We started to fall. In horror, Kohtel threw all his paper and books away. Immediately we rose upwards again. Soon I was able to leave him safely with Astor and Yammas. Chastened, he told them the tale.

THE EAGLE AND THE BUTTERFLY

I told Anya about the incident after I had returned to the cairn. She assured me she would not be so foolish, and our flight together went without mishap. She settled in the boat, overjoyed to have been granted the same mystic ferry journey again.

I turned from the ferry for the last time to fly back down for Zana, battling exhaustion. The cloud enveloped me like an obliging pillow. I succumbed to its temptation, relaxing back in its support.

The cloud released me over a cavernous gorge. As I hurtled down between jagged rocks, my stiffened wings refused to obey my desperate commands. In panic, I cried to the flower in my hand to save me. A restricting band broke away from my wings. The flower disintegrated into fine brown dust and slipped away between my clutching fingers.

I hovered to gauge my position and saw I was on the far side of Doudern Fell. Shamed by my foolish mistake, I slowly flew the four miles back to the cairn. There I found my fall to temptation had not only endangered me.

The cairn stood alone. Zana was nowhere to be seen. I called her name and heard a distant cry for help. A mile away, I found her pressed defiantly against a tall standing stone. A black-cloaked woman was coaxing her to come away. On my approach, the woman spun round to face me. It was Tamara.

'My Lady!' I cried, hurrying towards her.

'Stop, Eregendal!' Zana called. She left the safety of the standing stone to come between me and the black-cloaked woman. 'This is not the lady you seek! She is bad, as bad as Tamara is good, as black as Tamara is white!'

But the black lady had bewitched me. I had no choice of action. Mesmerised by those magnetic eyes, I ran towards her while time-stretched silence echoed through me. Then Zana caught hold of my clothes and clambered onto my back. My mind cleared at once.

'Fly, Eregendal!' she cried.

'But the flower…'

'I am the fifth flower. Now fly. Don't let Aramat touch you.'

I raised my wings, but they no longer had the strength to lift me from the ground. All my attempts to fly failed. Aramat laughed contemptuously, reaching out to touch me. I backed off in fear, knowing her touch would mean destruction.

Zana shifted her perch on my back and grasped my hands to keep her balance. With her small fingers entwined in mine, fresh energy pulsed through my hands and along my arms into my exhausted body.

Aramat saw the change and lunged forward to touch me before we escaped her. I fluttered aside. She stumbled to the ground with a cry, her hand touching the standing stone. It shattered into a thousand pieces through her power. Saved from her awful intent by Zana's mystic strength, I flew upwards from the fell for the last time that day.

The cloud oppressed once more. Zana whispered encouragements to will me on. Once again, I felt myself held back in mid-air. No matter how hard I struggled, I could rise no further.

'It is sunset!' Zana cried. 'If we don't get through now, we never will. For your enemy is mine.'

Her fear put desperation into my flight. I gained a few feet but flagged again soon after.

'Please get there,' Zana whispered in prayer, terrified.

'God, I am trying. Please help me,' I cried.

At once, a key on my belt shone silver through the darkness. We flew out of the fog into the light, to find we had been travelling up a column of the cloud. It had stretched out like an arm above the curve of the grey hemisphere.

'We are free!' Zana cried.

'Aye, but where is the boat?' I asked.

The last golden rays of the sun shafted across the purple-pink twilight sky and dazzled our eyes. Zana averted her gaze upwards and caught sight of the gossamer-winged boat.

'Up there, the light above us,' she cried. 'Come on, Eregendal. It's only a little way to go.'

Little it may have looked to her, but to my exhausted wings it seemed infinite. And with the coming of night, the cloud below us was growing. It snatched at us with smoky fingers.

'I will get through,' I chanted, though my body cried out in agony.

It was at that point, as the last of my energy was about to give out, that the end of a rope fell from the sky. Zana caught the rope and tied it round me, underneath my shoulders. When all was secure, she climbed off my shoulders and shinned up the rope into the ferry.

What bliss it was to hang suspended in mid-air and rest at last. The ending of the battle made even the bite of the rope under my arms a negligible discomfort. My companions hauled me up into the boat and made me a couch in the stern. I fell at once into a long, deep sleep.

I woke up feeling wonderfully refreshed at about noon the next day. As I stirred, my companions gathered around me. They showered me with apologies for the difficulties they had caused me in my flight and congratulated me for getting everyone through the enchantment.

Kohtel claimed he had been at fault for taking along unnecessary baggage. Yammas apologised for being fat. Astor regretted having mentioned the name of my adversary twice while telling the others about him. My reply to each was the same, that the trial should be forgotten because we had all survived it and were sitting safely in the ferry. I also took responsibility for the trial because it was my adversary I had fought, putting the rest of the expedition in unwarranted danger. Astor replied that if my adversary was trying so hard to stop me, I had all the more reason to keep going. Zana ended the discussion by asking me about the glinting belt and the five keys suspended from it.

I looked fondly down at the belt and picked up the five keys in my hands.

'I know little about this new friend of mine. It was given to me as I passed from the dreamlands to Berren through the Tarn of Mirrors. When I first noticed it, the belt was dull and lifeless. Now it is brighter, and four of the keys as well. Arzandel said the keys would open up the people's eyes. I rather think they mark the widening of my own vision. For the first grew brighter when I had to act cruelly to be kind, the second when through fellowship I helped Anya, the third when I swore despite adversity to rescue my Lady Tamara from my adversary, and the fourth when I prayed to God for help in fighting the black cloud.'

'And the last?' Zana asked.

'When I have the eyes to see, then it will shine.'

'What do you think it will be?' Anya asked.

'Something which will come no quicker for my attempts to answer such a riddle.'

Then the fifth key glowed brightly. The sun paled for a moment in its light. Yammas stared at it with hooded eyes.

'Ask no questions and you need no answers. They will all come when Fate decrees the time is right,' he said. 'Come, some food. We are amply provided for in this ferry.'

We sailed for three days, leaving the smoky cloud far behind. But whether we sailed north, south, east, west or straight upwards no-one could fathom. Thus the beginning of Kohtel's log of the expedition was little different to the records in Anya's diaries.

Chapter 9
The Landing

On the eve of the third day, the sharp eyes of Yammas first caught sight of land. He pointed out the darker smudge on the horizon to Astor. The rest of us did not see it until next morning when the ferry glided across the cloud into a natural harbour set in a forbidding coast.

We waded ashore through the cloud and climbed onto the rocky beach. Above and around us, black cliffs threatened, their faces unmarked by paths. A blustering breeze buffeted us. Kohtel called for Anya's advice.

'I am sorry. I cannot guide you. I did not come this way last time,' she replied. 'I am not sure if this is even the same place.'

'We have the rope,' Astor offered, unwinding it from his shoulders.

'I'll fly up and secure it at the cliff top,' I said. 'Then you should all be able to climb up without too much difficulty. The wind is too strong for me to take each of you in turn.'

Anya paled. 'I have no love of heights.'

'Nor I,' Kohtel replied. 'However, we do have a destination and we will not get there standing on this beach.'

I knotted one end of the rope around my waist and flew upwards. The weight of the rope pulled me downwards against the stiff breeze, but it was little enough in comparison with the grey cloud I had flown through before. Determination and confidence soon got me where I wanted to go.

The top of the cliff was smooth like glass. Nothing grew there. No rocks relieved the dark, flat expanse. I looked along the edge of the cliff for some slight overhang to tie the rope to but saw nothing. Disappointed at failing in my task after all my labour, I sat down for a while to gaze at the horizon. Inland, the plain vanished into a heat haze. Out across the sea of cloud, the ferry glided away. This was where we were meant to come.

'The rope was not long enough,' Astor said when I returned to the beach: 'Fifty feet too short at least.'

'There was no place to tie it at the top either,' I replied. 'The land above us is like a plain of obsidian.'

'But this is where we must begin,' Kohtel said. 'We must find some other way over this obstacle.'

'The tide is going out,' Zana said. 'Let's walk along the beach.'

She led the way. We followed, stepping with care across the

slippery black stones. I feared one of us would fall; and Anya did slip, but did not hurt herself. After that, I held her hand as we walked to help her keep her balance.

The tide went far enough out for us to round the first headland. We walked on in hope, only to find ourselves at the base of higher, smoother cliffs which extended into the distance along the coastline, getting higher the further away they stood.

'There is no use in following this path,' Yammas complained. 'Far better we turn back now than get trapped by the tide.'

'No,' Anya warned: 'In my travels before, I came across an obstacle like this, which grew worse the further I went. When I turned back, I was more the loser because the way I ended up taking was far harder than the way I chose not to go.'

'But how can we leave this shore?' Kohtel asked.

'There will be a way,' I said. 'If naught else, we have my wings.'

The wind buffeted against me, telling me my gift would be useless there. My companions realised this also, and all except Zana had a gloomy face. On we stumbled.

'The tide is turning,' Astor observed later. He anxiously scanned the cliffs. 'There is no way up. We will be drowned.'

'The way will be revealed,' I insisted. 'We were not brought here to die but to rise above death and adversity.'

I walked on. Zana followed me. The other four sat down in despair.

'Come, there is no sense in waiting to drown,' I called back to them. 'A heart so set will overcome, or drop at the last still fighting.'

Anya stood up and followed me, her shoulders bowed. The other three stayed seated, staring after us and seeing us as fools.

The three of us rounded the next headland to find the sea of cloud was already lapping against the base of the cliffs. Even my heart sank then. But Zana cried out in excitement, her finger pointing to the cliff.

'Look! A cave! Go, Eregendal. Tell the others we found the way.'

'What if it is only short? What if it ends below the high tide level?'

THE EAGLE AND THE BUTTERFLY

Anya asked.

'Ask no questions. That is what Yammas said,' Zana replied. 'We had to come this way, and this is the only way we can go.'

With that, she leapt nimbly over the submerged rocks towards the cave. Anya followed her reluctantly. I turned back to fetch the others.

Yammas was doubtful when I returned with the news, but Kohtel silenced him and led the way forward. He felt ashamed for letting a child and a butterfly take the lead. The four of us hurried as quickly as we could across the stones. As we rounded the headland, the tide surged in, knocking Yammas and me against the bottom of the cliff. Astor caught me and tied me to himself with his rope. Kohtel held Yammas by the shoulders and led the way.

Clouds rushed in, and a storm whipped up. The wind and rain severely hampered our stumbling progress. Had I not been roped to Astor, I would have been smashed against the cliffs many times. Through the struggle, I wondered gratefully how he managed to keep his own balance while supporting me. The cave seemed to be an eternity away. The wading felt so pointless that I wanted to leave myself to the cruel mercy of the elements, but for that lifeline linking me to Astor. At one point he led me with his arm about my shoulders; at another, I think he carried me. Had he not helped me, I would not have arrived at last at the blissful shelter of that cave. When I thanked him, he replied that had I not returned for them, the three of them would not have found any shelter from the storm.

Once in the cave, we collapsed on the black sand above the high tide line and rested for a few moments.

'Where have Anya and Zana gone?' Yammas asked.

'I shall go and look for them,' Kohtel said. He walked off, calling their names. His torch lit his way into the depths of the black cave. When we called to him, he did not seem to hear us. Soon his light and the sound of his voice had gone.

'I like this not,' Astor said uneasily, grasping the handle of his sword, Shartere.

We set off in the direction Kohtel had taken, lighting our way by Shartere and the key of bravery on my belt.

Yammas joked about Astor's fears, but we all felt uneasy in the heart of those black cliffs. The empty silence of the tunnels and caves seemed unearthly. The walls reflected no light but drew in all that shone upon them, making it hard to see our way. Our route kept leading downwards when we wanted to climb. The cave branched off into many side passages, vents and shafts. We soon realised we had little hope of either finding the others or our way back to the coast.

At last I could walk no further. I sank tiredly to rest on the sharp sand floor. Yammas sat down beside me. Despite our entreaties, Astor walked on ahead.

'There is a jinx in this labyrinth,' Yammas said. 'Something draws me on but I do not know where to or why, and that frightens me. So let us stay together: two heads are better than one.'

'Aye,' I agreed.

I fell asleep beside him. When I awoke, he had gone.

At first, I felt despair. Once again, I had lost my companions, the way I had lost the Four in the dreamlands.

Then I realised the labyrinth was a test each of us had to take in our own way. I searched about me for a lantern but found Yammas had left nothing behind. Blinded by the darkness, I stood up, wondering how I could win through the challenge. I tried blundering about in the dark, but that got me nowhere as I entered dead end after dead end. How could I succeed over the darkness and the unknown?

The keys glowed faintly on my belt, hinting. I touched them. They offered hope even in despair. Each key unlocked a quality, but in this situation endurance, fellowship, bravery and acceptance, could not singly help me through this trial. There was, however, one greater than the rest. I took up the fourth key, the key of trust in God, and prayed.

The key filled the cave with a brightness that dazzled at first. The

THE EAGLE AND THE BUTTERFLY

light showed me I was standing on the brink of a chasm, down which the light from the key seemed to point for me to go. I opened my wings and flew into the unknown depths.

The base of the chasm widened into a vast cavern, cathedral-like in its awesome architecture: a natural monument of worship and of death. I landed on the black sand floor and looked around me by the light of that key which dispels all darkness and shadow. Massive pillars of obsidian reached up into the heights above me, supporting the roof of the chamber. Around me dark boulders lay strewn in a pattern which looked too regular to be natural. The walls were incised with many tunnels and passages of all shapes and sizes. Which tunnel to take was a mystery.

I raised the fourth key aloft, trusting it would show me the way. The light shone directionally to a slight crack in the smooth stone wall. I changed the key to the fifth key of acceptance, whose more gentle light made it easier to follow the path. I squeezed through the crack and emerged in a narrow passage which led downwards. Logic said this path could only take me to the rocky foundations of the island, not to the top of the cliff and the light I desired to reach. A doubt entered my mind. I dispelled it by marching resolutely off down the passage. The dimming key brightened again in my hand.

For many hours I wandered through the maze of tunnels and caverns, fighting the nagging doubt that I would never escape those black-walled caves while hoping fearfully that each turning passed, each downward step taken, was not the wrong one. In such a place, it was easy to doubt. When I had wearied myself with walking and with mental debate, I sat down and wept. Exhausted by my grief, I slept, only to awaken some time later to face the same nightmare.

Sleep refreshes and eases the mind. What remained of my earlier defiant depression had become a numb and hopeless acceptance that my part was to walk through the maze to life or death.

From that moment, time because as meaningless as direction. By the dim light of the fifth key, I stumbled on, lost but no longer bewildered, hopeless but no longer halted, in a dream of a nightmare which felt as distant to me as Arzandel and the Tarn of Mirrors.

When at last I saw a distant spot of light, I felt dumfounded. I looked again. My eyes did not deceive me. Those distant reflected rays of sunlight shocked me out of my non-presence and filled my mind with confusion. All of my journey had been downhill. Why then should I suddenly find myself on the surface when I had thought myself to be in the depths? The light caused disbelief. How could I have found a way out of such a labyrinth? I begrudged the light for being there when I had felt certain of eventual release. I felt almost like turning my back on it and returning to the depths of oblivion.

Only one thing drew me out of the darkness into the light: a child's voice. Whose it was and what it said, I could not identify then; but the mystery and promise held in its excited tone, took hold of my feet despite my head, and dragged me out onto the top of the obsidian plain.

'Eregendal! At last!' a woman cried, embracing me.

I looked at her distantly without recognition. She held me away from her in concern.

'Do you not know me? I am Anya. And here are Zana and Astor and Yammas: all of our expedition but for Kohtel.'

I pulled away to sit on the smooth ground and recalled dreamlike images of an expedition. These slowly clarified in my mind until I recognised my companions again.

'What brought you through the Labyrinth of Lethee?' Astor asked.

I described my wanderings as best I could. Anya nodded in understanding as I spoke.

'Zana just followed her nose. She was the first to escape the Labyrinth of Lethee,' she said. 'Astor followed his sword. Yammas chose his route with a coin. I remembered an obstacle in my first travels here, where to get where I wanted to go, I had to travel in the opposite direction. You almost lost yourself in the labyrinth's spell. And

THE EAGLE AND THE BUTTERFLY

Kohtel?'

'We have waited here five days,' Astor said. 'I did not expect anyone else to come out after Yammas, two days back. But if Eregendal has now escaped, we should still wait on.'

'Nay,' Yammas disagreed: 'Eregendal left the cave only just in time. If Kohtel does not follow soon after, he will be gone forever.'

'Kohtel may need to learn that one must follow to lead, to be last to be first, but that is no reason to abandon him,' Astor objected.

'But we cannot waste more time. Five days have we spent in a cavern and waiting by a hole. Would you have us spend the rest of our lives so?'

'Friends,' Anya interrupted: 'Leaderless, our ways will part. We will lose the strength given each of us by being a part of the group. Your bickering alone proves it. Let us sit and wait a few days more in the hope that our leader will return.'

On the eve of the ninth day, Kohtel wandered out of the cave. At least, it was the body of Kohtel. His mind was not that of the leader with whom we had set out so joyously. The most obvious change was that he no longer spoke to destroy the silence. He seemed to wander through the corridors of his mind, having at last found the courage to set foot in them. He stayed in that exalted condition for several days, while we led him across the black glass plain towards the heat haze.

One morning, Kohtel awoke as if out of some treasured dream. A happy and relaxed smile transformed his face.

'Greetings, my friends,' he said. 'Never has peace lived within me before as it does now. Somehow I understand everything because I no longer know anything. Let us away to find the many new surprises this land holds in store.'

Kohtel did not leave his exalted state fully for another two days. When we finally found ourselves talking to a Kohtel more like the one we remembered, we knew that the challenge of the Labyrinth of Lethee and the waiting had been worthwhile.

Chapter 10
The Runner

Many days later, we arrived at the edge of the obsidian plain. Rocks and sand rose to earthy foothills and on up to a range of tall wooded mountains. We camped among the rocks, eagerly anticipating the coming morning's journey, which promised to be far more interesting than the tedious days spent crossing the obsidian plateau.

As the sun went down behind the mountains, the sharp eyes of Yammas caught sight of a silhouette against the skyline. He believed it was another traveller, though Anya insisted no party ever met another party on the island. Astor reminded her that in the Labyrinth of Lethee, she had convinced herself the place the ferry had brought us to was not the same land as that to which she had travelled before. He implied that her self-thought laws for the land were equally far removed from the truth. Kotel stopped their bickering and lit his torch to guide the stranger to our camp. He sat on the edge of our circle, holding the torch aloft as he waited for the person to arrive.

Near midnight, footsteps silenced our conversation. We looked up expectantly at the moonlit rocks. A few moments later, we saw the person running towards us, an unkempt young man with a fiery light in his eyes. He wore a belted wool tunic and carried no purse or bag.

'What news, stranger?' Astor called out to him.

The runner did not seem to notice.

'What news?' Astor repeated.

The runner tried to pass us. Astor caught him and held him back.

'Get behind me, wraiths!' cried the youth. He struggled against Astor with a fear-fuelled strength which equalled the soldier's own.

Zana gently took hold of the youth's shaking hands.

THE EAGLE AND THE BUTTERFLY

'Fear not,' she whispered, her innocent voice enchanting all our ears. 'We are travellers too. We won't hurt you.'

The youth relaxed in Astor's grip but still cried out defiantly, 'It doesn't matter what you say.'

'What do you run from?' asked Zana.

Her voice coaxed us to sit down and listen, and the stranger to stay and talk.

'There are a thousand evils on the way before you,' he warned. 'Return to the shore before they destroy you. Come with me and forget your foolish journeying.'

'We have not travelled this far to turn back,' Astor said.

Kohtel silenced him with a calm gesture.

'We all know our journey is dangerous,' Zana said: 'It's harder for you because you're all alone.'

'I wasn't always alone. But when one of our company disappeared and a second was found dead, the rest of us could not help but flee. Too much has happened that was bad, too little to help. We could not continue.'

At this the youth broke down and wept. Zana placed her hand upon his forehead.

'Come with us. Face the dangers again. It will be easier with us beside you.'

'But the path you take is too hard. Grown men fled. One killed himself. How can a child like you hope to succeed when people far more able than me were reduced to nothing in the face of such privations?'

'Friend,' Kohtel said, 'it is the innocent who have the easiest path in this land. This child is our truest guide, and myself our poorest leader. Come with us. Our expedition is no collection of exalted people but a group of those who wished to go whether alone or not. Perhaps with us you will succeed. As Astor says, it would be a pity to have travelled so far and faced so much, only to turn back through a little fear.'

The youth thought awhile and nodded uncertainly.

'My name is Epoh,' he declared, offering us his hand.

As I shook it, I realised his fingers were sticky with blood, though he had no injury. When I looked into his eyes, I noticed that the glinting fiery lights in them had hardened into sharp, disturbing spears.

'Why do you seek the Tree of Knowledge, Epoh?' asked Kohtel.

'I want to know my future,' he replied.

Anya and I looked at each other. We both knew he lied.

The camp settled for the night. I was the first to curl up in a nook of the rocks with my cloak over me. Anya came over to where I lay and settled with her head almost touching mine. Sleep soon took me away, only for Anya to chase it off again a while later.

'Eregendal,' she whispered, 'I cannot trust our new companion.'

'No?' I mumbled, shaking off the covers of sleep.

'No man would journey to the Tree of Knowledge only to find out about his future. That cannot be learnt there.'

'Then perhaps that is why he failed to get there.'

'He would not even have reached this land were that his cause. The ferry would not have come for him. I think he was lying.'

'What if he is? People's lies soon find them out. Let him lie until his need for pretence has gone.'

'But then it may be too late. Did you not see the blood on his hands and the light in his eyes?'

'Aye. What of it? If we are true to ourselves, our cause and our faith, we have nothing to fear.'

'If we are true to those things, certainly we need fear little. But as yet none of us except Zana could admit to such maturity of spirit.'

'Then let Zana guide us!'

My tone was firm, to end the discussion. As I fell back to sleep though, I sensed our talk had been overheard by the wrong ears and my heart became uneasy too.

We rose at dawn next morning and set off soon after. In the light of day, we could study our new companion more easily. He looked to be about nineteen but for the older expression in his eyes, and he moved with an uneasy mien. His voice, in contrast, was cheerful and his comments about the brighter dawn which our company had brought, ingratiated him with Yammas and Kohtel. Anya and I felt unconvinced. Zana's impressions were completely hidden by her innocent, smiling air and love for all things around her.

We halted after an hour as we needed to decide which foothill pass to head for that morning. Instead of choosing himself and telling us as he once would have done, Kohtel asked our company which way we thought was best. Epoh immediately pointed out a gentle-looking hill, describing it as an easy beginning to conserve our energy for harder times. Anya countered by pointing out a far more vicious-looking peak with the comment that the right road was never the easiest. Yammas gave no comment, and Zana was too busy studying a stone to voice her opinion. Kohtel turned to Astor and me.

Astor raised Shartere and pointed it slowly to each of the hills and mountains ahead in turn. The blade dulled to near black while it pointed to the rounded hills and gleamed brighter when pointed to the steeper slopes, though it dulled a little at the peak chosen by Anya. I grasped the key for trusting in God and scanned the horizon. When my eyes rested on a sharp peak near Anya's chosen one, the key burned so warmly in my hand I had to drop it.

'The peak to the north of Anya's,' I said.

Astor nodded in agreement, and Anya was happy to accept the recommendation. Yammas made his choice with a coin imprinted with a lamb and an ancient inscription. By tossing the coin, he chose first between hill and peak, and then peak and peak. He also reached our conclusion.

'Then by general agreement, that is the direction we will go,' Kohtel declared.

As I looked around the party, I noticed that Epoh's eyes were not on the mountains as the others were. They shifted between my keys, Astor's sword and Yammas' coin.

The journey through the rugged terrain of the foothills was without incident, and by nightfall on the third day we had encamped at the mouth of a gorge which separated the mountain Anya had chosen from our final choice. A deep river ran along the bottom of the gorge.

'Should we take the gorge or cross by the mountain slope above?' Kohtel asked when we had settled to write up our notes and diaries.

'Do not take the gorge,' Anya warned: 'It brings to mind an incident during my first journey here.'

She leafed through one of her five diaries until she found the page.

'Here is the entry: "Little had I thought when entering the pass that I would be so trapped by self-doubt in its miry bottom. Surely the quickest way on the map is not the best way".'

She stopped short and looked up. Epoh was staring hungrily at her diaries.

'May I have a look?' he asked with a hard little smile.

'No!' she snapped back.

'But we keep no secrets,' said Zana with an impish grin. 'Show Epoh your book. You showed me.'

Anya glared at Zana but handed over the worn leather-bound book. Epoh took it eagerly. As he leafed through the pages, his expression changed to one of bewilderment.

'There is nothing written here. The pages are all blank,' he said, puzzled.

Zana winked at Anya and turned to me.

'Eregendal, you once told us you got a blank letter from a person who couldn't see you,' she said.

'Aye,' I agreed, recalling the letter Tamara had given me in Halsanger market square. 'It was because I did not have the eyes to see, nor did he. It was as if we were both in the same building but on different floors.'

THE EAGLE AND THE BUTTERFLY

Epoh returned the book to Anya with a shrug. She read out another passage warning us of the dangers she had met in that pass similar to this gorge. Each of us decided, in our own way, whether to follow the gorge or climb above it on the mountainside. All of us agreed that the mountainside was the way to go.

We settled down to sleep. Anya again lay close to me, though she fell asleep without saying what concerned her. I fell asleep soon after. This time, Astor roused us all in the middle of the night.

'Shartere, my sword! It has gone!' he cried.

My hand went immediately to my waist. The belt was still there, but the five keys were missing. Anya opened her bag to check her diaries, but they too had vanished. Kohtel's torch had gone. We looked around us in dismay and saw, to our horror, two cloaks lying strewn across the ground.

'Epoh has gone, and Zana has disappeared,' Kohtel said.

Yammas checked for his coin. Even that had gone.

'So it was safe to let Epoh stay with us!' Anya exclaimed, glaring at me.

'Hush,' Kohtel calmed: 'This is only another trial on our way.'

'But now I can give no guidance,' Anya cried.

'And I no defence,' Astor warned.

'Then that must be the way we have to travel on, without protection or plan.'

'But what of Zana?' Anya demanded: 'Epoh has kidnapped her. We cannot leave her in his clutches.'

'Perhaps I can help,' Yammas said. 'Go fill your water-bags at the river and bring them back to me.'

We looked at him askance, but saw he was serious in his request. Dutifully we each took our own water-bag down to the river at the mouth of the gorge, with the moon lighting our way. We returned to find Yammas had placed his old cauldron in the centre of the camp circle. He poured all the water into the pot and bade us sit and watch.

MAGGIE SHAW

'I know you all wondered why I brought my little cooking pot. Now you will see why.'

The water in the cauldron boiled without heat. In the steam coming off the water, we could make out a blurred image. It looked to me like reeds near a waterfall. To Astor it was a gorge, and to Anya it was a reed bower. The image shimmered in the steam until the last of the water boiled away.

'Now you understand why my cauldron came with me in the flight from Doudern Fell. You have all seen something. I have seen far more.'

'What does the shimmering picture mean?' Kohtel asked.

'When I poured in the water, I asked the cauldron to show me where we can find Zana and our stolen belongings. They are in the gorge yonder, and we have to enter there to retrieve our treasures. But our leaving safely is another matter, if the bones and flesh there are to do with the blood which was on Epoh's hands before.'

'What of Zana?' Anya asked, fearing for her safety.

'She is safe and ever will be. We are the prey of that wraith.'

'But if that is so, why did he tell us to head for the rounded hills the morning we met?' asked Kohtel.

'It was his trick, to make sure we went the way he wanted. He knew some of us did not trust him.'

Nervous fear crept into our thoughts. Kohtel spoke to dispel it.

'We must make a plan. Yammas, you say we must enter the gorge.'

'Aye. At the far end, near where the river falls, is a reed hut. There we will find Zana and our belongings. They are the bait for the trap he has set to catch us.'

'Could we climb down the face of the gorge, and so avoid the danger?' Kohtel asked.

'Nay. The images were clear. The only way in is from the mouth of the gorge.'

'Or from the air?' I suggested.

All looked at me in hope, but then Kohtel shook his head.

'It is too dangerous for a butterfly to go there alone.'

'Without my keys I am weakened, but I do still have my belt, and that will protect me. Surely it would be better for me to face the gorge alone, than for us all to go, to suffer the same fate?'

Kohtel felt guilty about accepting my offer.

'Then it is planned?' he said in a reluctant voice.

'Aye. I leave tomorrow at first light.'

Chapter 11
Into the Gorge

Though I slept soundly that night, the others did not. They had no promise of death already hanging over their heads, which I had lived with since the day of Ashleigh's funeral. A few minutes before the sun rose above the black plain, Kohtel woke me and took my hand.

'Anya told me last night while you slept, of the dangers in front of you. Rest assured, whatever happens, our thoughts are for you and our hearts behind you.'

'Make them your prayers and I will succeed.'

My four companions embraced me in farewell. As I flew off across the mountainside, Yammas settled down to stare into his boiling cauldron while the others watched my progress from vantage points about the slopes.

Once in the air, the currents of wind helped guide my way. A chilling breeze reached dank fingers from the rocky gorge, dispelling the gentle, warmer air currents around the mountains which had come inland from the plain of glass. I skirted the cold current to the far end of the gorge, where I winged down to hover by the cliff edge.

Immediately below me streamed a high waterfall fed by a wide lake. The fall tumbled into a rocky, winding passage through a neck between the mountains. The steep, overhanging banks offered no grassy shelf to hold a reed hut for some distance.

I flew downstream a way, keeping above the cold air current. After about two furlongs, I dropped to hover again. Below me lay the place where the reed hut had stood, according to the vision from Yammas' cauldron. Yet there was nothing on the crescent of grass and sedge but two large rocks, a pile of leaves, a potsherd and some stones.

The vision from the cauldron had been convincing enough for me to investigate the grassy bank. As I landed, I thought how strange it was that there should be a pile of leaves in a place where there was no tree. I reached down and touched the pile.

At once a clap of thunder rent the clear sky. I found my fingers were touching not leaves but the pages of Anya's diaries. Beside them lay my keys, Kohtel's torch, Astor's sword and Yammas' coin.

As my right hand closed about the keys, a roar from behind made me turn, startled. The large rock had turned into a huge and horrible ogre. He faced me across a reed hut which had appeared around us. To my right stood Zana, tied to the centre pole. The floor between us was littered with half-eaten, maggot-ridden carcasses of recent travellers on the way.

My heart leapt with fear. In one swift movement, I passed my keys to my left hand, picked up Astor's sword with my right, and turned to face the ogre, strong again.

The ogre lunged at me. I parried with Shartere, struggling with my conscience as well as my foe, for I had never willingly raised a weapon against another. The ogre exploited my weakness and clawed my body with many blows. The angrier I got, the deeper the wounds he inflicted. Then he scored a deep gash in my side. I dropped Shartere and fell at Zana's feet, knowing the fight to be done.

'The flower,' she urged: 'See, by your hand, Eregendal; the zana. Quickly, eat it.'

I reached out with the hand that had dropped Shartere and touched a half-eaten carcass. Its cold flesh chilled my fingers and made me turn, repulsed and sickened, to look into the ogre's looming face. His wide claws hurtled towards me.

'Quickly! Eat the flower!' Zana ordered in a voice I could not disobey.

Time stretched as my hand reached over the rotting carcass and plucked the small green flower. Fresh strength flowed from it into my limbs. I rolled over out of the path of the ogre's claws and placed the flower in my mouth.

At once, the ogre and the reed hut vanished. Zana and I stood on a crescent of grass beside the rocky river. Around us lay scattered our stolen possessions.

I sat and held my head in my shaking hands, trying to understand what had just happened. Zana sat beside me and touched my forearm.

'He couldn't really kill you. He wasn't real,' she said.

'Then what are all these wounds on my body? And what were all those corpses on the floor?' I asked.

'You hurt yourself. The angrier you got, the bigger he got.'

Her explanation confused me, because I was still too close to the fight. I stood up and gathered our stolen property, attaching my keys and Shartere to my belt and putting the diaries, coin and torch in a leather pouch. Then I lifted Zana onto my back and stirred the air with my wings.

Something worked against me. When I tried to fly up out of the gorge, I could not rise into the air. It was not my load, for the weight was relatively little. I concluded that it must have been due to my injuries. Instead, I turned and waded downstream.

Each step brought me greater feelings of doubt. Although I had managed to find Zana and retrieve our possessions, I feared my injuries would prevent me from continuing the expedition. While the flower had strengthened me, it had not healed my wounds. My side was bleeding heavily into the cold water, my wings were torn, and I struggled to find the strength to wade even as far as the place where our companions waited for us. Above us, the high walls of the gorge crowded down. Soon I believed I would not even reach its mouth. Exhausted, I sat on the riverbank. Zana dropped from my shoulders and sat nearby. I lay down helplessly in the chill sunlight.

'Your key is shining,' Zana said.

I reached and touched the second key of fellowship. My defeat dissolved through the faith and prayers of my companions. I could hear their voices and even heard some of their words. They exhorted me to get to my feet. Their persuasion forced me up from the ground. Taking Zana by the hand, I stumbled on down the gorge. Rocky waterfalls and narrow steep-sided banks no longer dismayed me, nor did the sedge and mire deter. Through the second key of fellowship and my companions' prayers, we came out of danger to safety.

Anya was waiting for us at the mouth of the gorge. She bound up my wounds and led us up the mountainside to a sheltered dip in the slope. There the others had set up camp for our arrival, forewarned by Yammas' steaming cauldron. They embraced us when we entered the camp and asked us about our ordeal. I returned their stolen treasures, which they received with great joy.

For a while I drifted off to sleep. I drifted out again to find Anya seated beside me, wiping my brow with a cool, damp cloth. She talked abou my experiences in the gorge.

'The ogre you fought was none other than Epoh himself, guarding his strange stronghold in the Gorge of Self Doubt,' she explained. 'When Zana said, "The angrier you got, the bigger he got", she understood the ogre was feeding off you and us all. The angrier and more violent you became, the more deadly he became. Eating the flower dispelled your anger and so destroyed your foe.'

'So had I fought to kill, I too would have become one of the rotting corpses on the floor,' I said, and shivered.

'You would never have been able to kill him, though he could destroy you. Your defeat of him and your escape from the gorge are remarkable, the deeds of a hero.'

'Anyone can be a hero with the shield of Zana. But now this hero – or am I fool? – is spent. I can only hinder the further travels of our expedition. Leave me here in the morning and the five of you go on without me.'

Kohtel overheard my words. He knelt beside me, his face stern.

'After what you have done for us?' he asked. 'To leave you behind now would be the deed of ungrateful fools. No, we will carry you to a safer place and stay with you there until you recover. You have proved yourself worthiest of all to be a member of this expedition. Shame on me, that I could ever have questioned whether a butterfly would pull enough weight in our quest. But enough of that. Now you should rest.'

Later, Yammas carried me across the mountainside to the broad lake which fed the river in the gorge. We encamped in a glade of trees on the bank of the lake until time had healed the wounds I had sustained on behalf of my friends. All that while I fretted, sensing their impatience to be gone, which they resisted out of respect for me.

Chapter 12
Through Other Eyes

We set off again on a fine early autumn morning when the larches were turning and the forest put on its fresh russet and amber coat. The distant snow-clad peaks called to us with a voice we could not ignore. We headed towards a mountain pass picked out by Shartere. What lay before us, Yammas would not say, warning that one should not abuse one's powers. Disappointed by this, we left him to walk behind us, not realising that foresight is not always helpful.

The lower slopes of the pass were wooded with angular wind-blown trees which reached out to clutch us when we passed, as if we were foolish children and they our fretful mothers. Higher up, the trees became so clinging that we had to fight for every step. Astor brought out Shartere to hack through their twisting branches. With each cut, the trees cried out in agony. I called for us to go back and find another route rather than cause such unexpected suffering. Kohtel ordered us to fight on regardless, saying our expedition would suffer far more by turning back than by continuing. Only through Astor's persistence did we win through, but none of us were left unmarked by it. As we camped that night in the heart of the mountains, we were all subdued, our consciences troubled by the disturbing passage through the trees.

Next day, we climbed well above the snow line to follow the pass pointed out by Shartere. We did not feel the cold but were hampered by the effects of winter. An avalanche of rocks and snow had filled the narrow valley at the top of the pass. How dispiriting was the sight of that fall after our long and strenuous climb! Our only way forward was blocked, and our only way back to seek another route was through the fighting trees.

Kohtel asked me if I could fly above the avalanche to see how large it was. I shook my head and pointed to the clouds which raced above us. He understood. Although I had healed, my ragged wings were still too weak to fly against a strong wind.

Yammas stepped forward and placed some snow in his cauldron. We gathered around to watch. I saw little in the swirling image except a view of the avalanche that blocked us. Yammas saw more. Long after the snow had boiled away, he sat staring at the space above the pot.

'What is it you have seen?' Kohtel asked him in concern.

'There is a way through the avalanche if we are prepared to work,' Yammas replied distantly. 'It will be hard, and…'

'And what?' asked Astor.

Yammas did not answer. He walked in silence over to the fall and took out a handful of snow from beneath a long horizontal stone.

THE EAGLE AND THE BUTTERFLY

'This is where we begin,' he said, and dug with both hands into the wall of snow which loomed over fifty feet above our heads.

'But if we disturb the fall, it could slip again and engulf us all in rocks and snow,' Kohtel objected.

Yammas ignored him and continued digging. I joined him and dug with bare hands at that part of the snow face Yammas showed me. One by one, the others stepped forward to help too.

Our hard work became more light-hearted over time with snowball throwing and other games. An enthusiasm came over us reminiscent of our eager climb up Doudern Fell on the first day of our expedition, before the grey cloud came down.

My thoughts chilled. What was it Yammas had seen in that vision in the caldron's steam, which he would not tell the rest of us? I left my fears unmentioned rather than overshadow the other's raised spirits.

Working together as a team, we made good progress. Soon we had tunnelled several feet into the fall, with Astor, Yammas and Kohtel digging while Anya, Zana and I cleared the snow from behind them to keep their way out clear.

A shout from Yammas made us stop. He had uncovered an edge of blue slate he recognised from the vision in the steam. With a tense sigh, he struck the snow to the right of the slate with his palm. The last of the snow fell away, leaving a rock-bordered triangle like a window looking down into the valley on the other side.

'We're through!' Anya cried.

She pushed past to be the first to run out into the valley beyond. As we followed her through, she turned back in dismay.

'But it's the same place,' she whispered: 'Exactly the same.'

I looked across the land she saw. Below her pointing finger, at the foot of the snow-choked pass, rustled the same twisting trees through which we had fought. Beyond them dropped the same green foothills to the same distant plain of black glass. A chill hand clasped its fingers around my heart.

'What is the matter?' Zana asked several times, pestering Kohtel. He turned upon her in his anger at the frustration of this new setback.

'Stop making it worse! Use your eyes, child! Can't you see?'

'Yes, I can see,' she answered, unaffected by his anger: 'This is like the place on the other side of the snow fall.'

'It IS the place on the other side of the snow fall,' he corrected.

Zana looked at us. We nodded to confirm his words.

'But where are our footsteps in the snow?' she pointed out.

We looked and saw the snow ahead of us was pristine. Not one footstep had disturbed it.

'I'm tired. Can we rest here?' Zana asked. 'Then tomorrow I can show you this is not the same.'

We bivouacked a short distance from the fall, in the shelter of a shoulder of the hillside. It was an uneasy sleep we had that night. Zana was up long before the rest of us next morning. She joined us as we discuss the route we should take that day.

'Let's go climbing,' she suggested. 'We can use Astor's rope to keep us safe.'

As we had no better suggestion, and still did not know what to do about the mirror image valley, we agreed and followed her instructions, though each of us inwardly doubted whether her idea would achieve anything. We let her go first, with Astor behind to help her, myself next, followed by Yammas and Anya, and with Kohtel last.

Zana led the way to a jagged, snow-clad cliff. After studying the rock face for a few moments, she started to climb. She chose the snow-covered patches of rock for hand and footholds. To us she appeared to hold on to nothing, and where she had trodden, she left no mark. She settled on a perch some twenty feet above and called down to Astor to follow.

He stared at the rock face in bewilderment, not knowing where to begin. She called down to him, giving directions which he struggled to follow. He muttered several prayers under his breath. Despite his doubts, he soon pulled himself onto her narrow ledge which none of us could see. She asked him to lift her up to a foothold too high for her to reach unaided. From her new perch, she shouted directions down to me.

I scaled the cliff face with my wings open in readiness for flight in case I fell, but did not need them. As patient with the others as with me, Zana called out directions we struggled to follow, until all of us gripped invisible crannies in the rock face. Slowly, we edged our way upward in order, first one moving and then another.

When Zana reached the top of the vertical climb, she cheered. Startled by the unexpected noise, Yammas lost his grip and tumbled backwards towards the pass over a hundred feet below. The rope checked his fall. He swung back and crashed against the rock face. The sudden tug pulled Anya and me off the cliff too. Horrified, I struggled to fly against the stiff wind but held my fall long enough for Astor to join Zana and secure the rope at the top of the cliff. Then Kohtel fell from the rock face too. His added weight broke my strength and down I fell.

We hung from the rope with the sheer drop below us. The rock face was just inches too far away for us to reach out and recover our holds. Astor lay down to look over the edge and assess our situation. He called out directions to help us help ourselves.

First Kohtel climbed up the rope which held us all. When he had climbed past Anya, she promptly followed. After they had both clambered up past Yammas, he followed them up. When they had all clambered over me and reached the top, I opened my wings to help my tired arms scale the rope. At the top, I collapsed into the snow and let others untie the rope around me while I rested. As Astor undid the knots, the others debated the climb and the fall.

'But there was no way up there,' Yammas said.

'Aye, there was,' Astor disagreed: 'I climbed up it, though I could not see it. Only your doubt made you fall.'

'I cannot believe there was a way up,' Yammas insisted.

'But we are here,' Kohtel said. 'Judge it by the result, Yammas, not the method.'

'It can help so much to see the way through other people's eyes as well as our own,' Anya said: 'Sometimes we may not understand their way at all. No-one can see all things as they are to others. But that does not make their way less real or their success less probable.'

'We saw the cliffs, and we thought they had not changed,' Kohtel said. 'When we saw the similar valley, we closed our minds in disappointment. Only Zana took a second look and saw the truth. Once again, trusting innocence leads us better than cautious disillusion. Zana, take the leadership from me.'

We laughed, thinking that Kohtel was joking, until we realised he was not laughing with us. He was serious: he did not feel worthy of the leadership. We turned to Zana, who was smiling in that knowing way which seemed so much older than her years.

'You are our leader, Kohtel,' she said: 'We are all friends. But we only get on together because of you. We argued when you weren't with us at the Labyrinth of Lethee. If you had not come out, we wouldn't have been friends any more. We would never have got here.'

She reached down and picked a small green flower which had struggled through the snow into the light. I saw the love in her eyes as she pressed the flower into his hands.

'I'm not a leader, Kohtel. I'm just here to learn, and I see things in a different way. A leader unites people to follow him. Then he listens to them and lets them help him lead. That's what you do. You let Anya guide us, Yammas forewarn us, Astor defend us and Eregendal serve us. And you let me walk with you and learn. These are our parts.'

Zana stopped speaking, but we understood her unspoken message. For our success, we needed to keep to our roles, not deny them through our fear or doubt, nor take on others' roles to feed our own vanity.

'It was my worldly vanity which made me lead this expedition,'

Kohtel admitted.

'Aye, when we set out,' Astor agreed: 'But then few of us were worthy of our positions at the start. Now we are. So forget this foolish talk! We have a quest to finish.'

'True, Astor. Anya, which way should we go?'

She pointed up the steep mountainside to where thick clouds hid the summit.

'There it is – The Top of the World.'

Chapter 13
The Tree of Knowledge

The last climb was grim. None of us had imagined anything so arduous, so daunting, so difficult to overcome. We strove valiantly against the elements, but our progress was very slow. The cliffs, the ice-sheeted slopes, the crevasses and snow drifts which we negotiated in white-out blizzards, hailstorms, thick fog and high winds, prevented us from travelling more than a few miles each day. It was as if the weather itself was the guardian protecting our goal from all seekers.

At night we huddled together for warmth in what small crevices we could find on featureless slopes. We chewed our few salted provisions uncooked because there was no fuel to build a fire, and Yammas would not have his cauldron sullied by food for fear of destroying its power.

Anya kept us going on that relentless part of the journey. Ever hopeful, her reassuring smiles gave us the encouragement and endurance without which we would have lain down in the snow and given up. As natives of Berren and creatures, we were strangers to the vicissitudes of winter. Normally we would have sheltered in houses, barns and holes to hibernate or to prepare for the next spring. Now we struggled on while Anya, in her azure robes, encouraged our hopeless hearts, promising an end to the clouds and the cold when the warm spring sun would once more shine down from a clear blue sky. Yet the days passed with no relief, and that distant promise faded from all eyes but hers as we toiled, despite expecting the inevitable arrival of death.

Instead, one morning we walked out of the cloud and stood, dumfounded, on the plateau summit of the mountain. We looked down on the tops of other peaks that rose in immoveable splendour from their cloud-wreathed foundations, sharp columns of snow-clad granite defying all destiny.

Ahead of us, rising majestically above the naked mountain plateau, spread an ancient and massive tree. Its vast canopy spread out over a huge web of gnarled roots. Silver and bronze leaves shimmered and dazzled in the sunlight. But brighter still was the light emanating from the centre of the bole. The branches and leaves looked like the bars of a lantern silhouetted against that brilliant light.

With cheers of victory, we ran across the rock-strewn plateau, heedless of Anya's calls for us to keep together. We soon discovered our folly. The mountain had another guardian to protect the Tree of Knowledge from all seekers.

The rocks moved towards us, barring our way. Hatred and contempt swept through our senses, forcing us to cower on the ground, afraid. I knew from the cries of my companions that they were facing the same trial, but I could not raise my head to look for them.

The rocks piled up over me, their weight pressing down and crushing my breath. I strove to grasp my keys, but two boulders pinned down my hands. Summoning all my strength, I cried aloud and dragged my hands out from under the boulders. Before they could stop me again, I grasped the five keys in my left hand.

'Fellowship!' I cried, taking up the second key.

Light exploded from the key, shattering the rocks holding me. I staggered to my feet, free. With the burning key held aloft, I crossed the plateau to my companions. Rocks cleared from my path, their negative forces unable to withstand the positive power of our belief in each other.

I quickly freed my companions, and the six of us linked arms. Together, we walked that last short stretch to the Tree. We collapsed among its roots, crying tears of exhaustion and joy. A transforming warmth flowed into our bodies from the Tree, easing our minds and calming our souls.

'Where do we look to see?' Kohtel whispered.

'Sleep, friends,' Anya replied.

We slept. In our sleep, our dreams answered the questions we had come there to understand. I saw the world lying below me, like a garden of paradise being encroached by creeping evil. A cave in the heart of the Grey Mountains concealed Tamara. She sat weaving tapestries, unaware of the jackdaws flocking around her. I also saw how I had known the answer to my question all the time. Only my blindness had forced me to go through the trials of the expedition to realise it.

'This place is like the Island of Heart's Ease,' I whispered to my sleeping companions: 'It is not what we find when we arrive here: it is the journey to this place which brings us knowledge.'

The belt around my waist blazed into light, like a newly risen midsummer sun. The five keys became like silver stars outshining the gold with their purer light. The light awoke my companions but had gone before they were conscious enough to see it through the disintegrating tissues of their dreams.

Zana rose and picked her way through the gnarled tree roots to the massive trunk. She turned her head to look across at me and said the name of the fabled eagle Ladnegere from ancient folklore. Then she turned back and touched the trunk. I watched in awe as she merged into the Tree.

Anya leapt up, her sight focused on the dark skies to the south.

'Petros!' she cried, unmindful of my steadying hand. She ran off across the rock-strewn plain, along a dark and well-worn path.

'Petros?' asked Kohtel, still half lost in his own dreams.

'Aye. She met him here before. It was to meet him again that she returned.'

'But there is no-one there.'

'And neither are we.'

I pointed in a different direction, to where Yammas was strolling along a sheep track, singing an old country song.

'Are we to break up?' Kohtel asked.

He was watching Astor, who had sheathed Shartere and was taking a stony path away from us.

'There are certain things one can only do with others, and certain things one can only do alone,' I said.

'Aye.'

Kohtel got to his feet and walked despondently away from me, taking a second well-worn track into the darkness to the west.

I looked around me, knowing no track nor path was there for me to follow, although some earlier travellers had walked a similar way. As I walked off across the plateau, something made me turn to look back. It seemed to me as if the ancient Tree of Knowledge had burst into a dazzling array of silver-green flowers against its brilliant light.

The vision vanished ere I had time to see it, and the plain was cast back into relative darkness. I walked alone into the cloud.

Chapter 14
The Return

When I emerged from the great cloud concealing the plateau of the Tree of Knowledge, I was amazed. The storms against which we had striven had stilled and a bright summer sun shone down on me. The deep snowdrifts and thick ice had melted, and all around me flowers danced in a warm breeze beside a chattering beck. The mountain sang an exultant psalm of rejoicing, and I joined in, rejoicing and praising God too.

The land welcomed me. It opened its arms out to me. No longer was it an austere battleground. Now I looked down on hills wooded with laden fruit trees, and lush green valleys. Ripened wheat and flowers coloured a distant plain.

I strolled down the mountainside mazed but happy: I had succeeded in my task and the land blessed me for that success. In joy, I tried to fly down to the distant pass, but my wings could not carry my weight. Their mending wounds had been torn open again by the rocks about the tree. Undismayed, I walked on, filling myself with bilberries when hungry and drinking water from the beck when I thirsted. Both fruit and water had never tasted more beautiful than they did that day.

A few days later, I reached the woods where we had fought the thorny trees on our way up the mountain. It was most agreeable to stay there awhile, eating fruit from the trees and sleeping in hollowed roots made comfortable with lush grass. My thoughts congratulated me on my successful endeavour and told me to rest there until my wings healed. Then they told me to stay a while longer, because time where I was had no connection with time where I was to return to, and I did not need to hurry away from a hero's welcome to a choice of deaths. Then they told me I did not need to leave at all because Berren and the dreamlands would not miss me, and I had at last found paradise.

After that decision, my time sped past in pleasure. Unaccounted days passed without event. I did not regret the wasted time and had forgotten all the causes for which I had once sacrificed my existence. Life was a carefree round of eating and sleeping, dreaming and dancing, in a balmy summer season which seemed everlasting.

Late one evening, I heard human cries coming from the path to the pass. Out of curiosity, I strolled down through the trees, interested in meeting someone because I had seen nobody since I had left the Tree.

That scene in the wood mystified me. Three wraith-like people struggled slowly up the path to the pass, striking at nothing with their swords and sticks. Fascinated, I ran on ahead to watch their progress. They seemed to fight against powerful assailants, though their blows only crashed against the trees. Yet something unseen stayed their attacks, and that unseen presence cried out in many pained voices.

The three wraiths came upon me. They battered and slashed at me with their weapons. I retaliated at such unprovoked attacks, but my defensive actions make the three even more aggressive. Sorely wounded, I fell to the ground crying out with pain. Then I must have slept, for the next thing I saw was the sunrise.

Exhausted and sore with my injuries, I stumbled to a nearby beck and plunged into its bracing waters. My relieved cries resounded about me like an echo, though no echo could have lived in that wood.

The incident shattered the illusion by which I had recently lived. My desperate fight with the three wraiths brought to mind Astor's desperate fight on behalf of our expedition, when we had travelled through the wood together so long before.

Suddenly the past came back to me: memories of a dedication, a pledge to save my lady Tamara, whatever the cost. My conscience reeled with the blow. I had betrayed my quest, my faith, my dedication: my whole existence.

I threw myself out of the beck and ran headlong through the wood into a steep valley. The valley took me through the mountains into the higher foothills. I ran on, trusting Fate to guide my feet, resting only when the sun or the moon did not light my way. After the foothills were behind me, I crossed the verdant plain of wheat and flowers. I did not ease my pace until over a week later, when I reached the edge of the black cliffs which had so challenged the expedition on our arrival at those shores.

The sea mist rolled back from the beach, shaded in the rose colours

THE EAGLE AND THE BUTTERFLY

of evening. Down in the bay floated the mist-shrouded ferry boat which had brought us there. In its stern sat five people gazing out across the ocean of cloud. As I watched, the boat drifted out of the bay towards the horizon.

'Stop!' I cried, and again, 'Stop!' but my pleas were useless, and I knew in my heart that they would be even as I spoke.

I raised my wings and tried to lift myself into the air to fly after the boat, but the wind was against me and it was all I could do to flutter safely down to the rocky beach. Bemoaning my past complacency, I knelt at the edge of the high tide and prayed for help, yet knowing that through my own fault I could expect none. The night passed without sleep, but my penance did not bring back the ferry. As dawn blazed hazily across the cliff tops, I tried to think of a way to follow on alone.

The land still called me to stay, and the wind insisted. In desperation, I clutched the third key for bravery and launched into the air. A strong headwind blew me back inland against the cliff. I fell onto the beach, landing by a cushion of sea grass. Among the grass, a ribbon of leaf-green material had caught on a delicate silver-green flowering herb. With trembling hands, I plucked the flower and wrapped its short stalk in the torn cloth. A familiar warmth and strength returned to me as I held it. I wept.

Zana had wanted me to follow after her. She had left me her amulet, trusting that in time I would. Regrets forgotten, I clutched the amulet and my fourth key of faith, and took to the sky. The strength they gave helped me make headway against the wind and leave behind the enchanted Land at the Top of the World. I swiftly followed the path of the vanished ferry boat, and by evening had left the cloud-covered island far behind.

Night greeted my continuing journey with a beautiful rose sunset and bade farewell with a golden glow all around me in the clear air. I flew in a world with no up or down, with no land or ocean beneath me and no sun or stars above. Whether I headed in the right direction I could not tell, but trusted that something guided my flight. For three days and three nights, I travelled the void before my body demanded a rest. Still, there was nothing below me to land upon. I flew on, trying to ignore my body's cries. On the eve of the fifth day, my body stiffened with exhaustion and my flight changed to a glide. As I fell into a welcome sleep, the air gently lifted me, and the breeze took me in a different direction.

I woke refreshed to find I still glided through night, another night. Below me lay a deserted country of moonlit mountains, tall and pinnacled, standing tooth-sharp bright against the sky's ebon cloak. The air aloft was unnaturally still, but some warmer currents from the valleys below gave me an upward lift. Though the mountains below stretched without visible end, I rejoiced to see land beneath me once more and trusted I would find a way across the rugged landscape to distant Berren.

The new day was heralded by a grim red sky with bars of amber cloud. Through the day, the orange sun shone down on my flight with an unpleasant warmth and the atmosphere was unnaturally close. Towards dusk, my flight took me over land which became more gentle, with rounded fells marked by the snaking fingers of endless dry-stone walls. The cloud-covered sky darkened early, rolling lower with streaks of mauve-shaded smoke. In the more sheltered valleys, the fields of ripening wheat rippled like water, glowing with an eerie brightness. The few remote farmhouses were tightly shuttered and barred, and the haystacks had been rough-thatched or sheeted and tied down. The land was preparing for a storm.

It broke without warning. A gale-force wind blew up against me and the heavens split open in a flood of rain and hailstones. Lightning danced about me with spears which stabbed too close for safety. I had to find shelter.

Weary and wet, I knocked at the door of a farmhouse, hoping the chink of light between the shutters might be a promise of welcome. A gruff voice from behind the barred door told me the stranger's knock in the middle of the night was not welcome, nor would it be anywhere in the locality. I had no success elsewhere and spent the duration of the storm sheltering in the ruins of a barn.

The wind relented with the rising of the sun, and the rain lessened. It was still no weather for butterfly wings to take to the sky, but my need to return to Halsanger forced me to travel on despite this. That day I made little distance. However, late in the afternoon I thought I recognised the land below me from some chance sighting some distant year before.

As the sky darkened, the wind dropped and the rain stopped. The atmosphere became sultry, and the land filled with a foreboding silence.

That sunset was far grimmer than the one which had gone before. Behind the heavy dust-filled clouds gleamed a sun so deeply yellow it cast the full horizon with an ill-boding ochre. Tension charged the atmosphere and the smell of death was in the stifling breeze. When the full moon rose to chase the day away, its friendly face was a sickly amber colour veiled by the choking clouds.

Below the moon lay the long ridge of a mountain I knew well. At last I had arrived back at Doudern Fell. Seeing my goal gave my flight added impetus. I strove against the quickening wind to reach the cairn with the strength of one possessed. A mile from my destination, the wind became so strong it checked my flight to a battling standstill in the air.

The name of Zoust flashed across my mind. A dart of lightning flashed across my gaze. Blinded briefly, I spiralled downwards and with panicking hands again sought the fourth key, my faith in God. As my shaking fingers grasped the key, the air around me quietened to a charmed circle of peace amid the storm-wracked skies. A moonbeam lit the cairn on Doudern Fell to guide me. When I landed there, the mountain shook beneath me. Too tired to wonder at this, I sheltered by the cairn for the night.

Chapter 15
The Red River

The wind roused me at that darkest hour of night just before the dawn when all is silent. Its moaning cry, 'Eregendal, Eregendal,' chilled my soul.

I looked down the fellside into the valley of Sluthe Wood. A large fire blazed in the distance, a short way beyond Halsanger. Something in the heart of the glow told me I should waste no more time in sleep on Doudern Fell. With wings too tired from my last flight to carry me that short distance, I set off down the mountainside on foot.

My path took me past the shepherds' hut. My beloved refuge had been ransacked. The roof had been torn off, the shutters smashed, the door ripped off its hinges and the great stack of firewood burnt to a hollow shell. Sickened to see it wrecked, I hurried on along the path and took the long way to the Tarn of Mirrors to avoid Halsanger.

Sluthe Wood was uneasy. Its trees wanted to tell me something of grave importance, but I cannot understand trees. I heard only a faint essence of their message. They seemed to bid me hurry to the cave, but not to Arzandel. This worried me.

I reached the Tarn of Mirrors by early afternoon. The cave was empty and the fire circle destroyed. The only things left of Arzandel's presence were a few scattered hearth stones, and a green jade ring which I recognised from my earlier stay. When Arzandel placed the jade ring on his toe, the Green Lady of the Tarn of Mirrors rose out of the water to take all travellers home. As the ring worked only for Arzandel, I was trapped in Berren with no way of leaving until I found him, or when I died there.

Near the cave lay a scattered pile of baggage. It comprised the

THE EAGLE AND THE BUTTERFLY

possessions the expedition had left behind on Doudern Fell for fate to look after, when I had carried my companions to the cloud ferry. The baggage looked forlorn, unwanted in the bleak clearing.

I sat disconsolately on a boulder and stared at the blackened earth where the fire had always been. Scored into the ash was a three-pointed star breaking a circle: the sign of Zoust. Enraged, I scratched out the loathed symbol with a stone and drew in its stead the plain circle of perfection: the symbol Ashleigh had taught me so much about in my disruptive youth. Invigorated by that act of protest, I took flight and arrived at dusk in Halsanger.

The town was silent but not deserted. Too much fear radiated from within the stone walls of the houses for no-one to be there. Every door I knocked stayed shut and every cry I uttered was unanswered. I returned to the ransacked marketplace and prayed for a sign.

A silver-green flower beckoned to me from a wall. I plucked the flower, wrapped it in the leaf-green ribbon and pinned it to my robe. Behind the wall stood Tamara's white mare, cropping the grass. The horse carried a saddle and her halter trailed on the ground.

Someone had summoned me to the High Castle. I picked up the halter and led the mare up the hill. After a few steps, she refused to follow and nuzzled me as if expecting to be ridden. I sat astride her. Barely had I settled in the saddle than she raced away. She cantered up the hill and across the drawbridge into the castle courtyard.

The portcullis clanged down behind us. A farm labourer hurried out of the castle keep and led the mare to her stable. He waved to me to go to the keep.

The main hall was deserted when I entered. A chill silence brooded in the empty keep. I climbed the stone staircase to Ashleigh's turret room, my feet echoing hollowly. As I opened the heavy wooden door to his inner sanctum, the silence crackled with an electrical discharge like the atmosphere in a thunderstorm.

Standing by the window where I had once stood, was Maredudd

the Wise, one of the Judges' Council. His shoulders were bowed with the weight of responsibility, and his amber silk robes were covered in dust. His brown hair was unkempt, and his strong face looked haggard.

'You are Eregendal?' he asked suspiciously, as if he trusted no-one anymore.

'Aye, though I have little proof.'

He walked up to me and took from my pin the bright silver-green flower wrapped in the torn piece of leaf green cloth.

'I need no more proof, Eregendal,' he said, and returned the posy to me. I pinned it back on my robe for safekeeping.

'I must apologise on behalf of the Council. We did not realise how important you and your mission were until it was too late.'

'The great Ashleigh taught me it is never too late.'

'Aye? That was his philosophy.'

'And here the living proof.'

'Perhaps, but philosophies must wait. There are more pressing things on my mind, and we have little time before our meeting is discovered.'

'Discovered?'

'Aye. Halsanger is at war.'

Maredudd gazed at the view for a while before continuing to speak.

'Four days ago, you left with the expedition and my protégée Zana. No sooner had you all left Halsanger, than the town was plunged into a foul cloud of smoke. Then a great storm broke. When that abated, the forces of the enemy attacked. After your comrades returned, we understood the reason why. Ashleigh is dead, Tamara is their prisoner, Zana and you had gone. Though Zana returned within the day, she had been away long enough for them to attack with force. When you did not return with her, we knew our fate was - uncertain.'

He broke off, deep in thought.

'What of Arzandel?' I asked.

'He is - dead.'

THE EAGLE AND THE BUTTERFLY

Maredudd waved to a bier on the other side of the room. I crossed the floor to look at the only man who could be my liberator.

'Nay, he is not dead: he only sleeps,' I said, and placed the jade ring on the largest toe of Arzandel's left foot.

Maredudd shook his head in sad disagreement. But I knew I was right, for according to Ashleigh, Arzandel could not die.

'What of the expedition?' I asked.

'Your comrades returned three nights ago and are hiding in a safe place. They described their journey and gave you great honour. Their one regret was that the cloud ferry would not wait another day. Zana left you her sign, knowing that one day would make all the difference. She knew then how much we needed you.'

'Needed me? For what?'

'Arzandel told us ere he er, slept; of your vow to rescue Tamara from the er, enemy. How you would come back from the Land at the Top of the World to fight er, the leader of the enemy. When you did not return with the rest of the expedition...'

He stopped short, struggling to overcome the enemy he dared not name. The silence told me of his doubts about my continued dedication to that pledge now that the one witness able to bind me to it could no longer do so.

I walked over to the window to look out across Halsanger at the raging fire beyond. There I repeated my dedication and pledged myself anew to the pursuit of my quest, in the traditional song metres of Berren.

'My lady upon the white mare,
Robed in white yourself;
With purple orchids in your flaxen hair,
And in your hand a lover's ivy wreath,
And in your eyes a look of wistful care;
Your lips marked by a sorrow worse than death.

MAGGIE SHAW

'My lady, born inspiration,
In its High Castle;
When I returned and brought your father down,
You knew I heralded fair Berren's fall;
The jackdaws took you ere we could be warned
That Halsanger now faced the Last Battle.

'My lady, held by caves and bars,
I must seek you now.
I see your proud lands ravaged by this war,
And watch in dread here at your high window
While Zoust's great army gathers from afar.
Now, only you can save us from our foes.

'My lady, trapped, who should be free,
I too am fast chained:
Their blood-soaked bonds are now thrown around me:
See how my tired wings are rent and stained.
Yet still I must fight on for what must be,
To bring you to your castle once again.'

Maredudd regarded me.
'So you knew,' he said.
'Knew what?' I asked, turning back to face him.
He shrugged his shoulders and stared away to the sleeping Arzandel.
'Wait?' he offered. His mind had fractured to hear me name Zoust.
'No!' I cried and hit Ashleigh's desk with a clenched fist: 'To wait is to descend further. To wait is to give up flying against the wind and get blown backwards. Tell me to wait and I shall go my own way.'
'And what way is that?'
'To save my Lady Tamara. To go to the stronghold of Zoust!'

The tapestries rattled; the turret room dimmed. Maredudd turned away in a trance. I saw his soul disintegrate as he walked out through the door. Though I hurried after him, the quicker I walked, the faster he strode.

Maredudd left Halsanger and walked to a stone bridge across the river that fed Doudern Lake. I watched from the bridge as he strode down the steep riverbank into the water. The smoky haze lent the eerie scene an enchanted air. His body floated and drifted with the water under the bridge towards the lake. As he slowly sank, I realised that the river flowing beneath me was red: red with blood.

Chapter 16
The Battle

I followed the red river through the fields, my heart heavy with sorrow and fear. As I walked between the hedgerows, jackdaws rustled in the branches above me. Ahead sounded the clamorous dischords of battle. The noise came from the fields close to the fire.

Choking smoke and flying dust obscured the battlefield. The terrible cries of men fighting and men dying, rent the air. Citizens of Halsanger, clad in chain mail which once had been carnival rags, wielded weapons in hands which once had raised mugs of ale. The men fought valiantly against an undefeatable foe. The enemy, soldiers of Zoust, were far better equipped in every way. When one fell mortally wounded, he rose again immortal. The battle was futile. The Halsanger volunteers were mown down with no hope of advantage. Yet more and more volunteers stepped forward to fill the places left by their fallen brothers and sisters, wresting weapons from dead hands to carry on the fight. The people of Berren at least saw some hope in defending their beliefs with their blood and even with their lives in that futile battle.

The battlefield became so choked, the fighting paused for the bodies to be dragged away into the river. Zoust's sneering troops laughed at the dead army under their feet, comparing the battle-marked corpses with their own clean fresh ranks. Had I not seen them fighting, I would not have believed that they had once raised a sword that night.

I knew I had to end the battle somehow. Surely, one of Ashleigh's books would be able to tell me how. He had kept his library of wisdom in the keep of the High Castle.

I ran back to the bridge with jackdaws gathering around me. Each step I took, they fluttered the space of a step closer. When I reached the crossroads, they moved in and blocked my way. I opened my wings to escape them. They opened their more powerful wings and crowed exultantly to each other. They had trapped me.

Alone, I had faced and won lesser battles, but now the odds were so great against me that singly I could not hope to escape. To be alone was not the strength I had always believed it to be, for being alone there had left me powerless.

'Astor!' I cried, praying that the wind would call him to my side; 'Yammas? Arzandel! Tamara. Anya, Kohtel; Zana? Where are you? Can no-one help me?'

The only replies were the mocking cries of the jackdaws and the terrible song of battle. I took up the key for bravery and placed my foot on the turning to Halsanger.

The jackdaws dived on me at once, tearing my clothes and clawing my limbs. I fought desperately to ward them off. Rough feathers, grey wings, sharp curved beaks and savage spurred claws blocked my vision and filled my eyes.

Out of the bushes stepped a winged man holding a rusty sword. He attacked the surprised jackdaws with a force so powerful, I cowered too though the power was being wielded for my aid. The jackdaws fled. The man sheathed his sword and helped me stand.

'Come, Eregendal. Let us to Halsanger. There are things for you to see,' he said, opening his broad white wings.

'Thank you, sir, for saving me. But I don't think I can fly. The jackdaws have savaged me.'

'Then I will carry you, star of my life. Even though you once refused to carry me.'

He took me up in his arms and flew to Halsanger. There he set me down in the deserted market square and raised his wings to fly off again.

'Thank you, sir, for all you've done. Please forgive me, but I do not remember you.'

'Be not ashamed. We met but once. You helped me take my first step to liberation. Much has happened since then, and I have changed. See, my wings which you untied are now stronger than your own. But my love for you is still the same. Alas, I must leave you for other battles.'

He flew up into the cloud-covered sky. I tried to follow but struggled to gain the air.

'Winged Man, at least tell me your name,' I shouted after him.

'Arken, the fallen star,' he shouted back. 'Now go! Do what you must.'

I set off up the hill to the High Castle. One of the books in Ashleigh's library there would hold the information I sought. As I grew closer, I saw the stronghold had been sacked.

The battlements had been torn down and stones from the curtain walls filled the moat. In the courtyard lay the farmhand, dead. The white mare muzzled his shoulder in the futile hope of rousing him to feed her.

I climbed over the ruined walls and ran to the turret room. Ashleigh's study had been destroyed. The bureau had been smashed and the tapestries ripped. The books of wisdom I needed to read, had been pulled apart. Their pages lay scattered over the floor, covered in footprints and excrement. Upon the ceiling the three-pointed star had been painted in blood over the silver circle which Ashleigh and I had once studied together. Now his holy sanctum lay foully profaned.

MAGGIE SHAW

In horror I fled down the spiral staircase, unmindful of the stench underfoot, and hurried out into the courtyard. The white mare looked up at me and cantered off in contempt. With no food to offer her, I raised the portcullis so that she could go out and graze on the hillside. Then I walked away down the road to Halsanger. The mare overtook me and vanished into the ditsance.

Halsanger looked deserted, but I sensed fearful people hiding behind the bolted doors and shuttered windows. I stood outside the boarded tavern in the marketplace, my mind numbed by all I had seen since my return from the expedition.

'Arken?' I called in hope.

My call echoed emptily around the square. I called again.

'Arken, Arken.'

A cry from above made me turn. Arken fell from the sky with a flaming arrow through his chest. He had been wounded in many places and was covered in blood and dust. His blunted rusty sword was strapped to his belt, broken.

'I heard your call, and came,' he whispered.

I blew out the flaming arrow and knelt beside him on the cobbles to hear his words.

'Now I journey to true Heart's Ease at last. Eregendal, why did you call me?'

'I am an outcast. Yet all I want to do is help you all and put an end to this.'

'Do you not know why you are an outcast?' he gasped.

I shook my head. He tried to explain, struggling to breathe as he spoke.

'When you did not reveal who you were to the Judges, when your deeds caused the death of your teacher, you forgot your pledge, you drove Maredudd the Wise to his death, you caused the ravaging of Berren and the fall of Halsanger Castle? And still you do not see why you are an outcast?'

'I didn't realise. My actions had far greater effects than I foresaw.'

'Aye. Your eyes are open but they are blinkered. Even Arzandel has fallen, through you. Now Berren has nothing to trust.'

'Nothing? What of Za…'

'Stop! Say nothing more that may destroy. Your friends are safe, but only if you take care.'

'Then what should I do? I must have some advice. I have to end the battle so that I can rescue my lady from the stronghold of…'

'Stop! Wherever his name is said, there will he be! Though you have strength to hear it and survive, others do not. You have destroyed so much, not knowing that.'

Arken sighed and placed his hand on the arrow wound in his chest.

'This is the message your foolish champion pays for with his life. The battle shall not end until our lady returns. So go, fulfil your pledge quickly, before you drown in the blood which lies upon your head.'

The jackdaws descended upon him and ripped out his guts, gorging themselves. I turned away in revulsion and shame. When I looked back after the last jackdaw had flown away, all they had left of the winged man were scattered bones and feathers and a broken, rusted sword.

Chapter 17
The Stronghold of Zoust

I raised my damaged wings skyward and launched into the air. A following wind lifted me up from the market square, supporting my flight. I headed west towards the distant Grey Mountains, the land of Zoust. Soon, a train of jackdaws flew about me in the air. Some formed a skein ahead to make my flight easier. They rejoiced to lead me to their master's kingdom. They even hung back when I fell behind.

We passed the Berren border into Sulien. On the far side stood the vicious teeth of the bleak, uninhabited Grey Mountains. This region of towering peaks and precipitous gorges had once supported a great nation, the Elutha. They had been famed throughout the world in myth and legend for their courage, their power, and their love of peace. But that was before the jackdaws came. Now the Elutha had dispersed across the continent. They took their light to other nations, to save them from the jackdaws and their accompanying darkness.

Dusk had become night. Night stretched on, as if dawn would never come again. Further and further led the jackdaws. Then suddenly they vanished. I landed on the edge of the foothills between Sulien and the Grey Mountains.

In front of me drifted a grim grey cloud stabbed by brief random shafts of flame. I headed into its darkness and knew from the way the evil atmosphere choked me that I was in the right place.

The cloud led me into the heart of the mountains and stopped in a steep-sided gorge. Along the bottom of the gorge ran a turgid, oily beck, stifled by its foul pollution. The viscous beck oozed from a cave in the cliff at the end of the gorge. Its putrid stench was so strong that I knew it could be the only place to start my search for my lady Tamara. I waded through the stream into the cave, resolute against the stench which turned my stomach, the clinging fingers of the tarry fluids which caught my feet to hold me back, and the acidic water which burned whatever it touched. In the blackness which surrounded me, my belt and keys did not shine. I had entered a region where even God and virtue did not go.

My first experiences of hell were not the pits of fiery brimstone which had been the picture described to me in my childhood. That bright image holds none of the malignant unknown through which I stumbled blindly in that cave in the depths of the earth. Only my experiences in the Labyrinth of Lethee helped me keep going through all hell's rigours. To swim underwater in that putrid filth to pass under a submerged cave roof, to inch a way along jagged stone passages so narrow there was barely enough space for a person to pass through, to stumble over the edge of some deep chasm and search desperately with broken wings for a place to land, to find the way blocked by slimy cliffs on which roosted strange slug-like bats that swarmed about me when I disturbed them; to struggle with no light whatsoever to show the way, with evil eyes watching all the time, with demons mocking and mobbing, and with that chill malignant atmosphere forever provoking doubt and fear in my heart.

The intense loneliness, the hopeless backtracking, the discouraging passages leading back to the same hate-filled halls: how low they brought my spirit. Each time I thought I had gone through so much oppression I could no longer feel it, some new terror descended upon me to prove me wrong. Each time I thought I had exhausted the range of evils, some new vileness leapt upon my back and bore me further down.

One time I swam upwards through a pool of miry water towards a light, only to find when I surfaced that the light was a mirage created to lure me into a pit of screaming creatures which bit and stung and deafened. Another time I heard voices, one of which sounded like Tamara's, but when I reached the place from which the voices came, a small imp stopped its impersonations to throw a spiderweb net over me. The net held me for several hours while atrocities of many foul sorts were done around and about me. Sometimes I was hunted like game, sometimes abused, sometimes left so alone that I screamed for company, only to bring the hunters down on me again.

Eventually the agony forced me to my knees to crawl like a baby along passages I must have travelled at least twice before. My hope died of ever leaving that place and I searched out a chasm where, with a cry to God asking for forgiveness, I threw myself over the edge. What foolishness! No-one can escape Hell by death. A host of demons caught me in mid-air and placed me in a deep hole whose smooth walls I could not climb. There they pelted me with offensive missiles and mocked me with challenges to escape. By my own strength, I could not escape. I was forced to do the one thing which until then I had shunned in thought, let alone deed, to bring me out of that Hell.

'Zoust, by the sign of the circle, I call you hither,' I cried, my arms raised.

The ground trembled and tore apart beneath my feet. I fell down what seemed like an endless hole into a vast cavern lit by the fiery glow of a sea of boiling magma on the far side.

'Lo! Here is the one who can fight Zoust himself!' mocked an echoing voice: 'Aye, can fight us, but not a simple hole!'

The cavern filled with mocking laughter, which reverberated around me. The laughter did not dismay me. I had been through so much I no longer had any pride to care. As nothing I stood, not alive because I could no longer feel, but not dead because I could still hear and see. Life was naught and death was naught. Evil surrounded, but still the sign of the circle kept it from eternal destruction.

'I have come for my lady Tamara,' I said.

A cloud swirled out of the fiery sea and approached the dark shore. As it touched the grey rock, a shape appeared inside which became a tall, lean man with cruel, sarcastic eyes. He wore long flowing robes of orange and grey, the same fire orange and ash grey that Tuzos the tempter had worn when we had met at Halsanger carnival.

'Here is your lady,' he declared in a voice which had the power of thunder.

Towards me walked a lady dressed in black, the twin of Tamara but not her.

'I seek the Lady Tamara, not Ydal Aramat.'

'But she is the one you seek,' called a child dressed in robes of a deep blood red. She looked like Zana.

'Aye? Then you are Anaz, for I did not travel to the Tree of Knowledge with you.'

'In the eyes of men, I am the youngest of the expedition,' Anaz replied, her tone implying that I was lower than men.

'Aye? Then what am I?' Though I asked, her opinion did not matter to me.

'You are Arzandel's puppet. See, your downfall came only when he fell asleep under my spell.'

'That was not your work. He sleeps because the spirit worlds are at war. He will re-awaken when the bloodshed is over and the shattered world needs rebuilding.'

'And to end the bloodshed, you need your lady.'

Anaz glanced at the lean man, who nodded to her.

'If you take me back to Halsanger with you, your lady will be freed to walk with us as well.'

She winked at the lean man and smiled at Aramat. Her expression was that of an old man, not a young girl.

'Get behind me, demon: I shall not be your passport for the destruction of the world!' I cried; 'Become what you are, Anaz! I see through your mask, old man, and know not to trust your promises and deeds, for I see that behind them too lie only deception and death.'

Anaz raised a defiant fist but even as she shook it, she distorted in shape. She grew thinner, taller, more bent. Her hair became white, her face wizened and haggard, her mien decrepit. She glared at me, a bitter old man.

'Think not that you have the advantage, butterfly, though you have the eyes to see,' Anaz declared, calming his cracked and feeble voice; 'For I will be born when your young goddess dies. Every day I grow younger while she grows older. The day will come when I am stronger than her.'

'Aye,' I agreed, 'But before that day comes, Hell shall inherit all the dreamlands and Heaven all the sky; and the Final Judgement will take your victory cup from your lips.'

Anaz turned on his heel and walked angrily out across the sea of magma to disappear like vapour in its fiery light. Aramat watched him leave and then turned seductively toward me.

'And how knowest thou that I am not thy lady, disguised by our great…' she began, her lips curling slightly, like a vicious dog.

I recalled our first meeting on Doudern Fell when all the members of the expedition except Zana and I were safely in the cloud ferry.

'Get behind me, wretched wolf! You cannot even say the name of Zoust without revering him. Nay, nor dare you utter my Lady Tamara's name. She is the blessing, and you the curse. She inspires people forward to creativity, where you would lead them back to destruction. She spurs people to go beyond themselves, where you would imprison them in their vices and kill them in their beds for it!'

With an animal howl, Aramat threw off her black robes, unable to bear them over her rough fur. She dropped down to balance on all fours, writhing as her body changed shape. Before I had time to leap out of the way, the wolf had thrown herself upon me, struggling to tear at my neck with her savage teeth. I fell back with her on top of me, a few small inches from the edge of the magma sea. She struggled to bring me to the brink while I fought desperately against her. The fumes of the sea threatened to asphyxiate me, and the heat felt overwhelming. As my consciousness drifted away, thunder rolled about the heavens in my subconscious and seemed to form words.

'We do not kill you now, for should you die here you would surely take a path of virtue. Rather, we will let you return having failed. Our power in man's kingdom Berren will surely bring about a different result. For one, who has suffered to no avail and gone back to face only more contempt, will quickly sing a different song, as surely as my name is Stuzo.'

With the fading of his voice, the cavern shimmered, and its walls melted. The magma sank back into the earth and sedge sprouted up where it had been. The hot stifling atmosphere was blown away by an icy breeze whose freshness chased off even the worst of the foul smells. Hell had made way for Earth.

I sank to the ground in exhaustion, unable to appreciate quite where I was or the full meaning of my ordeal, but at least intensely relieved that I was free.

Chapter 18
The Return to Halsanger

Stuzo had left me stranded in a vast bog in the foothills of the Grey Mountains, on the edge of Sulien. I was sitting on a tussock, surrounded by peat water. My wings had gone, torn from me in hell. Now I only had weak arms and legs to cross the bog to safety. My back bowed under a heavy weight which pressed down on my shoulders. My robes were stained and torn in many places. No longer was I proud Eregendal, willing to face any foe to save another who needed help. Now I was the one who needed help, but no-one was there to help me.

I looked out across the bleak landscape, seeking a way to escape the bog. The nearest foothold to my tussock was a clump of reeds beyond a foul black peaty puddle. I misjudged the power needed for the leap. My momentum forced me to carry on leaping from tussock to tussock until my foot slipped. My legs sank into the mire up to my knees, but my body lay prone across a firmer gravel bank. At once, the evil-smelling mud tugged at my feet to pull them down. I struggled against the mud in panic, which only pulled my legs further into the morass. I grasped at clumps at clumps of sedge to stop my body sinking further lest the mire swallow me up completely.

Then I remembered the keys on my belt. I let go of the sedge with one hand and clutched the third key for courage. My fear fled and my mind cleared. I used the gravel bank to support my body and inched forward slowly, dragging myself across the firm ground with my hands while keeping my legs still. After some effort, my left foot pulled free.

The mud gurgled as it relinquished part of its prize. I fought on and freed my other leg too.

The mud returned to its former repose: no trace of our battle was visible afterwards. It had marked me though, for the slimy mire coated my legs and the smell it exuded was repulsive. The accident had also made me cautious about crossing the rest of the bog. This time, I took care to plan my path. I also steadied myself before making each leap. My tactics worked. By early afternoon I reached the edge of the mire. It felt so good to be back on solid ground that I cheered my victory.

The sound of hoofbeats made me look east., Tamara's white mare galloped past, a broken halter around her neck. I wondered what had brought her riderless to the Grey Mountains and who had tried to hold her back.

The misty Sulien plain stretched east across to Doudern Fell in the far distance, with some gentle foothills between. I turned my back upon the jagged teeth of the savage Grey Mountains and stumbled joyfully down a grassy track through the hills to the plain.

Late that afternoon, I arrived on the outskirts of a small market town. I washed myself in the nearby river before daring to set foot in the cobbled streets. The wide main street ran between tall thin houses which had been built as if everybody wanted to live overlooking the marketplace. Traders bustled around me, packing away their wares after a successful day at the autumn fair.

'Sir, that stale bread you are about to throw away: could you spare a piece?' I begged: 'Kind lady, that bruised apple you cannot sell: please could this hungry traveller… Young child, that water you draw from the well: could you give me a sip?'

The townsfolk threw me out of their town. I spent the night near where I had landed, in a dry ditch below a tall dyke on the roadside.

The sound of hoofbeats woke me next dawn. I stood up in the ditch to see who rode out so early. Coming towards me was the white mare. On her back rode my beautiful lady, Tamara, clad in white.

THE EAGLE AND THE BUTTERFLY

I pulled some ivy from the dyke to fashion into a rough wreath and climbed up onto the road. Tamara saw me and halted her mare.

'Who art thou?' she asked. Her voice and face were kind.

I saw the purple orchids in her flaxen hair and glanced down at the poor crown of ivy in my hand.

'My lady Tamara, dost thou not know me now?'

'Nay!' she returned and gathered up her reins to ride on.

'Wait, my Lady. Truly I went to Zoust to free you, but I failed. At least Halsanger will live again. When you return, the battle will end and Arzandel will re-awaken.'

She looked again at me. I bowed my head, a sorry figure in defeat.

'Who art thou, traveller, to know so much?'

'I am the one who sung the song thou didst inspire, and its curse lies heavily on my soul. So don this crown: even beggars can honour thee. And go! Return to Berren and end the pointless war.'

Tamara took the ivy wreath and studied it. She turned back to me.

'I charge thee to tell me thy name. Then will I don thy crown without further word and ride back to Halsanger Castle.'

'I am the one once known as the butterfly, thy father's former pupil, Eregendal. God speed thy journey. I will follow after thee.'

Tamara donned the crown and made to speak, but her promise sealed her lips. She urged on her mare and galloped off into the distance.

I walked after her along the dusty road. No travellers passed to offer help or company, but I did not want for food. An old untended orchard provided a pleasant lunch. I walked on more content into the afternoon.

An hour before sunset, a horse-drawn cart approached me from the road ahead. It halted beside me and an Eluthan couple climbed out. They were tall and broad shouldered, with the round faces and auburn hair typical of their race. He wore an inn-keeper's apron over his burgher smock. She wore a hand-woven leaf-green shift with an intricate beaded belt.

'Eregendal?' they asked with welcoming smiles.

'Aye, that I was, though I have no wings now.'

'I am Finian, and this is my wife Beatha. Come with us. A room awaits you at our inn in Dubrai, the next town.'

'But I have no money.'

'All has been provided for by a lady on a white mare.'

Finian helped me up on to their cart and Beatha turned it about to take me to Dubrai. At their inn, they treated me with great courtesy. They set out a large meal and prepared a room for me.

After we had eaten, they sat with me by the fire and talked.

'What happened to you in the Grey Mountains, Eregendal?' Beatha asked: 'I can tell from the way you stoop that you have been through a severe ordeal.'

I ventured to tell my tale. They listened with such sympathy and encouragement that I talked far more than I had intended. They heard me without judgement and helped me understand my experiences.

'I failed in what I had set out to do,' I admitted. 'My dreams of proudly leading Tamara on her white mare back into Halsanger, saving Berren and revoking the death sentence over me, proved to be the nonsense everyone else knew it all to be. I did not enter Hell. It was just an illusion created by the demons to torture me. I did not meet Zoust: I only saw his minions: Stuzo, Aramat and Anaz. And they did not return to their true shapes because I overpowered them, only because they had no further need to keep their guises. My only joy after all this is that Tamara is now free and is going home to save Halsanger.'

Finian opened a goatskin and poured me some wine in a silver goblet. He fetched tankards of ale for Beatha and himself.

'Truly, Eregendal, we are honoured to have you in our house, what though the town mocks us for it. No matter the result: you acted in honour, and we toast you for that.'

They raised their tankards to me. I sipped the warming wine and thanked them.

THE EAGLE AND THE BUTTERFLY

'What happened to Tamara?' I asked: 'Was she able to tell you?'

'The jackdaws treated the White Lady very well, for them,' Finian said: 'They kept her in a cave that had no light, but for a white crystal in the middle of the room. During the day, this crystal was bright and at night, very dim. The crystal showed her all that happened in Berren. When you stood at the turret window and sang, she was the one who whispered the words in your heart.'

'So that was the tapestry she wove. Why did she not recognise me on the road?'

'The crystal looked out only on Berren, the land of men. She could not see into the land of Zoust.'

I looked up, startled to hear someone utter the dread name.

'Fear not, Eregendal,' said Beatha: 'Zoust has our home, but never will he have our hearts and minds. We are exiles. We have no cause to fear him because he already has the one thing dear to us beside God – our homeland.'

'We armed Sulien against his coming,' Finian said: 'Because of Sulien, he could only trouble Berren at night when it was weak. Alas, Berren was weakened too much with the taking of the White Lady and the departure of the expedition. We can do nothing now but wait and pray for the time the White Lady returns to her castle.'

'How did Tamara escape?'

'When Zana and the expedition returned to Berren, her cell could no longer hold her. Nothing can stop the White Lady when people support her cause. But she needed her horse to make the journey back from the Grey Mountains. Instead, the Judges kept the white mare for her return, and used it for foolish errands. When you freed the mare, you caused great alarm in Halsanger. No-one realised your action would be for the good of the cause.'

'So still they doubt me. What hope is there for me when I return to Halsanger?'

'None can say.'

Finian's firm voice told me he knew but would not state it.

'Then it is only as I expected,' I said.

I slept there the night and rose early next morning to be on my way. Beatha had washed and mended my torn robes while I had slept. Finian saddled a horse for me and gave me some money for the journey back to Berren.

Three days' riding later, I reached the river border between Berren and Sulien, a tributary of the river which fed the lake at the foot of Doudern Fell. On the far side spread the muddy field where days before the battle had raged. Two women drove teams of oxen to plough the blood into the soil. By the river, a mason carved an inscription on an ancient standing stone to make it a monument to those who had died.

I forded the beck and reined in my horse to speak to a woman in sackcloth who was working beside the path. She stood back from her ditching to look at me with suspicious eyes.

'Greetings. How goes it in Halsanger?' I asked.

'Fear no longer walks the streets, and the song of mourning is silenced,' she replied in a bitter voice: 'The memory lives on though. That cannot be ploughed into the ground like blood.'

'Where can I find the Lady Tamara?'

'At the grave of her father, waiting on the one they call Eregendal.'

I thanked her and cantered off around the edge of the battlefield. After crossing the bridge, I took the path to the graveyard in the shadow of Doudern Fell. There Tamara knelt, by the grave of her father. I dismounted and walked over to her.

'Thou hast returned,' she said, arising.

'Aye, and I must thank you for the help you gave me on my journey.'

'Help only to see thee dead the sooner. Come: there are things to be done in Halsanger.'

We mounted our horses and rode together to the town. In the market square sat the Judges Council, now only of eight.

'We waited on your command, Lady Tamara,' said Micheldor.

The marketplace suddenly filled with people. In their hearts was a cry for blood.

'Honoured Council of Judges, here is Eregendal!' declared Tamara: 'Ye know the facts of the case. Now let them speak for themselves.'

Chapter 19
The Judgement

Judge Micheldor the Bulldog stood up, his face and voice grave.

'Eregendal, these are the crimes with which you are charged. The first charge: that you attempted to destroy Berren; the second charge, that you caused the death of Lord Ashleigh; the third charge, that by delaying the return of the Expedition to the Land at the Top of the World, you caused the deaths of thousands more in battle. Fourthly, that you betrayed your quest in the Land of Peace after reaching the Tree of Knowledge; fifthly, that you caused the death of Judge Maredudd; sixthly, that you caused the death of Sage Arzandel; seventhly, that you caused the sacking of Halsanger Castle; eighthly, that you liberated the white mare, the property of our Lady Tamara, against the wishes of the Judges' Council; ninthly, that you caused the death of Messenger Arken; and tenthly, that you failed in your pledge to free our Lady Tamara from the stronghold of the enemy. How do you plead?'

'Sirs, though I was involved with all those events, I did not cause them all. I ask for each charge to be heard separately, that I may be given a fair hearing.'

The Judges conferred and agreed to my request.

'The first charge, that you attempted to destroy Berren. How do you plead?' asked Micheldor.

'During this stay here? I am not guilty by intent. Why has such a charge been raised against me?'

'Our two witnesses, Lord Ashleigh and Sage Arzandel, are dead through your actions. As you have removed any evidence against yourself from your earlier stay, the Council finds you guilty of…'

'Stop!' commanded a woman from behind.

The crowd turned to watch the woman approach the Council. She had wrapped herself in a rough woollen cloak with the hood pulled low to hide her face and conceal her identity.

'Let me give my evidence,' she began: 'I was…'

'Your name, Madam?' asked Hapis the bull.

'My name is of no consequence. My words are. I met the accused on Doudern Fell the day after the carnival. We walked together to the shepherds' hut. We remembered each other from the time the accused studied here. The accused had stayed in the shepherds' hut winter six years back. It was the talk of the town at the time. Ashleigh was a hard teacher at times, as we all knew. The accused struggled to learn the lesson of patience in long-suffering and hid from the world to recover alone. None of us tried to help that troubled youth. So Eregendal returned that spring with a bitter heart we had not tried to ease. It is we ourselves who destroyed our land when we did not help one with the power to destroy it. So we ourselves who should answer this charge, not the accused.'

'First charge dismissed,' said Micheldor with a yawn. 'The second charge: that the accused caused the death of Lord Ashleigh.'

'I plead guilty, because Lord Ashleigh died through the consequences of my deeds. In atonement, I have already offered myself as the black rose wreath traditionally burnt at the Castle sepulchre to represent the honour and esteem felt for him by much of the town.'

'Dishonourable thing to use as a mark of respect,' remarked Sekma the cat in disdain.

'Third charge,' Micheldor continued: 'That by delaying the return of the Expedition, the accused caused thousands more to die in battle.'

'Why bother with all this?' shouted a man in the crowd: 'Eregendal has admitted murdering Lord Ashleigh. The scoundrel knows only death awaits.'

'Aye,' agreed another: 'What's all this for? To give a bad dog a good name?'

'Murderer! Burn the traitor! Stop the hearing!' the crowd demanded, surging forward.

'Stop! Come to order!' Micheldor commanded, projecting his voice so that all could hear him: 'Respect your court, or it will not respect you.'

The crowd halted and even drew back a pace, but the people were angry, and muttering went back and forth across the square.

'Let me stand as a witness for the third and fourth charges,' declared the woman in the rough woollen cloak. 'It is true that the charm of the Land at the Top of the World enchanted Eregendal to forget the pledge, but so it does all people, for that is one of many tests to overcome. Though that delayed the return of the expedition, it was only in dream time, which is immeasurable in real time: at the most a fraction of a second. And in Eregendal's defence, the Expedition faced many setbacks which we could not have overcome without Eregendal's help. Why, we would not even have left Doudern Fell.'

'Madam, if you are implying you were a member of that expedition, show yourself.'

'If I must.'

Anya drew back her hood, unpinned her cloak, and let the garment fall to the ground. She stood, proud and tall, dressed like a princess in azure blue. The people cowered to see her in her majesty and power: everyone but Tamara and myself. Anya turned to me.

'Why it is that I should return with the expedition in ease and be greeted with great honour, but you should return only through your own efforts, to face even more suffering; I do not know, dearest Eregendal.

But after all you have done for me, I could not leave you to be hounded by this merciless pack, who have destroyed many as good and better before you.'

'But I am fated to die anyway unless my lady Tamara decides otherwise.'

'Aye, and she is as hard a master as her father was before her! But these? O Eregendal, after all you have seen and done, how can you seek an honourable verdict from this pit of vipers? To be sure, if their books of philosophic law can answer their cases, then they are worthy enough. But the truly great Judge Maredudd the Wise, died trying to help you bring Tamara back here. So in this hearing you will find only closed minds, hardened hearts, pride and hatred. Come, let us away.'

'But we must close the case,' bleated Kanum the sheep.

'If that is what you desire, certainly,' Anya agreed: 'The death of Maredudd, your fifth charge, I have dealt with. Your sixth charge: surely you know Arzandel never dies but only sleeps, and even now awakens. The seventh, the destruction of the High Castle. Tamara herself inspired that by sending her thoughts there and with them Zoust's destruction. Well can we all remember the strange song which invaded our thoughts, sung by Tamara through Eregendal. Eight, the white mare. My Lady Tamara, you would not have spanned the distance between the Grey Mountains and Berren had Eregendal not freed your mare. Nine: Arken chose to die out of his gratitude to Eregendal, whom he wanted to help when no-one else was willing. That was why he volunteered to go. And finally, that Eregendal failed to free the Lady Tamara? O hypocrites! Did you even consider trying to rescue our lady from the stronghold of Zoust? That Eregendal returned from there is miracle enough in itself!'

'How do we know that Eregendal even went there?' asked Torpeth the Sage, waving his ear horn dangerously.

'Eregendal, kneel and bare your back so that the Council can see your shoulders.'

THE EAGLE AND THE BUTTERFLY

I did as Anya commanded, carefully lifting my singlet over the painful stubs where once my proud wings had been. Anya's cool hand traced a burning circle and three-pointed star between my shoulder blades, precisely where it felt as if I carried the heavy load.

'Tamara has the same mark, and so too did Ashleigh. So too did Petros the Martyr, an ancient prophet now forgotten by Berren. Thus, Council, you make a mockery of your institution, wishing to destroy that which you could never aspire to yourselves.'

I straightened my clothes and stood up, turning to Anya.

'You were right, Anya, and I was wrong. Let us leave them to their judgements. I know I have been as true to myself, my friends and my God as ever mortal creature can be. Let us go in confidence to Ashleigh's grave, where my pyre awaits me.'

Anya and I forced our way through the angry crowd in the market square. We walked off towards the graveyard. The people followed, but at a distance: Berren still allowed a person condemned to death the privacy to make peace with God. Soon the cobbled streets became a cart track and the bordering houses gave way to fields of partly harvested oats.

'Eregendal, why do you not go down to the Tarn of Mirrors and leave now, instead of facing more suffering?'

'I live in hope that Tamara will have compassion.'

'As much as her father.'

We walked a short distance in silence.

'Arzandel will not be there, and I need his help to pass through the Tarn of Mirrors.'

'He is there.'

We walked further in silence.

'I cannot go against my word. This is the path I must take, no matter how hard it may be. In my brief stay here I have learnt much. I now know that many things can only be learnt by the hard and painful way, and I must accept that as a law of living. I know that to tread the true path, I must expect adversity and face it with bravery, as many have done before me and more will do after me. I need to accept help from others as well as give help to them. And whatever happens, if I trust in God and listen to God as I do my best, I will do God's will. All is naught in the final counting. For God alone will judge, and not by our virtues or our vices, but on our hearts and our repentance, when we strive not to make the same mistakes again.'

'But those are the messages of your keys. What of the belt from which they hang?'

'Living by the virtues of the keys: experience, patience, courage, fellowship and faith in God; I will not have lived in vain, no matter what others may see me as, and no matter how strange my journey through the world appears.'

'But to face even death?'

'Is to touch the handle of the door into the next room. And to die is to fall asleep on a winter night and awaken to a spring morning; to pass from a world of dreams into a world of realities. To die is to continue on the circle that is life, and which will eventually rise to its summit of peace, having undergone its depths of sorrow.'

We reached the graveyard. Birdsong filled the air. The birds greeted us more warmly than I had ever heard them greet the day. Their song ended with the arrival of the people of Berren.

A circle formed about Ashleigh's tomb. Tamara and Micheldor stood on either side of the funeral pyre which had been built on the grave. A weary man pushed through the circle to stand before the four of us by the pyre. His long hair and beard were whiter, his skin blacker and his purple robes were deeper than before. I ran to embrace him.

'Arzandel, you have awoken!' I cried.

'Aye, I am awake; and full sorry too. For alas, I have not got the black rose wreath. It was taken from me in the storming of my cave. And those who stormed it first were not the forces of Zoust, for he would rather that the wreath was burnt than you, Eregendal.'

THE EAGLE AND THE BUTTERFLY

'Then why did he set me free?'

'Because he knew who does have the wreath; the person who fooled him with a mask of compassion. But Inspiration is never compassionate: it can only be as kind as its father, Experience. Lo, see the woman who bears your honour wreath and would also bear your blood.'

I looked at Tamara, the lady I loved so much, and saw in her hand the black rose wreath. Before I could speak, Micheldor raised his arms and silenced the crowd.

'Citizens of Berren, the Judges Council has conferred with Lady Tamara, daughter of the great Lord Ashleigh and has agreed this verdict. The condemned Eregendal shall be burnt on the grave of the victim, Lord Ashleigh. However, knowing how dishonourable Eregendal is, we cannot use such a criminal alone as our mark of respect for the deceased. Therefore, the black rose wreath will be burnt also.'

A cheer rang out through the crowd. People jostled me towards the pyre. Micheldor watched a space before he intervened. He raised his arms again.

'People of Berren, if any of you wish to speak your last words to the condemned before the execution, do so now.'

Many stepped forward, most to spit on me or deride or curse me. But one shook my hand and thanked me for rescuing his coin from Epoh. A second placed my hand around the haft of his sword, whispering, 'Shartere is at your command.' I refused, saying, 'I choose to go this way'; a third embraced me in tears and remembered our flight with the useless books; and a fourth, short and fully hooded, gave me a small green flower. She whispered, 'Take strength. This is the way it must be. Hold fast to the end, and you will see why.'

Finally, Anya embraced and kissed me before leading me to the stake. Soldiers stepped forward to bind me, but Anya ordered them away.

'One who has suffered the torments of Hell and who chose not to break a fatal pledge, will not fail you here in courage, though you doubt the butterfly still. Let me tell you, before this day is out, you will learn the errors of your ways. Eregendal, farewell. I will await your return, and trust it will come soon.'

She kissed me again and then stepped down. Tamara placed the black rose wreath as a crown upon my head and lit the kindling at the base of the pyre.

The flames curled up around me and it became difficult to breathe. I held the flower to me, and though I felt the heat, the burns and the smoke, they did not trouble me. I recall the people staring bewildered through the flames as I smiled back at them. A stranger called out to save me, saying one with my powers should not be martyred, but Tamara and Micheldor shouted them down. Even Arzandel said no.

The choking smoke overcame me and I fell on to the burning pyre. I did not realise that I died. The last thing I saw was the sky a sheet of flaming light, and then all went dark. My senses filled with a feeling of great peace, and consciousness vanished into a void.

Chapter 20
The Vision

For a timeless aeon I drifted in a fractured world of linking and parting images, a pattern of events somehow connected with each other yet completely divorced. After an agelong moment, my senses settled once again in a countryside scene. A crowd of people had gathered in a graveyard by a lake in the shadow of a long, rounded fell. The people rejoiced around a large fire in which a corpse was burning. I settled on the branch of a tree to watch, surrounded by carolling songbirds.

People were leaving the graveyard when a shout made them turn to look back. Something moved in the ashes of the funeral pyre. As we watched, an eagle shook out its wings. It looked small, dowdy and weak at first; but as it preened its feathers it grew in strength, stature and shade. Soon, it fully deserved the honour accorded its breed.

The eagle stretched and stood upright, six feet tall with its outstretched wings spanning fifteen feet. Its feathers gleamed like the golden sun, and its talons, beak and eyes shone like the purest silver. Its majestic presence overawed the crowd: many people ran away in fear.

'Ladnegere!' cried Tamara, shading her eyes.

The eagle lifted its head to the sky and uttered a terrible yet majestic cry. Lightning split the clouds and a thunderclap rent the air. The massive stone over the door of the Castle sepulchre slid slowly open.

Terrified eyes watched as a hand gripped the lintel of the tomb. Slowly, very slowly, a man stepped out of his grave and lifted his hands to the sky. Ashleigh had risen from the dead. Six pairs of hands helped the trembling man from the tomb while Ladnegere circled overhead. The people gathered around in awe, bringing water and food and a carriage for the man. Astor helped him climb into the carriage and Yammas drove him to Halsanger, while the crowd streamed behind, talking excitedly about the miracle.

Ladnegere flew to the river mouth on the lake, by Hearts Ease Island, in the shadow of Doudern Fell. As I caught up, it gave a second mighty cry which echoed across the fell slopes and out over the plain. Before the call died, the waters of the lake rolled back to reveal its bed. Out of the mud rose the soldiers who had died in the battle, now young, handsome and fit once more; marching in a column five abreast and singing songs of victory as they took the road to Halsanger. After the last five had marched out, Ladnegere circled the lake, bringing the waters together again.

The eagle flew over to the ploughed battlefield. Here its raucous cry turned the newly carved monument back into the ancient standing stone and filled the bare field with the crop of ripening wheat it had supported before the battle.

On the eagle flew to the bridge over the river where I had watched Maredudd the Wise drown. Its call brought the Judge out from the water as if the man had never entered it.

Ladnegere flew on up to the shepherds' hut where its cry made all return to its former neat simplicity. Even the fuel pile had filled again.

The eagle flew on to the Tarn of Mirrors. There, its cry did nothing except pull on me in a distant way. It seemed as if the destruction of Arzandel's home was as the seer had averred, not the workings of Zoust or his forces.

Having spanned the countryside, Ladnegere returned to Halsanger. The eagle alighted on the tallest turret still standing in the High Castle. Here its cry raised the walls, refilled the empty moat with water, and brought the farm labourer back to life. The sanctuary keep and Ashleigh's study returned to their former order and beauty.

The eagle flew down to the crowded market square. It gave a short cry which sounded as if it was holding back some great power that could destroy as well as heal. Its gentle call brought Arken back to life. The winged man praised the eagle and gave thanks to God.

Ladnegere flew to a column beside the Judges' empty tables. It balanced with open wings on the top of the column, while the blazing sun set behind it.

Dusk brought more people out onto the streets with torches to light the square. Many people looked fearful. They were those who had not been touched by Ladnegere's power. Those whom the eagle's voice had blessed, looked up with adoring eyes. Some pointed out to tearful wives and happy children, the benefactor who had brought them back to life. The untouched people talked in near-silent whispers with their eyes fixed only on each other or the ground.

A trumpet announced the arrival of the Judges' Council. The nine Judges walked to their places at the tables and sat. Behind them stood eight cloaked watchers dressed momentarily in shadows.

Micheldor the Bulldog silenced the people to deliver a speech. As he spoke, the eagle's shadow fell upon him. He talked of the wonderful victory over the enemy and the miracles that had happened that day, as if he himself had been the one who had led the land to that victory and had brought about those healings. His words were filled with self-conceit, and although they encouraged those whose eyes studied the ground, they sickened the reawakened.

Maredudd the Wise sprang to his feet in anger. He flung up his arms to silence his chairman. As he answered back, the moon came out.

'Hasty to condemn and murder, hasty to give yourselves the victory; hasty therefore will be those who judge you,' he cried in a new and powerful voice.

Ladnegere lifted its head to the heavens and gave a raucous call. A thunderbolt smashed down upon the Council's centre table, splitting it in two. Eight jackdaws rose screaming in agony and flew off into the night towards the distant Grey Mountains. One prince judge remained, upon his head a silver crown of beech leaves.

'And you,' Maredudd cried to the crowd: 'How many of you there were who came to this table to be turned away! To you is this land given. How few of you there were who came to this table to be judged fairly and to follow that judgement: to you is this city given. How great a number of you there were who were judged preferentially but gave nothing in return for what you were given. Dishonest as foxes, like scavenging crows, hiding like snakes among the rocks when your land called you, eroding your town's foundations like rats in its rotten core, bolting your doors and windows against the luckless stranger in the night, to come out at dawn like wolves to take that which was not yours. As you have judged and acted, so let it be judged and acted upon you.'

Ladnegere cried out and brought screaming confusion to the crowd. Between the feet of the new richly dressed ran foxes, snakes, rats and wolves; and fifty crows flew into the sky, fleeing from each other and the moonlit square towards the Grey Mountains. Those left raised their arms and cheered, but Maredudd silenced them.

'The night has just begun, and the last battle is only halfway through. Because of your faith and strength, you have saved our land, though our numbers are a small third of those who lived in Berren. Now has come the time to wait and hope and pray. Only by your united trust in God's power, will God save what is yours for you.

'Messengers have by now reached the stronghold of Zoust and told him about the liberation of Berren. Soon, Zoust and his forces will cross this border to win back our weakened country. So stay with me in this square. Unite your hope with mine, while those equipped to save you go to the battlefield.'

The eight black-cloaked watchers mounted horses and galloped away from the square towards the fell. The eagle soared above them. I followed and arrived with them all at midnight on the top of Doudern Fell. When I tried to speak to them, they could not see or hear me.

The night deepened as a heavy cloud hid the face of the moon. The nine gathered at the cairn, and eight conferred while the eagle watched.

First stepped forward a man with a torch which blazed through the cloud and lit up nine shadowed strangers cloaked in light ash grey.

'Lethok, come forward!' he cried. It was the voice of the expedition leader, Kohtel.

A crowned woman stepped forward, carrying a rod of darkening. They grappled for an hour in mental battle. She tempted him with promises of power and riches. Kohtel replied describing the servant who led, the poor man who was rich, the hermit beloved of all. When her persuasions failed to tempt him, she struck him with her rod in anger. The torch flew from his grasp. Exultant, she ran to grasp the torch with her left hand. It flared up in her face. She flung it from her with a scream and turned her back on its blinding light, to melt back into the dark cloud.

Kohtel lay for a while as one dead on the moor. A gentle breeze blew up from Halsanger, carrying the prayers of the people in the town. Their hope and strength raised his spirits enough to revive him. He crawled back to the cairn.

Astor leapt forward, brandishing Shartere. He was met in physical combat by a bronze-clad woman whose feigning tricks gave her the greater blood victory. Astor fought only to defend, parrying each blow with a waning strength that faded like the torch which lit the scene. Then the breeze returned. With a shout, Astor gave a mighty blow that disarmed the warrior but broke Shartere just below the hilt. Astor reached for her sword, but it leapt from his hand and smote him through the chest. As he turned and fell at the cairn, she too melted back into the cloud.

Yammas walked onto the field, carrying only the coin in his hand. His opponent was a strange monster, the Sammay, which had once helped the jackdaws drive the Elutha from their homeland. The Sammay struck viciously at Yammas, its claws and teeth glinting darkly in the torchlight. Its long, smooth-furred body tried to circle him.

A gentle wind swept across the moor. Yammas' coin grew into a shield which protected him from the Sammay's attacks. The torch grew brighter in the wind. The Sammay screamed with anger and began to attack itself. Yammas kept herding its movements with the shield until it perished by its own jaws.

The dark cloud became smaller and more intense, whereas the torch blazed brighter in the night.

Anya stepped forward to take the place of Yammas. She faced an ancient man dressed in the blazing robes of an enchanter. His incantations created a maze through which no human could find a way. In retaliation, Anya raised her hands in his face, describing a circle with her right hand and with her left the Mirror of the Hand by turning her palm towards him with her elbow as high as the fingers which guarded her face. Her counteraction made the enchanter's spells fall only on himself. He became entrapped within his own maze.

The dark cloud settled down on all and then floated back a space. It revealed Anya standing alone on the moor, a stone statue haloed by the circle her right hand had drawn.

All was quiet. Then Zoust called from the cloud that was him.

'But where is my next combatant, the one who thought to fight Zoust alone?'

It seemed as if the night suddenly chilled those left of the eight. One threw off her cloak and stepped forward.

'Eregendal is dead,' Tamara declared.

'Then who shall fight this other self instead?'

Arzandel stepped forward into the centre of the field.

'It was Tamara who killed Eregendal, fulfilling the ancients' prophecy, "From the funeral pyre of one shall come forth two: one but reawakening, the other newborn of the martyr's ashes".'

Ashleigh plodded forward. He looked as if he had already fought his battle. His appearance brought only scorn from Zoust.

'Why do three offer themselves with whom I am done? Where is the newborn? Ah, but such a babe must be too young to fight!'

Ladnegere raised its wings and cried. The torch flared up to reveal its opponent, a huge and terrible dragon four times the eagle's size. The dragon was slate grey, with the sheen of polished stone; long and thin, with spines along its back, four great muscular legs armed with barbed claws, and two leathery wings. Its neck was so long that it could coil it once and still face forwards with its long, dished face. It turned its sharp ears, protruding luminous eyes and flared smoking nostrils, towards Ladnegere. With a strange monstrous bellowing, it opened its fanged mouth. Fiery breath scorched the moorland grass.

The dragon lumbered up into the air, testing its wings as if it had not flown before. Ladnegere flew up after it and mobbed it viciously with little fear of retaliation. Of the two, the dragon looked the more newly born. It was a massive reptile with all the assets of other fighting beasts put together in a way that had sacrificed speed for strength. But with each movement, the dragon became more co-ordinated and its deadly weapons more accurate.

Berren stopped. All watched the two fighters in the sky. Neither looked to have the advantage. The dragon's flames could not harm the child of fire; weighty strength was matched by swift manoeuvrability; barbed claws and sharp fangs competed with hooked talons and curved beak against two equal hides and hearts of stone and metal.

After many blows, the dragon gained a slight advantage. A stray claw had torn Ladnegere's neck and his quicksilver blood dripped onto the ground. Weakened, and with one shoulder wounded, Ladnegere backed off from the dragon, who forced him into heading for the distant Grey Mountains. The people watched them tensely, giving the blows themselves which the two creatures gave, while distance distorted in all eyes and miles were scanned unnoticed. Each yard given by Ladnegere was ceded only with great effort and a lot of time. But time itself became endless: three o'clock had tolled in Halsanger several hours before the first quarter sounded.

Halfway across Sulien, the two fighters slowed down. Their movements became tired and more erratic. Now Ladnegere ripped at the dragon's wings, now the dragon's lunge forced Ladnegere back a yard. The half hour chimed. Ladnegere rallied its strength and fought more desperately. The dragon, more confident of victory the closer to the Grey Mountains they drew, began to tease as well as battle.

Far away on Doudern Fell, Zoust became more agitated, while the last cloaked one in the Berren party radiated more confidence. As if to distract the silent one from concentration, Zoust marched about wheeling the dark cloud like a cloak around his unseen body. When the third quarter chimed, the cloud moved into the centre of the battlefield.

'And where is the greatest of you who would aspire to conquer the truly greatest?' Zoust demanded.

'The time is not yet nigh,' Arzandel replied. 'Have you no confidence in your servant who even now has reached the border between Sulien and the Grey Mountains?'

Zoust did not appear to, for he threw balls of lightning across his cloud to distract the silent figure whose will was the only strength that kept exhausted Ladnegere battling on that distant border.

As Halsanger tolled in the fourth hour, Ladnegere looked stronger again and moved more swiftly. Now the dragon slowed. Zoust gave an angry roar which shook the earth. The edge of the eastern horizon glowed a dim pink with the first light of the coming dawn.

The fighters on the dark western horizon became more vicious, more desperate. They danced and darted in the air with terrifying passion. Now Ladnegere's darts found their targets. The dragon shed orange blood from its leathery wings and heaving sides. The dragon laboured in its twisting and began to give way to Ladnegere. The eagle forced the dragon to circle the horizon, travelling faster and faster with the strengthening light. On the first quarter, they had spanned a sixth of the horizon; on the second, they neared the half.

The circle of the sun rose from behind the purple-coloured mountains. It haloed the winged fighters in gold so blindingly that all but one averted their eyes. Zoust foamed and raged, but his thunder was sapped by the rising sun. Soon his cloud drifted in tattered shreds on the freshening wind.

In the short time the sun took to rise free of the land and light all but the most hidden valleys in the fells, Ladnegere had chased the dragon the rest of the way around the horizon. There in the west, above the sombre Grey Mountains, brave Ladnegere executed a brilliant feint across its adversary's eyes. The dragon twisted around and looped its neck, turned and darted its head, and strangled itself in a knot. It fell through the air and landed lifeless on the sinking Grey Mountains. Ladnegere glided tiredly back to Doudern Fell and dropped as one dead on the shining cairn.

At last the silent figure lifted the black hood and undid the cloak, dropping it to the ground. At once it seemed as if the sun itself was standing on the top of Doudern Fell. Zana called out to Zoust in a voice I thought nothing could disobey.

'Come, Zoust. My people fought yours in the depth of your night. Now it is your turn to fight, with me as your combatant, in the depth of my day.'

Zoust was far stronger than the world I knew. He took his shadows into himself and replied in a voice of low rumbling thunder.

'Nay, Zana. Even now I must leave thee before thy world takes me where I cannot face to go, the country of Ever Day.'

'Then for your flight and the staying of my hand, I claim this forfeit. I claim back all those people abducted by your servants and your jackdaws. I claim back all creatures imprisoned wrongly in your caves and jails. You will put them on the boats I send, so that I can return them to their rightful homes.'

'Aye,' Zoust agreed, willing to promise anything to save himself. He fled from the high sun towards where the last peaks of his Grey Mountains slipped below the horizon.

Zana looked around the field at her fallen champions. She asked Tamara to fetch a bowl of water, and knelt beside Kohtel. As she bathed his blooded head and wounded hand, he awoke. He leapt to his feet ready to fight on, but realised all was over.

'Where can this be? Heaven?' he asked, looking around.

Then he saw Astor lying with the sword through his chest and knelt at his side to weep for his friend.

'Aye, my trusty servant,' Zana declared. 'Now, shed no tears, for Astor lives.'

She pulled the sword from his chest and bathed his wound with fresh water brought by Tamara. Astor awoke as from a deep sleep and stared dazedly into Zana's eyes.

'My Lord' he cried, and struggled up to kneel at her feet, with Kohtel at his side.

'Rest, my defender. Sheath your sword: it will be of further use,'

Zana bade. She took the two parts of Shartere and returned them to the soldier, whole.

Zana blessed Yammas, who came out of his trance. She embraced Anya, who turned back from stone to flesh. She cleaned Ladnegere's wounds, reviving the eagle. Finally, she turned to address Tamara and Ashleigh.

'All has happened as fateful Arzandel foretold. Only make good the destruction of your misguided followers, and you are free to stay by the Tarn of Mirrors: yours shall still be the High Castle. For though experience alone is not the key to freedom, nor inspiration the only way to true enlightenment, yet still they have their parts to play. Now go!'

Tamara and Ashleigh mounted their horses and cantered off down the fellside.

Arzandel watched them go. He turned and spoke to Zana as her equal.

'Now is the time of the new heaven and the new earth.'

She nodded and smiled at him.

'Yes, Arzandel. Men say that you and I cannot touch. They say you are more lasting than I, for you were never born but came to be, and you are the older master while I am the younger.'

'Yes, Zana. Men believe many strange things.'

'They do. Arzandel, it is good that you will stay by the Tarn of Mirrors, where you have always been. Keep guiding those people on the last part of life's circle, with the Green Lady and the sky ferries. But before you return to your fire, please go to Halsanger one last time. I need your help at noon.'

Arzandel inclined his head to acknowledge her. He mounted his horse and rode off down the fellside towards the town.

Zana rode down from Doudern Fell soon after him. Anya, Kohtel, Yammas and Astor formed a guard of honour around her. Ladnegere flew above their heads, dancing in the air to please her. The people of Halsanger came up to meet them half-way, cheering their heroes. They adorned the victors with garlands of flowers and scattered petals to carpet the child-queen Zana's path. Glorious songs of wild beauty soared through the mountains' midst, and all around songbirds carolled and deer gambolled in greeting.

A wonderful feast had been set out in Halsanger market square, by joyful women and youths. Someone had wedged the broken Judges' table to make it more level. Zana took the place of honour at its centre. She brought the spring sun to the square, radiating youthful innocence, compassionate understanding and overpowering love. To her right sat Astor and to her left Anya. At the two other stone tables sat Kohtel, Yammas, Maredudd the Prince-Judge and Arken the Winged Man. Over the new order watched Ladnegere, perched upon the column. Before the three tables stood Arzandel. Around them all gathered people from Berren and beyond to witness the new ceremony.

The last to arrive before the ceremony began, were Ashleigh and Tamara. They entered the square looking chastened and went to join the crowd. Zana invited them to take the two empty places at the stone tables instead. As Ashleigh sat beside Yammas, his stern face grew younger and more gentle, softened by the light of Zana's smile. As Tamara took her place beside Arken, I saw how her beauty was but a reflection of the truer pure beauty of Zana. I realised that all my life, I had been striving to follow a lesser god.

Arzandel began the ceremony by reciting an old prophetic poem to welcome Zana. He spoke of how she had chosen to live among humans as a child, even though she was the source of all creation. He pledged the love and service of all those present, and voiced their happiness that she had now come to stay and would never leave. Then he asked her to accept their crown and become their queen.

Zana stood and replied with words from the same poem. She thanked the people for their help, their welcome, their love and their crown.

'Your home is mine: I come to stay with you, and will forever in this happy land,' she promised.

The people cheered to hear her pledge. They fell silent again as Ashleigh handed Arzandel a delicate circlet crown.

Arzandel held up the circle of white gold to frame the sun as he gave the blessing of fate. Then he placed the crown on Zana's silver-blonde hair.

A boy stepped forward from the crowd and sang a song in the ancient tongue. I had written that song myself five years before in another language. As the people chorused the refrain, 'For here with the people the daystar has come', I knew that all my past had been worthwhile, for that one moment.

The people cheered and called for more music. Arzandel raised his hands to quieten them again.

'People, not all the guests have arrived yet.'

He pointed across to the far side of the square. In rode a column of people from Sulien: the broad-faced Elutha and their friends. They brought more food and music for the feast. Then Arzandel pointed upwards to Doudern Fell, where ten pale blue sky boats rode on silver clouds.

Zana stood up to greet the latecomers.

'Here come those who were exiled for me and those who were imprisoned for me, and those who died for me,' she declared.

The people of Berren ran to welcome the visitors. Zana's smile took away all their pain and sorrow. The lines left their faces and they became young again.

Before the celebrations began, Zana had one last ceremony to perform. She called the members of the Expedition to come forward. First, she turned to Kohtel and took the torch from his hand.

'Kohtel, you brought light to the traveller and led the way. Let this torch burn always in remembrance of the people you represent, the spiritual leaders of the dreamworlds.'

She placed the burning torch on a pillar; and then turned to Astor, taking his sword Shartere.

'Astor, you defended the traveller with your sword, and only fought to protect. Let Shartere grow into a beech tree, the symbol of peace in this land, in remembrance of the people you represent, the defenders of the faiths of the dreamworlds.'

She placed the tip of Shartere's blade in the soil behind her seat. It grew up into a magnificent beech tree with silver branches and copper leaves. Then she turned to Anya and took her five diaries.

'Anya, you gave guidance to the traveller using the records you had written about your own lonely travels. Let these diaries become pillars for my new temple, in remembrance of the people you represent, the prophets of the dreamworlds.'

Zana placed the five diaries on the ground beside the beech tree. They grew into tall marble pillars. Behind them, a beautiful temple formed from a great white mist. Then Zana turned to Yammas and took from him the cauldron and the coin.

'Twice blest Yammas, you were the diligent shepherd, knowing when to follow chance and when to use foresight. Let this cauldron become a window looking out on the flocks of the dreamworlds. And let this medallion become a statue at its head, in remembrance of the people you represent, the faithful shepherds in the dreamworlds.'

She placed the cauldron in front of the centre table on the square. It changed into a marble-edged pool of clear water. At the foot of the pool she placed the coin, which grew and changed into a life-sized statue of the lamb depicted upon it.

Finally, Zana looked into the pool. I looked with her through its misting waters and saw myself sleeping in an overgrown clearing beside a tarn.

'Eregendal, you were the willing servant who suffered hell and death to do what your conscience knew was right. Though you do not yet live with us in Berren, the child born of your ashes, Ladnegere, represents you in our land. Your belt and keys have become part of our temple. Each key has opened a chapel. Each chapel is linked by the belt which now supports the dome. Here in my house, all will remember the people you represent: the believers in the dreamworlds.'

My vision moved from watching my sleeping self through the pool, and travelled into the magnificent temple. The beautiful house centred around a vast domed hall. Five chapels led out of the hall, their wrought silver gates standing open. Each chapel was decorated to show the virtue held by one of the five keys. The posts of each gate fitted into a crown of stone which supported the great dome. The crown was covered by a gold-cloth tapestry, embroidered with the portraits of many people: some famous, most not. My last view was of a small tortoiseshell butterfly, embroidered on that part of the tapestry where the dawn sun would first touch.

Chapter 21
Arzandel's Farewell

I awoke to a misty dawn which tinted Sluthe Wood grey. Although it seemed as if I had slept for many days, I knew it was only a few hours after I had come by the clearing. I lay there for a while, thinking about the experience. So much had happened in those few hours, and the events had seemed so real to me while I was taking part in them. But now they threatened to slip from my memory the way all my past had done during my endless searching. This I did not want to happen.

I felt lost and also hurt at not being allowed to stay in Berren. Others had been brought back there from death, but I had not. My conscience shamed me for these thoughts. I knew I had much to do in the dreamworld before duty could permit me to return to Zana's side.

With a sigh, I turned to look into the mist-grey waters of the Tarn of Mirrors but saw only my reflection. I thought of calling the Green

THE EAGLE AND THE BUTTERFLY

Lady but did not. My part was not to run away from my responsibilities, even though life no longer held the charm and promise which once had prevented me from hastening my journey along life's circle from the dreamworld to Berren. I told myself that life is a precious gift, not a mountain to face through a misguided sense of duty. But a man who once had a palace cannot see immediately the beauties of his cottage.

My horse was grazing nearby in the clearing. I mounted and turned his head away from the Tarn of Mirrors, back in the direction I had come along the forgotten grassy lane. The Four who followed after me would perchance have arrived at the village where I had last stayed. Talking with them would help me remember the events and understand them more.

By mid-afternoon, I arrived back at the village and found a room at the inn. After a meal, I walked through the cobbled streets asking those I met whether four strangers had passed that way. The answer to all my questions was a shake of the head.

I felt very lonely as I returned to the inn. There was little company for me there. The local people were engaged in farming talk and had no time for a tired, dishevelled traveller with troubled eyes and a warm but empty heart.

The inn keeper's daughter ate supper with me, recognising my loneliness and wishing to ease it in her good-natured way. She chatted gaily about this and that, and asked me where I had travelled from, where I was going and how long I thought to stay in the village.

'I am waiting for some friends to arrive,' I replied: 'They said they would follow after.'

'Oh, no-one ever comes here. So my father says. Mother says we are silly running an inn in a place where no-one ever comes. Hark at that wind! 'Tis a sure sign that winter's on us again. You won't be travelling far now, I'll warrant.'

'No. I hope to find a cottage somewhere and wait for winter to pass.'

'If you care to do for yourself, I know a farmer with a croft standing empty. He would be pleased to let it.'

'That would be good. I have work to do, which requires me to settle for a while. And perhaps the Four will find my trail again before the winter is out.'

So that winter, I lived in a small two-roomed croft which stood in a sheltered valley overlooking the village. By day, I assisted at the inn. During the evenings I sat beside my peat fire writing about Berren and my second visit there, while violent gales howled around the gable ends and buffeted the squat stone walls.

Writing about my experiences helped me understand them. I saw how I had had to die to self, in order to rise in glory. I saw how my reborn self was able to make good the damage I had caused in my immaturity. I saw how interwoven creative inspiration and experience are. And I saw how merciless a tyrant my false god creativity became, uncoupled from the true creativity of the author of the universe.

Though the winter was long and hard, I hardly noticed. The day I penned the last word and set down my quill, I felt great satisfaction in having written down all the tale. I celebrated by going for a walk.

Outside, the sun shone and the air felt warm. The beck was an angry torrent swollen with meltwater from the snowy fell pastures. The grass in the fields was a fresh emerald green, and newly opened leaf buds sprouted on the bare branches in the hedgerows and the trees. Spring had come at last, and in my heart too was a new season where hope and joy could flourish once again.

I stayed for a while longer, but when the first cuckoo heralded summer, my thoughts turned again to travel. The Four had not arrived there, and it seemed certain they never would. I resolved to retrace my steps of the autumn before and try to find them.

I stayed next in the large market town which served that village, living in a garret room which overlooked the theatre square. It seemed a good place to wait for the Four and ask other travellers if they had seen them. After biding there some time, I realised I would never see the Four together again. As Arzandel had said while the Song of Time danced around us at the Tarn of Mirrors, the Four were naught but illusions, people who had never come, were not coming and never would come this way. Zoust had not summoned their images: he had had to rely on voices alone to tempt me out of the charmed circle.

There comes a time when our hearts distort our memories into strange fictions, far removed from the truth of the events we think we remember. To protect ourselves from future pain, we veil the pain experienced in the past. Our images magnify into extremes without detail, where they drift like kites, based on truth but supported by nothing. No challenge is great enough to bring them down. Even when they fly before the sun and shade it from our eyes, we still let them soar. Thus did I discredit half my dreamland wanderings; or would have done had I not looked out of my high garret window.

The night-lit streets were alive with glittering coaches carrying veiled ladies. Around the half-domed theatre's entrance, a throng of people jostled to arrive for the evening performance. In the myriad of faces, one looked up at my darkened window. He stood still a moment and stared at me while the people milled around him. I gazed into his eyes and felt my body chill.

There below me stood one of the Four, in dress still the same, but oh, how he had changed. Understanding eyes had become bored, contemptuous. His once hopeful expression had turned to a belligerent sneer. Sympathetic smiling lips had become thin and cold. There stood the reason Zoust had not used his image or the images of the other three to tempt me. The dreamworld had so changed them that had they ever reached the Tarn of Mirrors, my eyes would not have recognised them. Only their voices had withstood that sad but inevitable change.

Times change, and we change too, and where we go is beyond our redirection; but we could have stood firm in our doubt and stayed true to our dedication. Now, the ashes of our friendship lay scattered in the street, trodden into the mud between the cobbles. Now Berren called me back with a stronger voice. Exhausted conscience could no longer fight against my adamant will.

I sat down at my table and opened an antique silver locket I had bought in the market that day. The trinket reminded me of Arzandel's locket. It tempted me, promising to keep alive something of that fading memory. I cupped it in my hands and gazed through the mirror into darkness.

Reeds waved by the banks of the Tarn of Mirrors, and the cold moon shone down. Three people walked up to the water's edge, where the Green Lady waited to guide them through the circle. She took their hands and led them in turn down through the water, bringing them safely to the shores where the Song of Time forever plays. Here stood Arzandel by his roaring fire, inviting the travellers to rest a while, and giving his blessing as they passed through.

The first traveller was obese and bullish, with a sour expression on his jowled face. He did not want to wait and hurried off in the first direction Arzandel described to him, towards where Halsanger had once stood. Only Doudern Lake lay there now though, I discovered as I followed the traveller to its banks. On the dark waters, shrouded in a smoky cloud, floated a fiery orange boat weighed down by unseen passengers. They had been arguing about seats and greeted the traveller with curses. Once he had climbed aboard, the boat lurched into movement, throwing all the passengers onto their seats. The boat drifted across, yet through, the lake for some time before I realised its destination was the Grey Mountains. I turned aside with a shudder and flew back to the Tarn of Mirrors.

The second traveller was also well fed, but his eyes were compassionate and his face reflective. He listened to Arzandel's directions and took the steep path which climbed Doudern Fell. By the cairn at the summit floated one of Zana's pale blue cloud ferries, wreathed in the mists of springtime dawns. I hurried forward to climb aboard too, but the man had already settled in his seat. The boat glided out of my desperate reach. It sailed across the sky to the place I knew I could not yet go. I returned to the tarn and joined Arzandel and the third traveller where they sat sipping wine beside the fire.

'You do not need to travel these lands again. You have been here before,' Arzandel told the third traveller. 'Do not tire yet, child. Your time is almost done. To give up now would be to sacrifice all your past.'

'Aye, I know. But I had to return, to sustain me in this dark hour,' said the traveller in a familiar voice.

As the thin hand lifted the frayed hood from the tired face, I looked and saw me: the gaunt, dark frame which was all that was left of my hopeless inner self. Thus, with conscious and subconscious divided, I saw the scene through two pairs of eyes and saw two different scenes. It bewildered me so much, I barely understood its meaning at first.

'Others I would send to the Tree of Knowledge, but you have already been. I can only direct you back to your home.'

The traveller glanced away to hide shaming tears.

'And this directing,' the traveller shortly asked; 'Is this your eternal work?'

'Not this alone. I also direct the paths of those in the dreamworld.'

'Then could you – call me here? Arrange it?'

'It was arranged long ago, my child. All the travels that brought you here were written in the Book of Days. You were brought without choice to the start of the events. But all the choices were yours when you faced them: then you acted alone.'

'And you control all the dreamworld in this way?'

'I could.'

'Then why all the wars, the violence, the pestilence?'

'My child, you already know that yourself. War is born of human desire. Violence is the uncontrolled release of natural emotions in people. Pestilence is born of nature. These challenges, and the many others which plague the dreamworld, are fires which prove the metal and give it new properties.'

'Aye. But Zana is omnipotent. How could she allow wars to happen in the dreamworld? Why doesn't she end them?'

'One with great power must use that power with great care. People love most truly when they love of their own free will. In seeking truest human love, God gave people complete freedom in their dreamworld. Only I stand apart from this, a dabbler in dreams from a more ancient cult. Can a person change a dream as he dreams it? Moreover, does a person want to, however bad it is, when in his mind are all the nightmares he fears he might dream instead?'

The traveller who was me whispered, 'Nay,' in vague answer and thought a while. Then came the question I was thinking.

'What of me? What will my future bring? Tell me, please, you who sit in the place where all time is one and one time is all. You can see.'

'I can, but you must discover it for yourself. Otherwise, life might become too challenging or too mundane for you to persevere to the end.'

'And what of the loss of the Four?'

'In Berren you had few friends other than the keys on your belt. You faced many of your challenges alone. You will be able to face the dreamworld alone.'

'Aye, but I am getting so tired.'

A shout from the edge of the clearing made us look up. A young woman strode across from the trees to the fire. She wore a rough wool tunic and leggings. Her olive face was framed by straight black hair.

'I understand now. I am at peace,' she declared with joy, and sat down beside Arzandel.

'You have travelled to the Tree of Knowledge? How was it?' asked the one who was me of the newcomer.

'Heaven knows. What matters that, when I can now go on at last?'

The one who was me sighed and drained the cup of wine.

'Alas, I cannot return to the Tree of Knowledge, though Anya once did. I pray that Zana will show me the right path to take. And then, one day, I will find my true friends again and come back to the land I love.'

Arzandel smiled and turned the green jade ring he wore on the largest toe of his left foot. The tarn rippled. The Green Lady rose out of the water.

'Come, my friends,' she said: 'It is time for you to return to the land of your birth. Your work here is done, and you have seen what needs to be seen. Come back with me, to those who await you at the end of the road.'

The young woman and the one who was me took the Green Lady's outstretched hands. Arzandel followed to the water's edge and took out a handful of stars from his pocket. As the travellers descended, he sprinkled the stars on the water. They glinted brightly. All too soon they faded and died.

'Fate's hardest charge is the duty of death. None can stay here long with me, for the mind's house has an insistent call: it falls without its tenant. Farewell, my butterfly. Life still holds three stars for you.'

I saw his thoughtful face in the locket mirror as my room became apparent to me again. Then I blinked and he had gone. His last words lingered in my mind, recalling memories of another time. I crossed to my window.

'Time gave me three stars,' I told the theatregoers below. Emotion forced me to stop.

Beneath my high window, a woman cut through the crowd and stood for a moment, staring up at me. I had seen her olive-skinned face before: a vision of moonlit reeds and dying stars framed her image, the young woman with whom I had just returned. She had aged by some ten years, yet had hardly changed at all.

'Time gave me three stars, which I held in this hand,' I stated.

I looked again. Her place was empty. She had gone. Hopes just raised, fled just as fast. My shoulders sagged. I sat tiredly on my windowsill.

MAGGIE SHAW

'The stars reached out and destroyed the rising sun,' I whispered, to her memory.

'Leaving you in present darkness?' she asked.

She entered my room like a sister who, though seldom seen, is always welcome.

Our eyes met. I knew at once that Arzandel had sent her in answer to my prayer. The night's dark shadows chased away as the heavy cloak of loneliness disintegrated at my feet.

'Sit, eat, my friend,' I invited, drawing out a chair for her.

She sat at my table and handed me a present, a small parcel which contained a length of gold ribbon and five uncut keys.

'I have sought you many years, Eregendal, though you knew me not,' she said. 'My name is Selene, Daughter of the Moon. All this time I have been led by a dream. I was lost. I could not find my sun. I travelled and found the Tree of Knowledge. There I slept, in its gnarled roots. A young child came to me as I looked down on the world. She wore a dress of green and silver. "Take this gift to my servant Eregendal," she commanded. I obeyed. No matter that the gift is worthless, no matter that you might not exist: I obeyed. Strange that such a dream, such a child, should so change my life.'

'No. It is more strange that others don't heed her voice. For we all hear it. But human beings have the right to choose.'

I held the ribbon to my cheek and looked up at a drawing I had once sketched, of Zana as I liked to remember her, holding out the fragile green flower which is her symbol. A distant whisper echoed in the air.

'Well done, thou good and faithful servant. Now go out into all the world in the name of God: seek justice for the poor, defend the oppressed, and set the captive free.'

THE END

About the Author

Author Maggie Shaw creates her stories from her many and varied life experiences. A teenage runaway who made good despite undiagnosed Autistic Spectrum Disorder, Maggie writes as one who has walked the walk in recovery and spiritual development. Her degrees in science, divinity and church music, and her career as a Mental Health Dietitian, give a solid framework to the exciting adventure stories she loves to tell. The Scottish hills and Lakeland fells where her grandparents farmed often feature as landscapes in her work.

She is also a church musician, composer and song writer, and many of her songs are inspired by the stories she writes.

Maggie has published three other books through the micropublishing firm Eregendal: *The Vision and Beyond* (2018), *Diviner's Nemesis I: Avenger* (2019) and *Diviner's Nemesis II – Retribution* (2020). Her music and short stories have been broadcast by Radio Carlisle, Cat Radio, and Red Shift Radio; and articles of hers have been published in the West Cumbrian Arts Co-operative magazine Raven, The Whitehaven News, Amateur Photographer, and The Crewe and Nantwich Chronicle. Online, Maggie publishes through ArtSwarm, YouTube and Sound Cloud.

Maggie lives in Cheshire with her husband Alan.

MAGGIE SHAW

The Eagle
and
The Butterfly
(abridged version)

by

Maggie Shaw

eregendal.com

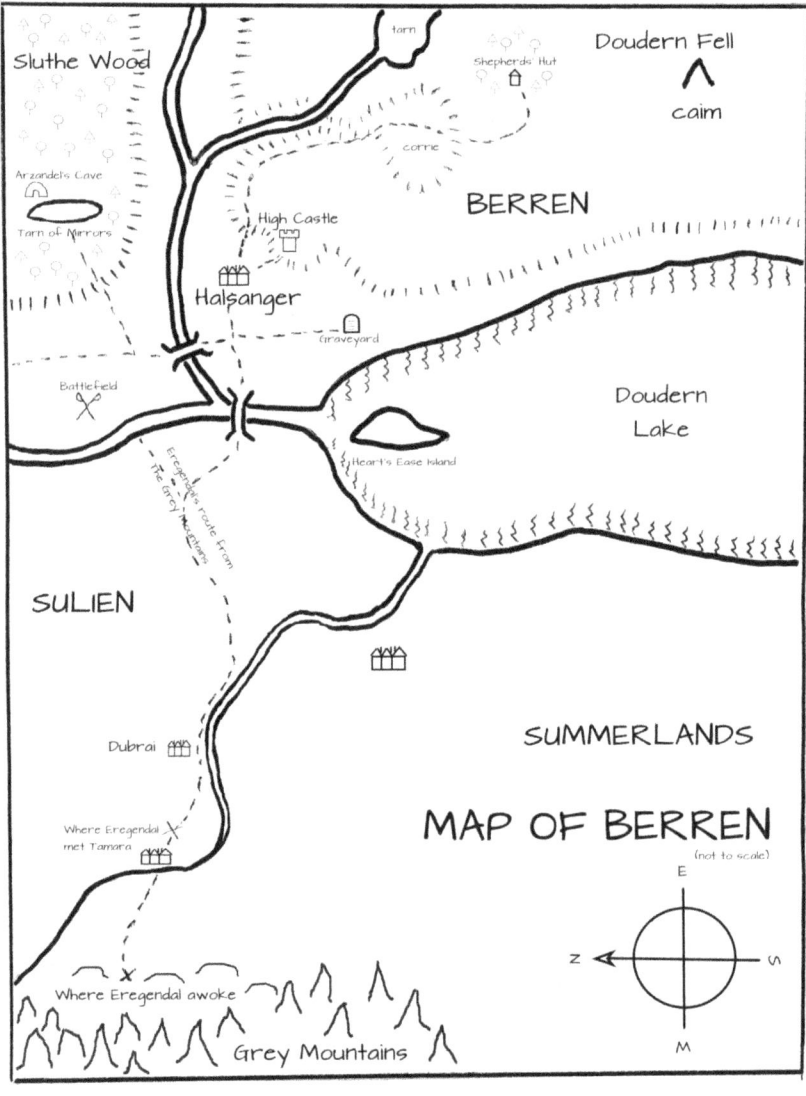

Sluthe Wood

tarn

Shepherds Hut

Doudern Fell

∧

cairn

Arzandel's Cave

Tarn of Mirrors

corrie

BERREN

High Castle

Halsanger

Graveyard

Battlefield

Doudern
Lake

Heart's Ease Island

Eregendal's route from
The Grey Mountains

SULIEN

Dubrai

SUMMERLANDS

Where Eregendal
met Tamara

MAP OF BERREN

(not to scale)

Where Eregendal awoke

Grey Mountains

Contents

Introduction and Acknowledgements

The Eagle and The Butterfly tells the story of a person who passes through a thin place into the mythical world of Berren, and becomes the butterfly Eregéndal. To atone for the past, Eregendal must face hell and death to help save Berren from Zoust and the forces of evil in the Last Battle. Eregendal's sacrifice helps the child-goddess Zana attain her throne.

This is the abridged version of the novel, with a reading age of about 9 years and up. It follows the original story but omits much of the violence and reflection. Because its themes include the battle between good and evil, and death and resurrection, some parents may not think it suitable for younger children.

The novel was written in the long hot summer of 1976, when I was twenty-one. I wrote it in two weeks, piecing the story together from a series of poems I had written over the previous few years. It is steeped in the folk lore I have always loved, and includes many symbols drawn from North European myths and legends.

As always, I would like to thank those who helped with the book in any way, including Rev. Edward Robertson and the artist Heather Bolton. Any faults in the work are mine alone.

0: The Calling

The night sky was dark and cloudless. The air tingled, as if something important was about to start. Three bright new stars shone in the constellation of the Northern Crown. The sign had appeared at last.

The old wizard Arzandel left his cave. He had a long dark face and a long white beard. He wore long purple robes trimmed with scarlet and gold.

Arzandel banked his fire with ashes. He walked down the moonlit path to the Tarn of Mirrors on the edge of Sluthe Wood. This was a thin place, where dreamworlds touch. The trees looked eerie in the moonlight. The rushes on the edge of the tarn rustled in the cool breeze.

Arzandel raised his arms over the water. In his left hand, he held his wand. In his right hand, he held a silver locket.

The rustling wind died down. A strange, haunting tune filled the air. The trees, the tarn, and distant Doudern Fell shimmered in the moonlight. A haze drifted across the water.

Arzandel opened the silver locket. The picture inside was of a small tortoiseshell butterfly. It looked so little, yet so much depended on it.

Into the haze above the water, Arzandel chanted the spell to call the butterfly home.

1: The Night Rider

It was night. I was riding my bay horse along a grassy lane through a ghostly wood. The gaunt trees reached out gnarled fingers to catch me. The leaves rustled in a chill breeze. They seemed to say, 'Go back.'

I had ridden that road since noon, looking for the inn at the centre of the wood. As I did not want to sleep in the bracken that night, I rode on by the light of my lantern.

Four friends had set out with me on a quest three years ago. Now they had stopped riding with me. I felt hurt because they had left without telling me why.

The lane led into an ancient region of the forest. Oak and sycamore mingled with the rowan, the hawthorn and the gorse. In a gap between the trees, I saw three strange glinting points of light. I dismounted and doused my lantern to look at them. Around me, the trees shimmered in the eerie light of marsh gas Will-o'-the-wisps.

I stood on the bank of a deep peaty mere. The three glinting lights were three stars, reflected in the water.

A shining green figure rose from the water, her blue-edged robes quite dry. Frightened, I knelt on the bank and bowed so low, my forehead touched the water.

'Greetings, traveller. Arise and welcome,' said the strange spectre: 'Don't you know where you now kneel?'

I stood up and stumbled back in fear, shaking my head.

'Open your eyes! This is the Tarn of Mirrors. You fled from here six years ago to ride in the dreamlands. Don't you

recognise this place or this pool?'

A veil lifted from my eyes, as if a spell had been broken. Suddenly I recognised where I was.

'The gate to Berren. At last!'

'Welcome back,' said the Green Lady: 'The land of Berren has not forgotten you.'

She took my hand in her cold fingers, to take me away from the dreamlands. We walked across the water. At the centre of the mere, we sank down into its warm, dark water and rose out on a different shore. Then she sank back into her depths, her work done.

I stood on the bank, quite dry. The glade looked like a mirror image of the place I had left. But here, a fire burned in a stone hearth, and a cave stood behind it.

An old wizard stood by the fire with his back to me. He had a long white beard, a long dark face, and long flowing robes of purple trimmed with scarlet and gold. He raised his arms. In his left hand, he held a wand.

The clouds released the moon, and the haunting song of all time filled the glade. He turned and stretched out his right arm as he set me a riddle.

'Time gave me three stars, which I held in this hand. But the stars reached out and destroyed the rising sun, leaving me with nothing.'

'Your three stars shine still: on men, Arzandel. They are the past, the present and the future. If you have nothing, how came I here?'

He smiled in welcome, but his eyes were sad. We sat

down together on the fireside stones.

'Friend, you have been away a long time. Welcome back to Berren, Eregendal. Will you stay this time?'

I shook my head.

'I cannot promise that, my friend, as you know.'

'Yes, I know how you must live, little butterfly.'

Arzandel waved his wand across the shimmering vision. As the wand finished its circle, the haunting tune turned into a joyful song. The vision became real. The song became a dawn chorus with bells ringing and music playing. A choir of angel voices sang:

'Eregendal, welcome home.'

2: The Carnival and the Letter

All morning, the wind carried music and the sounds of children's cries and women's laughter. I stood on the bank of the Tarn of Mirrors, staring at my reflection. New robes covered my human body in bright reds and yellows with brown bars. They matched the gaudy patterns of my new wings, which had just shed their pupa case. I flexed them to help them expand and dry. I longed to join the party in the town.

'Arzandel, why can't I go now?' I asked again.

'You must wait until the smell of the dreamlands wears off you, Eregendal,' he ordered. 'Come sit and eat. You may go at noon.'

I sat near him by the ashes of the fire and picked up a wooden bowl of fish and oatcakes. My thoughts were not on the food. I listened for the midday bell in the nearby town.

'Eat, or your wings won't be strong enough to reach Halsanger.'

I finished my food and went back to the tarn to stare at my reflection. My looks had changed so much overnight. The way I had looked in the dreamlands seemed just the drab underside of myself, like the underside of my butterfly wings.

At last Arzandel said, 'There's the noon bell. Now fly!'

I stirred my wings and rose into the air above the treetops. It felt so free to leave the ground behind. I waved goodbye to Arzandel and followed the music in the breeze to the carnival.

Halsanger was a quaint old town with narrow streets. Half-timbered cottages with thatched roofs stood next to stone shops and a clock tower with slate roofs. A few red brick buildings with tiled roofs stood among them. High on the hill nearby stood a stone castle with a moat around its curtain walls. Inside the walls stood a keep with four turrets.

People had come to the town from all parts of Berren. They had crowded into the cobbled market square to watch the colourful carnival parade.

I wandered happily through the crowd. A young woman with ribbons in her hair, smiled to coax me to buy from her tray of fruit. Outside the tavern, three gruff farmers supped ale and talked about the prices they had paid. A

dainty mermaid with sparkling eyes offered me her fishing net: I threw in a small coin. Around me, laughing children sang and played with the dancing clowns.

'What brought you here? Was it the music, like me?' asked a stranger, shouting to me above the noise.

'Yes. Are you from Berren?' I asked him in reply. His clothes looked like clothes from the dreamworld. They were in shades of smoky grey and fiery orange.

'Nay. I'm from beyond Sulien. I can hardly hear you.'

'I can't hear you either. Let's go to the inn.'

We opened the heavy oak door and left the bright warm sunshine. The inn was dark and welcoming. We sat at a window table where we could watch the carnival.

'My name is Tuzos, a traveller. You look like a traveller too.'

I nodded and looked at him more closely. He was about as tall as me, fat, and with laughter lines on his kindly face. On the index finger of his right hand, he wore a large signet ring. Its seal was a three-pointed star over a broken circle. My eyes kept being drawn to him.

'I am Eregendal. I am staying here for a while.'

'You are THE Eregendal? How lucky I am to have met you. What are you doing back in this town?'

'I don't know. I got here by chance just last night. Tell me about yourself, Tuzos. What made you travel here?'

He laughed.

'Ah, travel! It frees me from the boredom of the daily round. I love change. I thirst for things that are new. Weren't

you like that too, when you first stayed in Halsanger? You wanted change. You wanted everyone to take a new road.'

'Aye. And that is still true for me, but now I know it isn't right for all, just for some.'

'A philosopher still! But surely you don't admire these carnival folks! They can't see beyond today and their own needs.'

'Yes, I do. They are happy to trust their leaders. That I could never do, because I see how selfish their leaders can be. How they betray their trust!'

'You could become the Teacher in the High Castle. Then that would stop.'

I laughed.

'No, Tuzos. That's not the place for me!'

'But think of the power, the honour, the wealth.'

'What is wealth to a true philosopher? Or power? Or honour?'

'They are all important in the dreamlands you've escaped from.'

I looked sharply at Tuzos. How did he know where I had come from? I did not like the turn of his banter and became more wary.

'That is why I am so glad to be here, Tuzos.'

'But you could change things in the dreamlands too. You could go back and tell them you have seen through the vale of death and stayed in the world beyond. They would listen to that. You could travel from kingdom to kingdom preaching salvation.'

'Stop, Tuzos. There are enough false prophets without me joining them. Let me be as I am.'

Tuzos nodded and scowled. His kindly face had vanished.

'So be it, Eregendal! Enjoy yourself while you can.'

He finished his drink and stood.

'Remember what I have said, when you sit alone in your grim garret, looking out on a world that ignores you. For today you could have held that world or this in the palm of your hand, but you let the chance pass you by.'

He left. I stared at the closed door long after he had gone.

'The Carnival Queen is going by!' the landlord cried.

He threw open the tavern doors. I hurried out after him into the crowded street.

The Carnival Queen's float passed slowly through the crowds, pulled by two dappled grey percheron horses. The emerald clad Queen waved gracefully among the banners and confetti. Her long chestnut hair lifted in the gentle breeze. The crowd's happiness lifted my own spirits. When they cleared the square for dancing, I joined some of the townsfolk in an eightsome reel.

The dance ended and the dancers re-joined the crowd. A white mare crossed the square, ridden by a beautiful woman with a sad face. Though her white robes were costly, she wore a crown of purple orchids in her blonde hair. She reined in her horse and held out a gold-sealed letter to me.

'Thine elder sent thee this letter from yonder High

Castle,' she said: 'Dally here no more and spread thy wings. My dear father said, "I must speak with Eregendal".'

I took the mare's bridle and led the lady through the crowded streets. As we climbed the hill to the High Castle, I broke the gold seal and opened the letter.

'What is the meaning of this?' I asked.

'As it is writ,' she said.

I handed her the paper. Not a mark was on it.

3: The Man in the High Castle

The High Castle stood on the side of Doudern Fell and looked down upon the town. We crossed the castle drawbridge and entered the courtyard. The lady told me to go to the castle keep while she stabled her horse. I crossed the cobbled yard with dragging feet. I had been that way many times, and the last time had not been good.

The distant carnival music mocked me as I entered the tower keep. The cold stone staircase echoed my slow footsteps. I opened the door to the turret room at the top, like a fearful child expecting to be told off, but heard nothing. That silence was worse than words.

By the window sat the person who had invited me, my former teacher, Ashleigh. He was a tired old man, and his dark green robes were too large for his bent body. He nodded to me in greeting and then stared through me as if I was not there. I sat down and waited. After some time, I spoke.

'Your pupil sits here, holding your letter. But I cannot read my master's words.'

'And I, I too look but cannot see,' he replied from afar. 'Although Eregendal sits here, the real butterfly is not with me. I sit alone, waiting for my old friend. That Eregendal left Berren six years ago, thinking they had learnt all a student needs to know. They did not realise one never stops learning. You are naught but a shadow.'

'Great Ashleigh, what laid ghost do you seek? Six years have passed. I have changed from that foolish child into this lost adult. Here I am, to find myself again. Here sits your student Eregendal.'

The old man looked into my eyes. His heart spoke more plainly to me than a library of words. I sat with him as the sun set over Halsanger.

His daughter Tamara, the lady in white, called us to the dining hall below to eat. She helped her father walk down the stone staircase to the hall and sat him at the head of the table. After she had said grace, she served us with a meal of fish and oatcakes, plus bread, meat and other treats from the carnival town.

Tamara ate a morsel but then pushed her plate away.

'I maun thank thee for coming at least, Eregendal. I had not trusted thee to do so.'

I looked at her father. He sat alone at the head of the table, unaware of us and the food before him. He was lost in that maze around the Tarn of Mirrors when the Song of Time is sung.

THE EAGLE AND THE BUTTERFLY

'Aye, that is your great Ashleigh!' Tamara said. 'My father lives in the past. He has seen no present for six years, since the day thou camest back from the shepherds' hut on Doudern Fell. I had hoped thy six years in the dreamlands had mended thee, but thou art not the one he seeks. So this dark spell canna be broke. I'm sorry I brought you here. It had been better if thou hadst not come at all.'

'Forgive me, my lady. Had I but known.'

My apology drew a bitter reproach from her.

'Aye, well shouldst thou wear the mask of shame! The day thou didst leave, thou cursed this world thou'dst seen – the land that had taught thee, guided thee, nursed thee – walked away saying "Ashley the deceiver has run away and Berren is no more", when 'twas thou the deceiver who ran away, and thy vision alone which was no more.'

Ashleigh stirred. He chided his daughter with a gentle rebuke.

'Tamara, butterflies must ever flutter on. They seek those flowers where happiness still blooms. They cannot help what happens after they leave.'

'Aye, Eregendal,' Tamara said, ignoring him. 'I saw thee flitting here and there once free. I saw thee discard thy riches, choosing to be poor, renouncing our lands, and condemning my father to that same dread black night from which he'd saved thee once!'

'Is there nothing I can do to save your father now?' I asked.

'Nay! Do no more, Eregendal. Again, thou'lt flutter

away, so proud of thy gaudy wings, thou'lt see no colours less bright.'

'Hush, Tamara,' Ashleigh bade. His voice was calm, as if he had made his peace. 'Eregendal, it is no fault of yours, that you must follow your fate.'

He slowly closed his eyes and leaned back in his chair. His head dropped back with eyes and mouth open, and did not move again.

'Father! Father, where art thou!' Tamara cried.

She took him up in her arms. I reached across and touched his cold hand.

'He has travelled on to the next land in the circle, my lady. Even now he passes through the Tarn of Mirrors.'

Tamara hugged her father as if to hold back what had already gone.

'Please go, Eregendal!' she ordered me.

I stood up. Though Ashleigh had forgiven me, I took up the guilt his daughter had placed on me, instead.

'Though you think my hand is stained, my lady, it is at your service, should you ever need me,' I pledged.

I sent a servant to help her. Then I left the High Castle to fly back to Arzandel's cave.

The wizard sat as he always sat after dusk, beside his smouldering fire. He listened to the evening's drowsy hum and dreamed in the twilight warmth. The first moonbeam tiptoed over the fell to the clearing. As I sat beside him, he sighed.

'A drink?' he asked and raised an earthenware jug to

pour a golden dandelion cordial into a goblet-shaped cup.

I thanked him and sipped the sweet drink. After some time, he sighed and spoke again.

'Eregendal, I was the one who called you back to your old home. All has changed. Nothing now is as it appears to be. You have always owned the keys to true vision, but you must open your eyes to see the locks that must be turned. Yet all you do is dart here and there as the fancy takes you.'

I thought about his criticism. While it was not true for my deeds that day, it was true for my life the past six years.

'Why do I choose this path, Arzandel? Why must I act this way?'

He smiled and stirred the embers of the fire. It felt as if I had passed an unknown test.

'Eregendal, work awaits you in Berren, which was the reason for your birth. Take the wind again tomorrow. Look at what is happening to the people. You have the keys to unlock their prisons. So take up your keys and use them.'

I looked down and saw that I was wearing a dull gold belt with five silver keys. When I held the keys in my hand, they radiated a dim light like the light of the moon.

'These keys are given to you in trust, Eregendal. Don't squander them on yourself. Use them to help those that are poor.'

His words lit a new fire in my heart where the ashes of years of guilt had lain.

'I will go at dawn,' I promised.

4: The Winged Man and the Cloaked Woman

I followed the dawn breeze south next day until I saw a stranger standing all alone at the river mouth on Doudern Lake. When I landed nearby, I saw he was a winged man with his white wings taped to his sides. He was tall, slim and dark-skinned. His cream silk tunic gathered at the waist under a thick leather belt. He smiled at me and walked closer with his hands outstretched as he asked for help.

'Friend, a lift, please, over this deep wide river. On that island over there lies Heart's Ease.'

'Untape your wings. Fly yourself over the river,' I replied.

'What wings?'

I plucked out one of his long white feathers. His face told me he had felt it.

'Who taped your wings to your sides?'

'I'm not deformed. It's your eyes that cannot see!' he cried. Then he saw the feather in my fingers and dropped his head in shame.

'Others don't have wings. I was born this way,' he said.

'Sir, you have a gift. Has it not been that to you?'

He turned to look across the water at Heart's Ease Island as if he had not heard me.

'Others don't fly.'

'So you don't?'

'How could I? They taped down my wings because they

were jealous. They told me it was better for me, to live the life they live.'

'Sir, gifts are to use, no matter what others say or do.'

I untaped his wings and lifted them up until the wing tips reached into the blue sky.

'Now fly, my winged man!'

He tried to flutter his wings. They were pitifully weak with misuse. I opened out my own bright wings and took his hand.

Upwards we rose, hand in hand. The sun's golden light haloed him, and a key's silver light on my belt haloed me. Together we flew to Heart's Ease Island. He landed with a glad cry. I released his hand and hovered low.

'Eregendal! I didn't recognise you before,' he cried. 'Stay here and talk with me a while. People say you walked in darkness. On Heart's Ease Island you will find light.'

He tried to catch my hand. I drew back.

'Friend, it is not the journey's end which gives this island its name. It's the way we travel to it. I don't seek heart's ease, so I don't need to land here.'

'But I love you, Eregendal. Please don't leave me now.'

'You love me because I freed you. I freed you because of my love for all creatures. Good luck in your new life.'

I stirred my wings against the wind. He called after me as I soared upwards.

'Farewell, Eregendal. If ever you need help, call me and I will come to you. Just call my name, Arken.'

I flew off with a heavy heart. He had looked hurt when

I had refused him. I had not wanted to hurt, but to help him. Just like Ashleigh had been hard with me sometimes, so I too had been hard with Arken. Then I felt able to forgive Ashleigh. My own eyes opened a little, and I saw my dull gold belt glint faintly in the sunrise.

The whispering breeze told me to follow. It led me to Doudern Fell. I landed on a path in a bleak corrie to rest awhile and ate some bilberries growing there.

A rattling stone made me look up sometime later. Below me climbed a cloaked figure with a hooded face. The woollen winter clothes were too heavy for the warm sunny day.

'Hello, friend. Where are you going?' I asked.

'Go, gaudy stranger. You are no friend. Alone must I travel, for I am the outcast of the pack,' said the stranger, a woman. She sounded like a friend I once knew, but bitter instead of kind.

'Then you too walk to the shepherd's hut?'

'Aye. Do you also wish to stay there?'

She sounded disappointed. I fell into step beside her. Although she wore a cheap, coarse cloak, the slender wrist that held it bore three gold bangles, and four aquamarine rings glinted on her fingers.

'No, I will not stay at the hut tonight,' I said; 'But once I did stay there, that long winter before Ashleigh's fall.'

'Then you also know the pain of life, for all your gaudy silks.'

'Aye. Riches bring sadness when they are not used wisely. While we may find contentment in poverty when

little is enough.'

We walked on in silence. The steep path dropped down into a sparsely wooded gully. There stood the shepherd's hut, my past refuge from the world.

'You light a fire with fuel from the woodpile behind the hut, while I gather sticks to refill the store,' I said.

'Aye,' she agreed, and busied herself with the task.

Soon we sat snugly in the old stone hut, lit by a blazing wood fire.

'Are you Eregendal, the one known as the butterfly' she asked.

'Aye, I am. And aren't you Anya?'

She nodded and pushed back her hood. I held out my hands to her.

'Oh, joy of joys! My old friend Annie. I have missed you so much. What brings you here?'

'It will seem little to you, but it is a big thing to me.'

She undid her cloak pin and draped the cloak about her shoulders, showing a little of her sky-blue dress. Her graceful manner had not changed, but her face looked lost and sad. She tucked her long black hair behind her ears.

'I came here because I found my lessons too hard to learn,' I said. 'I thought my teacher Ashleigh was too hard. Now, I understand sometimes he had to be that way to teach me.'

'What brought you back to Halsanger after staying here that long winter?'

'Sadly, my bitterness. I went back to ruin my teacher

and change Berren. Then I fled through the Tarn of Mirrors, back into the dreamlands.'

Anya nodded.

'So you know hurt, so perhaps you will understand me. I mocked a very rich man to let others know about his evil deeds. Since then, the jackdaws have mobbed me. It was so bad, I went to the Judges' Council. They just laughed at me - I was not in their charmed circle. They said my existence was nothing, my riches were naught. So I put on the poor man's cloak and came here to stay awhile and plan my new life. First, I shall bury my wealth. Then I shall become one of the townsfolk.'

'No, Anya: that doesn't work. When riches are like thoughts, they may burn and rot, but their metal still remains. Your winter season is not here to stay.'

'What can you know of my winter when you live in summer?'

'I know that the world turns, and the tides follow their cycle, and the butterfly lives its circle. All circles travel through different planes, but when all finish, they start again. As the egg becomes the larva, which in turn becomes the pupa, out of which flies Eregendal.'

'All this is about Eregendal. Naught about Anya.'

'Nay? I know you have seen winter before. You told me once about your journey to the Tree of Knowledge, where you met a man who helped you choose the way you should take.'

'Aye, winter came then. Petros walked back into the

limelight of a well-trodden road. He didn't have the courage to follow my rugged little path. It was after that, the jackdaws began their attack. Somewhere still that great tree stands, lit by its own pure silver shadow. I would so love to return there. Perhaps, if I went back and chose a different path, I could succeed at last.'

'We can't retrace our steps, Anya, for we ourselves have changed. But maybe there is a different way, if you are willing to search for it.'

'I've spent all my life searching, and I am so tired.'

'Then come back with me to Arzandel's cave. He might show you where to start. Perhaps he can find you some help to protect you from the jackdaws and the Judges.'

Anya's face brightened She reached out and clasped my hand.

'Thank you, Eregendal, for giving me some hope. I will go, as you say, but I am too tired to travel any further tonight.'

'Take off your cloak, and I will carry you.'

She stood up against the firelight and let the cloak fall. It seemed as if daylight had entered the darkened room. Her sky-blue gown shone in brilliant splendour, and her long black hair gleamed like the star-spangled sky outside.

I tidied the shepherds' hut, ready for the next traveller. Then we flew back to the Tarn of Mirrors. I carried Anya in my arms. lit by the silver light of the key of fellowship. The twinkling belt around my waist gave me the strength I needed to get there.

Arzandel was sitting by his blazing fire waiting for us

when we arrived late that evening.

'The wind told me you were coming,' he said. 'Come, sit and eat. You both have much to do in the morning.'

We ate by the fire and slept in the bracken-strewn cave. Arzandel sat outside, like an eternal sentry, as one who never sleeps.

In the morning, a youth arrived at the tarn. He wore the tunic of a townsman and spoke very fast. He sought help to plan an expedition to the Tree of Knowledge and the Land at the Top of the World. Arzandel sent Anya off with him. When I tried to go too, Arzandel held me back.

'No yet, Eregendal. Today we have something more important to do, in Halsanger.'

5: The Funeral

Halsanger was dressed in mourning. The people who lined the streets wore dark clothes. Behind the draped bier walked those who had respected Ashleigh.

Tamara rode beside Ashleigh. A long dark blue shawl covered her white dress and blonde hair. A mantle of dark blue silk draped over her white mare. She looked at nothing but the peaceful smile of her sleeping father.

Arzandel and I led the people through the town to the burial ground. Both of us wore black. I kept my wings folded to hide their bright pattern. Arzandel wore a crown of black roses on his silver head.

The burial ground lay in the shadow of Doudern Fell, a mile from Halsanger. As we came near, we heard the people there singing a lament. Stringed viols and reed pipes played.

The Castle Tomb was an old stone building with a granite slab for a door. Ten strong men dragged the slab back to open the tomb. The people gathered around. Beyond them gathered a flock of jackdaws.

Arzandel stood in front of the dark opening and raised his hands to the grey skies. He sang prayers for Ashleigh in an old dialect. At the end of each prayer, the people bowed their heads. As they said, "God hear us", another pair of jackdaws joined the edge of the circle.

The jackdaws soon surrounded us. That worried me. I wanted to raise the alarm, but I felt too guilty to stop the service.

The escort placed the open coffin in front of the tomb. Arzandel stood on Ashleigh's left. He told the mourners about the great man's life. Then a young boy came forward, stumbling on his long black robe. He sang a song of sorrow which stabbed my heart with guilt.

I threw myself to the ground by Ashleigh's coffin to show my remorse. Then I stood up to face the people.

'In the legends of Berren, Llyrin hero of Halsanger slew his father by chance. When he realised what he had done, he threw himself of the mercy of the Judges' Council. He offered himself as the black rose wreath from the people of Berren.'

As I paused, a distant horn sounded in the tense silence.

'In the same way, I now realise the wrong I did to my

teacher Ashleigh. So as Llyrin did before me, I offer myself as the black rose wreath. For your dear teacher is dead because of what I have done.'

The shocked crowd gave a sharp intake of breath, knowing what I had just pledged to do. At that same moment, the jackdaws sprang up into flight, a black cloud against the sun. They cast a dark grey shadow over the tomb.

'My lady Tamara!' I warned, too late.

The jackdaws fell from the sky. The mourners threw themselves to the ground. The largest jackdaws grasped Tamara with their claws. Some forty of them lifted her up off her horse. I launched into the air to chase after them. At once, two dozen birds beat me down with their wings.

The distant horn piped again. The flock of jackdaws soared back into the sky with their prize. They circled the graveyard widdershins, and all flew off to the west. We watched, confused and helpless, as we struggled to our feet.

'Arzandel?' I asked, helping him to stand.

'You wove the spell, Eregendal. Only you have the key.'

He took the crown of black roses from his brow and stared at its thorns.

'You have offered yourself as the black rose wreath. You cannot go back on that.'

'Nor do I mean to. My guilt forces me to accept my fate.'

'But Eregendal, by tradition the black rose wreath is burnt on the tomb by the nearest relative, when it is resealed. Ashleigh's daughter Tamara will have to choose now, between this wreath in my hand, and you.'

Everyone around us was listening. I spoke so that all heard my reply.

'I am not afraid of death, Arzandel. It is but a journey through the Tarn of Mirrors. It is a border between one land and the next. I brought Ashleigh and Berren to this. And I knew the jackdaws were about to attack, but I didn't warn you. I must accept the consequences. So I will go rescue my lady Tamara from her captors. Then she can finish the ceremony and Ashleigh can go safely on to the next world.'

'Are you a fool?' demanded a shepherd: 'Better for you to burn alive on this tomb than be found in the jackdaws' stronghold!'

'Better to suffer true hell and pay for my wrongs, than walk the coward's path of ease.'

'Eregendal!' Arzandel called sharply to stop me before I said more. 'Go back to the Tarn of Mirrors. You can do no more here. I will talk to you when I get back.'

I threw off my black robes and flew away. I left behind a crowd of people blinded by the gleaming light of my belt and the third key.

6: In the Enchanted Circle

Arzandel came back to the Tarn of Mirrors at dusk. He lit his fire with a wave of his wand. I set out some food and drink for us both and sat beside him on a stone in the circle around the fire.

The wizard waved his wand again. The clearing shimmered around us. We travelled without moving, back through the Tarn of Mirrors to where the Song of Time sings without end.

'Do not leave the fireside circle,' he warned. 'We are in an enchantment. If you leave the circle, you will return to the dreamlands or travel on with Ashleigh through the maze of circles.'

'I shall not move. Now let us eat.'

Arzandel sipped from his earthenware goblet. He looked into the distance as if he was watching or listening for something.

'This is the safest place I can take you to, though even here is not safe from them. All time meets at once here, and each second is all time. So those from the past and the future can do the work of those we hide from in the present.'

Two large birds disturbed time's trembling music with an awkward landing on a nearby tree stump.

'Ignore them. They can't harm you, though we can hear them. Today, Eregendal, you won yourself a place in the annals of Berren. If you go now, you will avoid much pain, but you can never return.'

'Why should I go? I have a task to do: to rescue Tamara.'

'That will not be easy.'

'As I swore over Ashleigh's grave, I would rather suffer Hell than run away like a coward.'

'Is there no sense in you? To rescue Tamara, Hell is where you have to go.'

A clamour of voices struck up outside the circle. Some screamed to be saved; others plotted to destroy us. I tried to ignore the voices by thinking about the food I ate.

'Eregendal, you are weak. Butterflies can weather no storms.'

'Talk like that never won battles, Arzandel. Better you said nothing than try to persuade me to quit.'

'Then your heart is set to go?'

The clamouring outside the circle faded. Instead, I heard the Four calling from the paths of the dreamlands. They sounded desperate to find me. I leapt up to answer them. Arzandel grasped my hand and held me back.

'Don't die for shadows. They are not real.'

'But they need me. The Four: my friends who follow after me in the dreamlands; we have found each other again.'

He pulled me down beside him.

'Friend, if they were the Four, you would see them. That would have tempted you much more. Past, present and future are one here. Zoust has not summoned the Four in person, but only copied their voices. Know then, that the Four who follow after you never came, are not coming, and never will come this way.'

The news shocked me. I stared sadly at the fire and mourned the loss of my friends.

'Then I have all the more reason to rescue Tamara,' I said at length.

The voices stopped. The Song of Time filled the clearing. The sound of rippling water blended with it. The Green Lady

rose out of the Tarn of Mirrors, her clothes and hair dry.

'Come, my friend,' she whispered, her voice soothing: 'It is time for you to return to the land of your birth. Your work here is done, and you have seen what needs to be seen. Come back with me to those who await you near the end of the road.'

I looked at Arzandel, who shook his head.

'She is a wraith. Do not trust what you see,' he said.

The Green Lady multiplied until the whole black pool was hidden by green images rising out of the water and whispering their muddled invitations. When I did not obey, they each slowly sank back into the tarn, whispering until the water silenced them. Arzandel and I turned back to the fire.

'Zoust is interested in you, Eregendal. Has anything happened during your stay to tempt you away from Berren?'

'No. Except perhaps the traveller I met at Halsanger Carnival. He helped me understand things more. He showed me all the things I could be. But it didn't seem right, so I said no. As he left, he said something which sowed doubt in my mind. *Remember what I have said, when you sit alone in your grim garret, looking out on a world that ignores you. For today you could have held that world or this in the palm of your hand, but you let the chance pass you by.'*

'Why didn't you tell me about him? Had I known! But no, the wheels turn and will not stop. This traveller, what was he like?'

'Friendly, well fed, with clothes like those from the dreamlands, in grey and orange. He wore a signet ring

marked with a star breaking a circle. His name was Tuzos.'

'So Zoust saw some easy prey. It is well you did not fall for the silver tongue of his minion Tuzos. What he offered was not his to give, and he would have taken far more in return. Use faith to overcome the doubt he sowed. And take heed: you may meet up with others – Stouz and the rest.'

'Then you think Zoust fears my attack?'

'Nay. If you free Tamara, he only needs to destroy the black rose wreath to stop you. No, it is your destiny he tries to stop. Do not think that he would fear.'

'My destiny? If that is bound with Berren: good. I would like to stay here when my quest is over. Tomorrow I go to the jackdaws' stronghold. Can you tell me the way?'

The air filled with a fearful screeching. Outside the charmed circle, a hundred jackdaws dived towards us from the skies. I cowered by the fire to avoid their mobbing, even though I knew they could not touch me.

'As you are, you do not have the strength to face them on their own territory,' Arzandel shouted. 'It is better we return.'

He waved his wand. The clearing shimmered, the screeching stopped, and we were back in the peace of a tranquil night in Berren.

Arzandel brought out his heavy silver locket and opened it. He chanted a spell to the mirror inside. The reflection clouded over with a mist in fire-lit darkness. I thought the mist twisted into the shape of a woman's face for a moment. The image faded and Arzandel closed the locket.

'They do not wish us to find Tamara.'

'Then what should I do tomorrow?'

'Go to the Judges' Council. Seek their advice. If they will give it.'

7: The Judges' Counsel

I arrived at Halsanger market square shortly after dawn next day. Several people had got there before me, and many more came during the morning. I sat near three stone tables where the Judges' Council would meet.

The Judges arrived at noon with a fanfare of trumpets. They took their places with much ceremony. Four of them were like me, a curious mixture of human and beast. The Chairman, Micheldor the Bulldog, sat at the centre table. His ugly canine face looked fierce and threatening. Kanum the Sheep sat to his right, with a fleece for hair. Hapis the Bull sat to his left, front hooves firmly planted on the table. At the table next to Kanum, sat an old woman who kept knitting and two youths who played cards all afternoon. At the table by Hapis sat Sekma the Siamese Cat, human in form but cat-like in movement, Maredudd the Wise, and Torpeth the ancient Sage who used an ear horn to hear.

Micheldor chose the order they heard the cases. The judges called their friends' cases first, and they usually won. People not in that clique were heard with contempt and scorn. Only one won their case. I watched and said nothing,

though the unfairness of it all made me angry. Many people left before they had been called, put off by how the judges had heard other cases. As dusk set in, I was one of just four people left waiting.

The man whose case was heard before mine was a wealthy trader from the Summerlands. He pleaded the cause of his sister, who had lost her inheritance in marriage. As he spoke, the judges barely hid their amusement. Before he finished, Kanum bleated with laughter. When he bowed to hear their final verdict, all the other judges but one laughed too. They laughed and laughed and until he could face them no more. Outraged, he mounted his horse and galloped back to the Summerlands.

The Judges heard my case last. I stood before them, fearing how they might treat me. They looked at me with interest when I stood up and gave my name.

'State your case,' Micheldor ordered.

'Your honours, I have pledged to rescue Tamara, Lady of the High Castle, from the jackdaws. They abducted her yesterday from the funeral of her dear father, Ashleigh. I need your help to find out where the jackdaws have taken her. And I need to know quickly, for there is little time to lose if I would bring her back unharmed.'

The Judges whispered to each other. They pointed at my wings and shook their heads. Micheldor hushed the others and sneered at me.

'So you would fight jackdaws alone?'

The other Judges laughed and some clapped at his

words. They hushed when he gave their judgement.

'Go, little insect. The Council has no love of riddles. Nor will it be tested by some worthless butterfly.'

I opened my mouth to speak. Before I could say anything, the nine Judges stood up, turned their backs on me and walked off into the night. They left me standing alone in the market square. I flew back to the Tarn of Mirrors, furious.

Arzandel was sitting by the fire outside his cave. He had set out a meal for me. His long beard and hair looked even whiter against his dark skin in the firelight. I sat down beside him. He covered my pale hand with his dark fingers.

'Be brave, Eregendal. Don't give up just because the Council of Judges mocked you. This is only your first setback in a quest that will be full of them. When it is all over, the Council will come to know your worth.'

'I don't know that I want their approval. They hear only those in their own circle, and they're self-seeking and rude.'

'You do not see the full picture. It may not be clear to you, but those within their circle may have better reasons to win their cases than those who do not.'

'And what of me?'

'You are learning, Eregendal, but you have not yet learnt.'

'Then I AM just a little insect, a worthless butterfly, and all my being IS only vain riddles, and my words ARE just so much wind.'

'No, Eregendal. You are able. But you need a cause finished, you need something worth saying. Then you will

break through into the inner circle.'

'What is worth saying if "help me save my Lady" is not? Oh, how I regret wasting this day!'

'Impetuous child! Your day was not wasted. Now you have seen for yourself how much Berren has changed. And while you were away, I asked about for people to help you. Your friend Anya will come here shortly to speak with you.'

Anya joined us at the cave at midnight. She gave me a hug and sat beside me. She pushed her long, black hair from her heart-shaped face and tucked it behind her ears.

'How can I thank you for your help, Eregendal? Yet here I come seeking more, without having repaid you yet.'

'Forget repayment, Anya. Whatever you want, if it is in my power, I will do it.'

'Better hear what it is before you commit yourself. I am going on a new expedition to find the Tree of Knowledge. Kohtel is leading it: the youth who came here yesterday. Three others are also going. They asked me to be their guide as they don't know where to start. I have diaries I wrote when I went to the Tree of Knowledge before. We set off tomorrow, at dawn.'

'What a great quest! What can I do to help?'

'It's not a little thing. The first thing we must do is to fly to the top of the world. But none of us have wings.'

'How did you get there before?'

'I was walking by the cairn on Doudern Fell when a mist came down. In the mist floated a flying ship, carrying sail but unmanned. I stepped aboard and off it flew, high above the

world on an ocean of cloud. Whether I travelled north, south, east or west, I do not know. Nor do I know how far it took me, for it sailed many days. I'm sure such magic can only happen once in life, so I know the boat will not come for me again. That's why we need your help. We want you to join our expedition because we need your wings to take us the first part of the way.'

'I'm sorry, Anya,' I said, my head bowed: 'I would love to go with you to find the Tree of Knowledge. But I have a quest myself, to rescue Tamara from the jackdaws who kidnapped her at yesterday's funeral. I have wasted a day already and I still don't know where to find them.'

'What better reason for coming with us! At the Tree of Knowledge, you can look down on the world in your mind and see whatever you want to know. And you need not worry about time, for time there is apart from time here.'

I looked at Arzandel, hoping for his advice, but he said nothing. The decision was mine to make alone, and he was not free to guide me. Then I recalled he had asked Anya there to help me.

'I shall be ready at dawn,' I agreed.

8: The Expedition Sets Out

The expedition met outside the inn on Halsanger marketplace as the cocks crowed in the dawn next day. The other four members looked glad that I had joined them. We

set off in great spirits to climb Doudern Fell.

Kohtel led the expedition. He was an excitable young man of twenty with ginger hair and a hooked nose. He wore a purple jacket over his bronze silk tunic. Whenever we stopped talking, he quickly chatted about nothing to fill the air with sound. He wanted to change the system run by the Judges' Council and was going to the Tree of Knowledge to find out how.

Kohtel's right-hand man was a soldier called Astor who was about forty years old. He was a swarthy, muscular man with a clean-shaven face and cropped black hair. Over his rough wool tunic, he wore chain mail and burnished leather. His job was to protect the expedition from danger. He longed to end war and bloodshed, which had made the Judges' Council laugh. He thought the Tree of Knowledge would show him the best way to work towards world peace.

Our cook was a grizzled old shepherd called Yammas. He wore a woollen smock and leggings and a copper-coloured coat. His wise old eyes missed very little. He wanted animals and humans to live together in peace. Anya was our guide, returning to the Tree to choose a different path to the one she had chosen before. They had given me the tasks of helping with travel and finding places to camp.

The sixth member of our expedition was a nine-year-old girl called Zana. She had white blonde hair and wore a leaf-green dress. She was the last person I had expected to come with us. I waited for a chance to ask about her.

We climbed to the summit of Doudern Fell in blazing

sunshine. Below us, a murky cloud covered the Berren lowlands. That evening, we camped by the summit cairn. After our meal of fish and oatcakes, I took Kohtel to one side.

'Kohtel, why did you bring Zana on our expedition?'

'Why. Don't you like children, Eregendal?'

'No. I just fear for her safety. Why should she face the dangers of a journey to a place where only people like you and I need to go?'

Kohtel laughed.

'Why didn't you just ask straight out to be told my vision? We keep no secrets here, for we are all grey within however we look outside. All except Zana, of course.'

I apologised and sat down beside him at the campfire. When he started his tale, Yammas stopped playing his haunting reed pipe. The others moved closer to hear the story again.

'I was walking by Doudern Lake, thinking about the expedition. Suddenly, I found I was clinging to the edge of a cliff. Horrible creatures mobbed me. I cried out to God three times to save me. On the third time, a misty light appeared on my right. It grew so big, it chased the evil creatures away. Out of the light walked a silver angel. He took my hand and returned me to the lake. I awoke and found Zana smiling down at me. She said, "I am coming with you." So she came.'

'Then what are you, Zana?' I asked in awe: 'Some angel? A good magician in a changed body? A guardian spirit to guide us on our way?'

Zana smiled with eyes full of mischief, shattering my

awe. She sat by Yammas and asked him if she could play his pipe.

'No,' Kohtel answered me: 'Zana is well known in Halsanger. She walked into the marketplace about five years ago and chose to live with the good judge, Maredudd the Wise. No-one knows where she came from. They called her Zana because she looks dainty, like the little zana flowering herb. Maredudd says a sweeter child never walked.'

'And he let her go on a journey like this?'

'He said she is free to go as she came. If she wants to go, he can't stop her.'

As the others slept that night, I read one of Anya's diaries to learn which direction we should take next day. In the morning. Yammas woke the camp for breakfast.

It was still dark. Yet we all felt we had slept longer and thought the sun should be quite high. The air was so still, only our deadened voices stirred it.

'This is not good,' said Astor. 'Something already tries to stop us.'

He unsheathed his sword Shartere and cut the air with the blade. At the highest point, it gleamed like quicksilver.

'Shartere speaks,' he said, and sheathed the sword. 'This night is a spell to stop us. I can't fight it because I don't know who caused it or what they want to stop.'

'Perhaps my torch will show the way,' said Kohtel.

He took out a glazed cone of patterned china and lit the resin inside. By the light of his torch, we could see some way through the cloud. The sun was high above the long ridge of

Doudern Fell. Much of the morning had passed.

'I will fly up,' I offered, and stirred the air with my wings.

At first, I flew upwards with ease. The higher I climbed, the harder it became. I pressed on, determined to break through the cloud. At last, through the smoky fog shone the dull yellow-grey disc of the sun. I put all my strength into a final surge upwards. The cloud arced and a shaft of lightning struck me down. I fell to the earth, stunned.

Anya revived me with some smelling salts.

'What happened?' asked Kohtel: 'How deep is the cloud? What is it made of?'

'Stop, Kohtel. Let Eregendal rest a while,' Anya chided.

'Nay. We have no time for rest,' Astor warned. 'When night comes, the spell will strengthen. The cloud may stifle us.'

Zana wandered over to us, holding a zana in her hand. It was a small, dainty green flower with a silvery sheen. She offered me the bloom with childish pride.

'See: I have found one of my flowers. They are magic flowers. They grow in magic places. There are some around the cairn.'

I took it from her. My mind cleared and my bruises eased.

'This flower is indeed magic! If I held this as I flew, I would break through the spell.'

'Fly from the cairn. That will bless your flight,' Zana said.

I did as she said and climbed the cairn. Then I put my trust in the frail flower and flew upwards a second time.

Though the sulphurous cloud pressed in on me and lightning flashed past me, I flew through all unharmed and came out in bright sunshine. The noon sun gleamed on a distant object gliding towards me. It was a pastel blue boat, moving through the sky on a puff of cloud, its gauze sails unfurled. Anya's sky ferry was coming for us.

In joy, I plunged back into the yellow-grey cloud. Now it would not let me get back to the ground. I held the flower close and felt my strength return. Soon I landed a short distance away from the cairn. Zana ran over to me ahead of the others.

'What happened?' she asked.

'I made it to the other side, but only because of your flower.'

'The zana is dead.'

As the others joined us, I looked at the flower in my hand. Its stalk had withered and its petals were brown.

'Awesome power is raised against us,' Astor said.

'I won through the cloud. On the other side I saw the sky ferry Anya took before.'

'That's good news,' Kohtel said. 'Eregendal, can you carry us up to the ferry on your back?'

'One at a time, with the help of the flower, yes,' I said.

'Then let's work out an order to go,' Kohtel said. 'Astor, you go first: the ship may need defending. Yammas, you go second: then the heaviest of us have gone and Eregendal's

task gets easier.'

'Then you should go third, Kohtel, I go fourth and Zana goes last,' Anya said.

'No, I should go last as leader of the expedition.'

'You don't know how to pick the flowers,' Zana said. 'I shall go last. The flowers only come out when I call them.'

Something in Zana's voice made us agree to that.

'What about the baggage?' Yammas asked.

'We cannot ask Eregendal to make another journey just for that,' Kohtel said.

'I wouldn't have the strength. I cannot take anything except the person and vital things, like Anya's diaries. It was hard enough for me to fly alone.'

'But we must have our baggage. The tents! Our food!' Yammas protested.

'My books, our papers,' Kohtel added.

'Would you risk everything for a few worthless objects?' Astor demanded. 'When we came into this world, we had no baggage. And we will take none with us when we leave. Take only what is vital. Leave the rest to Fate.'

Kohtel and Yammas protested. Astor and I walked away and climbed the cairn. When the soldier had settled on my shoulders, Zana handed me a zana flower. I launched into the air, struggling at first with the extra weight. Then I found the best wing-beat pattern and was able to rise upwards.

Once back in the choking grey cloud, I forgot Astor. I had to hold the flower to my lips to breathe.

'What is wrong?' he asked.

'The cloud… is trying to… choke me,' I gasped.

'But I feel nothing. So this enchantment must be for you alone, Eregendal.'

'Zoust!' I spat: 'He is the one against me – Zoust!'

The skies flashed and thundered at the name.

'So that is who we fight, and for the sake of you! That devil's picked a good one! Take heart, Eregendal. I see the sun ahead.'

Lightning flashed as we came out into the sunlight. The pastel-blue ferry floated across the azure sky towards us on its couch of silver mist. Astor climbed aboard in wonder. He pressed me to join him for a rest. I refused as I still had a lot to do.

'Then good luck. And be warned,' he said. 'Do not mention your enemy's name, for wherever that is said or writ, there will he be. When you go to fetch Zana at the end, I will tell the others. It is better the child doesn't know.'

I gave him a wave and plunged back into the cloud to fetch my next passenger. My flight with Yammas was not too hard, despite the large cooking pot he insisted on wearing on his head. Kohtel's journey was not so easy. When we had risen halfway through the cloud, I could go no higher, however hard I tried.

'Kohtel… what are you carrying… that is useless?' I asked.

'Nothing. All very essential.'

'What books?'

'Some spiritual papers, a couple of political pamphlets

and a review of religions.'

'Throw them away!'

'What?'

'If you… want to… get there.'

We started to fall. Kohtel panicked and threw all his books and papers away. At once we rose upwards again. When I left him safely with Astor and Yammas, he told them about his mistake.

I felt tired when I went back to collect Anya, but took her up to the ferry without mishap. She settled in the boat, overjoyed to be riding in it again.

I turned to fly back down for the last time, feeling exhausted. The cloud wrapped around me like a warm blanket. I fell for the temptation and lay back in its support.

The cloud dropped me over a deep gorge. I hurtled down between jagged rocks. Panic flooded my dull mind and my stiff wings could not obey my desperate commands. I cried to the zana in my hand to save me. A restricting band broke from my wings, letting me fly again. The flower crumbled into dust.

I got back to the cairn to find Zana had gone. When I called her name, I heard a distant cry for help.

Zana stood with her back to a tall standing stone, about a mile away from the cairn. A black-cloaked woman was coaxing her to go with her. I called out. The woman spun round to face me. It was Tamara.

'My Lady!' I cried and ran towards her.

'Stop, Eregendal!' Zana called.

She left the safety of the standing stone to come between the woman and me.

'This is not Tamara, Eregendal! She is bad, as bad as Tamara is good, as black as Tamara is white!'

But the black lady had bewitched me. I had no choice but to run towards her, while time stretched around me.

Zana caught hold of my robes and climbed onto my back. My mind cleared at once.

'Fly, Eregendal!' she cried.

'But the flower?'

'I am the fifth flower. Now fly. Don't let Aramat touch you.'

I raised my wings, but they had no strength to lift us from the ground. Aramat laughed and reached out a hand to me. I backed off, fearing her touch.

Zana shifted her seat on my back and grasped my hands to keep her balance. With her small fingers entwined in mine, fresh energy pulsed through my hands and along my arms into my exhausted body.

Aramat saw the change and lunged forward to touch me before we flew. I fluttered aside. She stumbled and touched the standing stone instead. It shattered into a thousand pieces. I flew up from the fell, saved from her awful power by Zana's mystic strength.

The cloud oppressed me again. It held me back in mid-air. Though Zana urged me on, I could rise no further, however hard I tried.

'It is sunset,' Zana cried: 'If we don't get through now,

we never will. For your enemy is mine.'

Her fear made me strive harder. I gained a few feet but flagged again.

'Please get through,' Zana prayed, terrified.

'God, I am trying. Please help me,' I cried.

At once, a key on my belt shone silver through the darkness. We flew out of the fumes into the light and saw we had been travelling up a column of cloud. It had stretched out like an arm above the curve of the cloud's grey body.

'We are free!' Zana cried.

'Aye, but where is the boat?'

The last gold rays of the sun shafted across the purple-pink twilight and dazzled our eyes. Zana looked upwards and spotted the gossamer-sailed boat.

'Up there, the light above us,' she cried. 'Come on, Eregendal. It's only a little way to go.'

Though it looked little to her, for me it was a flight too far. The cloud below us grew and snatched at us with smoky fingers.

Just as the last of my energy faded, the end of a rope fell from the sky. Zana caught the rope and threaded it under my arms. She knotted it around my chest. Then she climbed off my back and shinned up the rope into the ferry.

What bliss it was to hang in mid-air and rest at last. Even the bite of the rope under my arms felt nothing. My companions hauled me up into the boat and made me a couch in the stern. I fell at once into a deep sleep.

9: The Landing

We sailed for three days, leaving the grey cloud far behind. Whether we sailed north, south, east, west or straight upwards, no-one could tell. So the beginning of Kohtel's log of our expedition was little different to what Anya had written in her diary.

On the eve of the third day, we caught sight of land. On the morning of the fourth day, the ferry glided across the cloud into a natural harbour set in a rocky coast.

We waded ashore through the cloud and climbed onto a stony beach. Above and around us, black cliffs loomed dourly. No paths marked their faces.

'Anya, what does your diary say about this place?' Kohtel asked.

'I'm sorry. I can't guide you. I didn't come this way last time,' she replied.

'We have the rope,' Astor offered. He unwound it from his shoulders.

'I'll fly up and secure it at the cliff top,' I said: 'Then you should all be able to climb up.'

I knotted the rope around my waist and flew upwards. The rope's weight dragged me back against the stiff breeze, but it was not as tough as the grey cloud I had flown through before. I soon landed on the edge of the cliff.

The ground behind the cliff was smooth, like glass. Inland, the glass plain vanished into a heat haze. Nothing

grew there. No rocks stood out against the dark, flat expanse. Nothing lay there to hold the rope. I returned to the cliff edge and saw the ferry glide away towards the horizon. Then I flew down to the others on the beach.

'The rope was not long enough, at least fifty feet too short,' Astor said.

'I couldn't see anywhere to tie it to at the top either,' I replied. 'The land above us is a plain of obsidian.'

'We need to find another way to scale this cliff,' Kohtel said, looking at the rest of us.

'The tide is going out,' said Zana: 'Let's walk along the beach.'

She set off, and we followed. The black pebbles on the beach were very slippery. After we had slipped a few times, Anya, Zana and I held hands to keep our balance.

The tide had ebbed far enough for us to round the first headland. The cliffs beyond were higher and smoother. They went into the distance, getting taller the further away they stood.

'There is no point going this way,' Yammas complained: 'We should turn back now before we get trapped by the tide.'

'No, don't do that,' Anya warned. 'In my last journey, I faced an obstacle like this, one that grew worse the further I went. When I turned back, the way I ended up taking was even harder than the way I didn't go.'

'But how can we leave this shore?' Kohtel asked.

'There will be a way,' I said: 'If naught else, we have my wings.'

The wind buffeted against us, warning everyone my wings would be useless there. Zana and I walked on along the beach. The other four sat down on the shore.

'There's no sense in waiting to drown,' I called back to them.

Anya stood up and reluctantly followed us. Yammas, Astor and Kohtel sat on, looking at us as if we were fools.

We three rounded the next headland. The sea of cloud already lapped against the base of the cliffs. Even my heart sank on seeing that. Then Zana cried out in excitement, pointing her finger.

'Look! A cave! Go tell the others, Eregendal. We have found the way.'

'What if the cave is only short? What if it ends below the high tide level?' Anya asked.

'We had to come this way, and that is the only way we can go,' Zana replied.

She leapt nimbly over the submerged rocks towards the cave. Anya followed her, and I turned back to fetch the others.

Yammas doubted my news when I returned to them, Kohtel told him to stop complaining and led the way along the beach. He felt embarrassed that a child and a butterfly had taken the lead from him.

As the four of us rounded the headland, the tide surged in. A big wave threw Yammas and me against the cliff face. Kohtel and Astor tied us to themselves. They carried and dragged us through the cruel waters to the safety of the cave.

We fell onto the black sand above the high tide line and rested for a while.

'Thank you, Astor, for saving me,' I said.

'It is you we should thank, for risking yourself to come back for us,' he replied: 'If you hadn't, we would have been lost in the tide and the storm.'

'Where have Anya and Zana gone?' Yammas asked.

We looked at each other, surprised that we had not thought of them after our own ordeal.

'I'll go and look for them,' Kohtel said.

He lit his torch and walked off into the depths of the cave, calling their names. We watched until his light and the echo of his voice had gone.

'I don't like this,' Astor said. He grasped the handle of his sword, Shartere.

We set off to explore the cave. Shartere and my key of bravery lit our way.

The silence in the caves seemed unearthly. The walls reflected no light but drew in all light that shone on them. It was very hard to see our path. All the passages headed downwards when we wanted to climb. Many tunnels branched off the cave. We lost all hope of finding the others or our way back to the coast.

I sat down on the sharp sand floor to rest. Yammas sat beside me. Astor walked on.

'Astor, don't leave us,' I called.

He did not turn back.

'There is a jinx in this labyrinth,' Yammas said. 'Let's

stay together, Eregendal. Two heads are better than one.'

'Aye,' I agreed.

I fell asleep beside him. When I awoke, he had gone.

At first, I felt despair. Once again, I had lost my companions, the way I had lost the Four in the dreamlands.

Then I realised the labyrinth was a test each of us had to take alone. I took up the fourth key on my belt and prayed. The key filled the cave with dazzling brightness. Its light pointed towards a deep pit, telling me that was the way I had to go. I opened my wings and flew into the unknown depths.

The base of the pit widened into a vast cavern like a cathedral, a natural monument for worshipping God. Massive pillars of obsidian reached up into the heights above me, supporting the roof of the chamber. Around me, dark boulders lay strewn in a pattern which looked too regular to be natural. Many tunnels and passages led away through the walls. But the key did not direct me down one of those. Instead, it guided me to a slight crack in the stone wall. I squeezed through into a narrow passage which led downwards. Though I thought it was taking me the wrong way, I followed the passage down further into the labyrinth.

I wandered for several days through that dark maze, until I felt that I no longer had a life outside the labyrinth. It felt my destiny to walk its passages for the rest of my life.

When I saw a distant spot of light at last, I felt dumfounded. All my journey had been downhill, into the depths of the earth. Why then should I find myself near the surface? I wanted to turn my back on the way out and return

to the depths of oblivion.

A child's voice drew me out of the darkness into the light. I did not know whose it was or what it said. The mystery and promise in the voice, took hold of my feet despite my head, and dragged me out onto the top of the obsidian plain.

'Eregendal! At last!' a woman cried. She hugged me.

I looked at her but did not know who she was at first. She held me from her in concern.

'Do you not know me? I am Anya. And here are Zana and Astor and Yammas: all of our expedition except Kohtel.'

I recalled dream-like images of an expedition. These became more real to me as the fog in my mind from the caves became less. Soon I knew who my companions were again.

'How did you find your way through the Labyrinth of Lethee?' Astor asked me.

I told them how I had used my keys but had struggled to follow their guidance. Anya nodded as I spoke.

'Zana just followed her nose. She came out first,' Anya said. 'Astor used his sword as his guide, and Yammas chose his way with a coin. I remembered being in this land before and facing a similar trial. To get where I had to go, I had to walk in the opposite direction.'

'What of Kohtel?' I asked.

'We have waited here five days,' Astor said.

'Eregendal left the cave only just in time,' Yammas said. 'If Kohtel does not follow soon, he will be lost forever.'

'Kohtel may need to learn that one must follow to lead,

but that is no reason to abandon him,' Astor said.

'We cannot waste more time here! We've spent five days on this hole. Must we spend the rest of our lives here also?'

'Friends, stop bickering,' Anya said. 'Without our leader, we'll all fall out. Let's wait for him a little longer.'

Kohtel wandered out of the cave on the ninth day. He did not leave his dreamy state of mind for several more days. His experiences had changed him. No longer did he talk to fill the silence.

'I've never felt so peaceful before,' he told us. 'I seem to understand everything now, because I realise I know nothing much at all.'

We saw the change for good in Kohtel and knew that the challenge of the Labyrinth of Lethee had been worthwhile.

10: The Runner

Many days later, we reached some earthy foothills at the edge of the obsidian plain. Beyond them stood a range of wooded mountains. We set up camp for the night.

As the sun set behind the mountains, Yammas' sharp eyes spotted a distant traveller on the horizon. Kohtel lit his torch to guide the stranger to our camp. Some time later, the stranger arrived.

He was a red-faced young man of about nineteen and had a fiery look in his eyes. He wore a belted wool tunic and

carried no purse or bag. When we stood up to greet him, he backed away in terror.

'Get behind me, wraiths!' he cried, cowering.

Zana took hold of the youth's shaking hands.

'Fear not. We won't harm you. We are travellers too. What are you running from?'

'There are a thousand evils on the way ahead,' he warned: 'Go back to the shore before they destroy you.'

'We haven't travelled this far to go back now,' Astor said.

Kohtel waved at him to say no more.

'We all know it's dangerous,' Zana said. 'It's harder for you because you're all alone.'

'I wasn't always alone,' said the youth.

He tried to tell us about the fate of his friends, but broke down and wept. Zana placed her hand upon his forehead. Her touch calmed him down.

'Come with us,' she said: 'It will be easier with us beside you. What is your name?'

The youth thought awhile and nodded.

'My name is Epoh,' he said, and offered us his hand.

As I shook it, I felt a stickiness on his fingers. He smelled of blood but had no wounds.

'Why do you seek the Tree of Knowledge, Epoh?' asked Kohtel.

'I want to know my future,' he replied.

Anya and I looked at each other. We both knew he lied.

As we settled for the night, Anya and I talked over our

doubts about our new companion. I sensed the wrong ears had overheard our whispers.

We set off soon after dawn next day. Our new companion seemed to get on well with Yammas, Kohtel and Astor. Zana, in her innocence, gave him the respect and love she showed for all creatures. Only Anya and I doubted him.

Kohtel stopped us after an hour and asked us which way we should go. We stood in a broad valley leading to several foothill passes. To our left lay gentle rounded foothills. To our right and ahead towered steep mountains.

'That's the way to go,' Epoh said, pointing to the left.

'No. That's the way,' Anya countered. She pointed out a tall, dangerous peak to our right.

Astor raised Shartere and pointed it at each of the hills and mountains in turn. The blade dulled when it pointed to the rounded hills. It gleamed when pointed to the mountains.

I grasped the key for trusting God and scanned the hills around us. When I looked at the sharp peak next to Anya's chosen mountain, the key burned so warmly in my hand that I dropped it.

'The peak north of Anya's,' I said.

Yammas took out a coin pressed with a lamb and an ancient inscription. By tossing the coin, he chose first between hill and peak, and then between peak and peak. He chose the same mountain I had.

The others agreed to go that way. But while their eyes looked at the mountain ahead, I saw Epoh's eyes look greedily at my keys, Astor's sword and Yammas' coin.

We walked towards the mountain for three days. At nightfall on the third day, we camped at the mouth of a gorge which separated the mountain Anya had chosen from mine. A deep river ran along the bottom of the gorge.

'Should we walk along the gorge tomorrow, or cross by the mountain slope above?' Kohtel asked.

'Don't take the gorge,' Anya warned. She opened one of her diaries and read an entry to us. 'Little had I thought, when entering the pass, that I would feel such self-doubt in its miry bottom.'

She stopped short and looked up. Epoh was staring hungrily at her diaries.

'May I have a look?' he asked with a hard little smile.

'No!' she snapped back.

'But we keep no secrets,' Zana said with teasing eyes. 'Show Epoh your book. You showed it to me.'

Anya glared at Zana but handed over the worn leather-bound book. Epoh snatched it from her. As he leafed through the pages, his expression turned from greed to bewilderment.

'But there is nothing written here. The pages are all blank,' he said.

Zana winked at Anya and turned to me.

'Eregendal, didn't you say you once got a blank letter from a person who couldn't see you?'

'Aye,' I said, remembering the letter Tamara had given me in Halsanger market square. 'It was because I did not have the eyes to see, nor did he. It was as if we were both in the same building but on different floors.'

Epoh returned the book to Anya with a shrug.

We each decided in our own way whether to walk along the gorge next day or climb above it on the mountainside. All of us agreed that the mountainside was the way to go. We then settled down to sleep.

Astor woke us in the middle of the night.

'Shartere, my sword! It has gone!' he shouted.

My hand went to my waist. My belt was still there, but the five keys were missing. Anya looked for her diaries in her bag. They had gone. Kohtel's torch had gone too. Even Yammas' coin had disappeared. We looked around in dismay and saw, to our horror, two cloaks lying on the ground.

'Epoh has gone and Zana has disappeared,' Kohtel said.

'So it was safe to let Epoh stay with us!' Anya said, glaring at me.

'Hush, Anya,' Kohtel said: 'This is only another trial on our way.'

'But now I can give no guidance,' Anya cried.

'And I no defence,' Astor warned.

'Then that must be the way we have to travel on, without protection or plan.'

'But what of Zana?' Anya demanded: 'We can't leave her in the clutches of her kidnapper, Epoh.'

'Perhaps I can help,' said Yammas. 'Go fill your water-bags at the river and bring them back to me.'

We looked at him in surprise but saw he meant what he said. Each of us took our own water-bag to the river to fill it, with the moon lighting our way. Yammas placed his old

cooking pot in the centre of the camp circle. He poured all the water we brought into the pot.

'Sit and watch,' he said.

The water in the cauldron boiled without heat. In the steam given off, we saw a blurred image. It looked to me like reeds by a waterfall. To Anya it was a reed bower and to Astor it was a gorge. The image shimmered in the steam until the last of the water had boiled away.

'Now you know why my cauldron came with me when we flew from Doudern Fell. You have all seen something. I have seen far more.'

'What does the shimmering picture mean?' Kohtel asked.

'As I poured the water in, I asked the cauldron to show me where we can find Zana and our stolen treasures. They are in the gorge yonder. We have to enter there to get them back. But whether we leave there safely is another matter. If the bones there are to do with the blood that was on Epoh's hands when we met him.'

'What of Zana?' Anya asked in fear.

'She is safe and ever will be. We are the prey of that wraith.'

'But if that is so, why did he tell us to head for the rounded hills the day we met?' asked Kohtel.

'That was his trick, to get us to go the way he wanted. He knew some of us did not trust him.'

Kohtel nodded. 'And is he in the gorge now, with Zana and our belongings?' he asked.

'I think he lies between us and them,' Yammas said: 'At the far end of the gorge, near a waterfall, stands a reed hut. That's where Zana and our belongings lie. They are the bait for the trap he has set to catch us.'

'Could we climb down the face of the gorge to avoid him?' asked Kohtel.

'Nay. The vision was clear. The only way in is here, by the mouth of the gorge.'

'Or from the air?' I suggested.

All looked at me in hope, but then Kohtel shook his head.

'No, it is too dangerous for a butterfly to go there alone.'

'My belt will still protect me, even without the keys,' I said. 'Surely it is better for me to face the gorge alone, than for us all to go, and suffer the same fate?'

'Then it is planned?' Kohtel said, reluctant to accept my offer.

'Aye. I leave tomorrow at dawn.'

11: Into the Gorge

Kohtel woke me a few minutes before sunrise.

'Anya's told us about the dangers you face today. Know our thoughts are for you and our hearts behind you.'

'Make them your prayers and I will succeed.'

We hugged each other in farewell. As I flew off across the mountainside, Yammas settled down to watch me in the

steam from his caldron. The others watched from the slopes above.

The currents of wind guided me. I flew above the cold air from the river to the far end of the gorge. Then, I dropped to hover by the cliff edge.

Below me, a waterfall cascaded from a wide lake. The fall tumbled into a torrent running through the neck between the mountains, and gushed between the overhanging rocks. No grass banks lay there.

Two furlongs downstream, I found what looked like the grassy bank where the reed hut might have stood. The grass was bare but for a pile of leaves, some sedge, two large rocks, a broken pot and some small stones. It seemed strange to see a pile of leaves in a place where there were no trees. I landed and reached down to touch the pile.

A clap of thunder rent the clear sky. I found my fingers touched not leaves, but the pages of Anya's diaries. Beside them lay my keys, Astor's sword, Kohtel's torch and Yammas' coin. I picked up the keys and fastened them to my belt.

A roar from behind made me turn, startled. The large rock had turned into a huge and horrible ogre. He faced me across a reed hut, which surrounded us. Zana stood tied to the centre pole. The floor of the hut was littered with the bodies of other travellers.

My heart leapt with fear. I picked up Astor's sword Shartere to defend myself. I had to fight my conscience too, because I did not want to raise a weapon against another

creature.

The ogre lunged at me. I parried with Shartere. The ogre clawed and hit me, trying to spur me to fight back. My anger rose. The angrier I got, the deeper his claws slashed me. Then he scored a deep gash in my side. I dropped Shartere and fell at Zana's feet.

'The flower,' she said: 'See, by your hand, Eregendal: the zana. Quickly, eat it.'

I reached out and touched the cold body of a past traveller. Sickened, I turned and saw the ogre's looming face. His wide claws hurtled towards me.

'Quick! Eat the flower!' Zana ordered.

Time stretched as I reached over the body and plucked the small green flower. Fresh strength flowed from it into my limbs. I rolled over out of the path of the ogre's claws and put the flower in my mouth.

The ogre and the reed hut vanished. Zana and I stood on a crescent of grass beside the rocky river. Around us lay our stolen treasures.

I sat and held my head in my shaking hands, trying to understand what had happened. Zana sat beside me and touched my arm.

'He couldn't really kill you. He wasn't real,' she said.

'Then what are all these wounds on my body? And what were all those bodies on the floor?'

'You hurt yourself. The angrier you got, the bigger he got.'

I gathered up our treasures and lifted Zana onto my

shoulders. When I opened my wings to fly, something stopped me from taking off into the air. I felt weak and useless at having to walk through the gorge instead.

In many places, our path forced me to wade through the cold river. Above us, the high walls of the gorge crowded in. They made me feel small. My wounds hurt and my strength had gone. I lay back on the riverbank and wanted to give up. Zana sat near me.

'Your key is shining,' she said.

I reached down and touched the second key for fellowship. The air filled with the prayers of our four friends at the mouth of the gorge. They told me to get to my feet, to keep going. My feelings of defeat left me. I stumbled on to the end of the gorge and brought Zana back to safety.

Anya waited for us at the mouth of the gorge. She hugged Zana, bound up my wounds, and called Astor to carry me to our camp. They gave me a hero's welcome. I thought it was undeserved.

'Anyone can be a hero with Zana as their shield.'

My friends rejoiced to get back their stolen treasures. We discussed the day's events as we ate supper.

'The ogre you fought was Epoh himself, guarding his stronghold in the Gorge of Self Doubt,' Anya said. 'When Zana said, "the angrier you got, the bigger he got", she meant the ogre was feeding off your anger and hatred. The angrier and more violent you became, the deadlier he became. When you ate the flower, your anger died, and so did your foe.'

'So had I fought to kill, I too would have become one of

the bodies on the floor,' I said, and shivered.

'You could never kill him, though he could destroy you. When you defeated him and escaped from the gorge, you proved yourself a hero.'

'Yes,' said Kohtel: 'Shame on me, that I ever doubted a butterfly could win through.'

They set up a camp near the broad lake above the gorge, in a glade of trees on the lakeside. There we stayed until my wounds had healed.

12: Through Other Eyes

We set off again on a fine autumn morning when the larches were turning and the forest put on its fresh red and amber coat. We headed towards a mountain pass picked out by Shartere. Yammas had looked in his cauldron to see where we were going. He refused to tell us what he had seen. Disappointed, we made him walk behind us.

Angular, wind-blown trees covered the lower slopes of the pass. They reached out and clutched at us as we walked through them. Higher up the pass, the trees clung to us and held us back. We had to fight for every step. Astor used Shartere to hack through the twisting branches. The trees cried out in agony with each cut.

'Let's go back and find another way,' I said, upset by the cries of the trees.

'No,' Kohtel replied: 'We will suffer far more if we turn

back than if we fight on.'

Only through Astor's efforts did we win through. As we camped that night in the heart of the mountains, we heard again in our sleep, the cries of the trees that day.

Next day, we climbed well above the snow line. Though we did not feel the cold, the effects of winter held us back. A large fall of rocks and snow had filled the narrow valley at the top of the pass.

'Eregendal, can you fly above the fall to see how large it is?' Kohtel asked.

I shook my head and pointed to the clouds racing past above us on the stiff breeze. Although my wounds had healed, my wings were not strong enough to fly against such a wind.

Yammas set up his cauldron and placed some snow in it. We all gathered around to watch. I saw little in the steam apart from the snow that blocked us. Yammas saw more. Long after the snow had boiled away, he sat staring at the space above the pot.

'What have you seen?' Kohtel asked him.

'There is a way through if we work hard. But...'

'But what?' asked Astor.

Yammas did not answer. He walked over to the fall and took out a handful of snow from below a long horizontal stone.

'This is where we start,' he said, and dug with both hands into the wall of snow.

'This fall is fifty feet high. If we disturb it, it could slide

and engulf us,' Kohtel said.

Yammas ignored him and kept digging. I joined him and dug with my bare hands too. One by one, the others stepped up to help us.

Working as a team made our hard work more fun. Soon we were throwing snowballs and playing other games while we dug. Our joy reminded me of our eager climb up Doudern Fell at the start of our expedition. Astor, Yammas and Kohtel dug. Anya, Zana and I cleared the snow from behind them to keep their way out clear. Soon, we had tunnelled several feet into the fall.

Yammas cheered. His hand had punched through the snow beneath an edge of blue slate. Snow fell away, leaving a rock-edged triangle like a window looking down onto the valley on the other side.

'We're through!' Anya cried.

She pushed past to be the first to run out into the valley beyond. As we followed her through, she turned back in dismay.

'But it's the same place,' she said: 'Exactly the same.'

I looked out across the land beyond her pointing finger. Below the snow-choked pass stood the same twisting trees. Beyond them dropped the same green foothills to the same far plain of black glass.

'What's wrong?' Zana asked Kohtel.

He turned upon her in frustration.

'Use your eyes, child! Can't you see?'

'Yes, I can see,' she said calmly: 'This is like the place on

the other side of the snowfall.'

'It IS the place on the other side of the snowfall,' he corrected.

Zana looked at us. We nodded.

'But where are our footsteps in the snow?' she asked.

We looked and saw the snow ahead of us was unmarked. Not one footstep had dented it.

'I'm tired. Can we rest here?' Zana asked. 'Tomorrow I can show you this is not the same.'

We made camp a short way from the fall, in the shelter of the hillside. Zana woke up long before the rest of us next morning. She joined us as we talked about our route that day.

'Let's go climbing,' she said: 'We can use Astor's rope to keep us safe.'

We agreed as we had no better suggestion. Though we each thought her idea would not work, we still did what she said. She led the way with Astor behind to help her. I went next, followed by Yammas and Anya, and with Kohtel last.

Zana led us to a jagged, snow-clad cliff. She studied the rock face and then began to climb. She used snow-covered patches of rock for hand and footholds. To us, she seemed to hold on to nothing, and she left no mark. She settled on a perch about twenty feet above us and called down to Astor to follow.

He could not see where to start. She had to call down directions to him. He followed fearfully, muttering prayers as he did so. Despite his doubts, he reached her narrow ledge. She asked him to lift her up to her next foothold. From there,

she shouted out directions to me.

I scaled the face with my wings open but did not need them. Zana was as patient with the others as she was with me. Soon all of us were clinging onto the rock face. We slowly edged our way upward in order, first one moving and then another.

Zana cheered when she reached the top of the cliff. Startled, Yammas lost his grip and tumbled backwards towards the pass a hundred feet below. The rope checked his fall. He swung back and hit the rock face.

That tug pulled Anya and me off the cliff. I struggled to fly in the stiff wind. That held my fall long enough for Astor to join Zana and secure the rope at the top of the cliff. Then Kohtel fell from the rock face too. His added weight broke my strength and pulled me down.

We hung from the rope with the sheer drop below us. The rock face was just too far away for us to touch it and recover our holds. Astor lay down by the edge to see what had happened. He called instructions to us to help us save ourselves.

Kohtel climbed up the rope from the bottom first. When he had climbed past Anya, she followed him. After they had both clambered past Yammas, he followed them too. They all climbed over me and reached the top. Then I half climbed and half flew to the top. I rested in the snow and let Astor untie the rope around me while the others talked.

'But there was no way up there,' Yammas said.

'Aye, there was,' Astor replied: 'I climbed up it, though

I couldn't see it. Your doubt made you fall.'

'I can't believe there was a way up,' Yammas said.

'But we are here,' Kohtel pointed out: 'Judge it by the result, not the way.'

'It can help so much to see the way through other people's eyes as well as our own,' Anya said: 'We may not understand their way at all, but that doesn't make it less real, or wrong.'

'We saw the cliffs and the valley, and we thought they hadn't changed,' Kohtel said: 'We were so disappointed, we closed our minds. Only Zana looked again and saw the truth. Once again, you lead us better than I do. Zana, take over the role of leader from me.'

We laughed, thinking Kohtel was joking. He did not laugh with us. Zana took his hand.

'You lead us, Kohtel. We are all friends. But when you aren't with us, we all argue. If you hadn't come out of the cave, we wouldn't be friends any more. Thanks to you, we're here.'

She saw a small green zana flower that had struggled through the snow into the light. With childish delight, she picked it and handed it to Kohtel.

'I can't lead: I just see things in a different way. I'm here to learn. You are a good leader. You listen to us. You let us help you lead. Anya guides us. Yammas warns us. Astor protects us. Eregendal serves us. And I learn. That's why we're here.'

Kohtel's head dropped.

'My vanity made me lead this expedition,' he admitted: 'Nothing else.'

'Aye, when we set out,' Astor agreed. 'Few of us were worthy then. Now we are. So forget this foolish talk. We have a quest to finish!'

'True, Astor. Anya, which way should we go?'

She pointed up the steep mountainside to where thick clouds hid the summit.

'There it is – The Top of the World.'

13: The Tree of Knowledge

The last climb was tough. We fought bravely against all that tried to stop us. The obstacles made our progress very slow. We conquered cliffs, ravines, ice, snow, hail, thick fog and high winds. The weather itself seemed to protect the Tree of Knowledge from all visitors. Though each of us played our part in that stage of the journey, Anya was the one who kept us going. She gave us hope to carry on when we felt like giving up. Knowing that she had been there before, helped us believe in those hard days that we could get there too.

One morning, we walked out of the clouds. We stood, dumfounded to have got there. In front of us stretched the flat summit of the mountain we had climbed. Behind us rose the tops of other mountains, rising proudly from the clouds.

At the heart of the rocky plain grew a massive tree. Its vast canopy spread out over a huge web of gnarled roots.

Silver and bronze leaves shimmered and dazzled in the sunlight. But brighter still was the radiance at the heart of the tree. The branches and leaves looked like the bars of a huge lantern with the light shining through them.

We cheered and ran across the rocky ground. Anya shouted to us to keep together, but we did not listen. That was our mistake.

The mountain had another guardian to protect the Tree of Knowledge from all visitors. The rocks around the Tree moved towards us and barred our way. They tripped us up and piled about us. Their weight pressed down on us and crushed our breath.

I heard my companions' cries and longed to help them. My keys were inches from my fingers, but boulders had pinned down my hands. With a great cry, I dragged my arms out from under the stones and caught the five keys in my left hand.

'Fellowship!' I cried and held up the second key.

Light burst from the key, shattering the rocks which held me. I held the burning key high and ran to help my friends. The rocks cleared from my path and fell away from those they had trapped.

The six of us linked arms and walked with each other that last short stretch to the Tree. We fell among its roots, crying tears of joy. The roots filled us with a healing warmth which eased our minds and calmed our souls.

'Where do we look?' Kohtel asked.

'Sleep, friends,' Anya said.

We slept. In our sleep, our dreams told us the answers to the questions that had brought us there. I saw the world lying below me. It looked like a garden of paradise, but evil was creeping across it. Tamara had been hidden in a cave in the heart of the Grey Mountains. She sat, weaving tapestries with jackdaws all around her. The vision made me realise I had known the answer to my question all the time.

'This place is like Heart's Ease Island,' I told my sleeping companions: 'It's not what we learn when we get here. It's our journey here that brings us knowledge.'

The belt around my waist blazed into golden light. It shone like a newly risen midsummer sun. The five keys shone like silver stars, brighter than the gold with their purer light. The light awoke my friends, but it had gone before they had left their dreams.

Zana rose and picked her way through the gnarled tree roots to the massive trunk. She turned to look and me.

'We will meet again, Ladnegere,' she said. The name was that of an eagle in an old myth.

Zana turned back and touched the tree trunk. I watched in awe as she became one with the tree.

Anya leapt up, her eyes looking towards the dark skies to the south.

'Petros!' she cried. She ran off across the rocky plain along a dark and well-worn path.

'Petros?' asked Kohtel, still half-lost in his own dreams.

'Aye. She met him here before. She returned here to meet him again.'

I pointed in a different direction. Yammas was strolling away along a sheep track, singing an old country song.

'Are we to break up?' Kohtel asked.

He looked at Astor. The soldier had sheathed Shartere and walked away from us down a stony path.

'Some things one can only do with others. Some things one can only do alone,' I said.

Kohtel nodded and sadly walked away. He took a second well-worn track into the darkness to the west.

I looked around me. No track or path was there for me to follow, though some earlier travellers had walked a similar way.

As I walked off across the plain, a change in the light made me look back. The ancient Tree of Knowledge had burst into a dazzling array of silver-green flowers against its brilliant light.

The vision vanished before I had fully seen it. The plain became dark. I walked alone into the cloud.

14: The Return

The world had changed when I walked down out of the great cloud hiding the Tree of Knowledge. Instead of the storms we had fought on the way up, a bright summer sun shone down on me. The snowdrifts had gone. All around, trees and flowers danced in a warm breeze. The mountains sang a happy psalm of praise. I joined in, praising God too.

The land welcomed me. I walked through hills wooded with laden fruit trees and lush green valleys. When I was hungry, I ate bilberries and apples, and when thirsty I drank beck water. Both fruit and water had never tasted so lovely.

After a few days, I reached the woods where we had fought through the branches on our way up. Now the trees were my friends. They gave me food and a place to sleep at night, in a hollow between roots padded with lush grass.

I stayed there for some days while my wings healed after being torn by the rocks. Then I stayed a while longer, because I knew time there had no link to time when I went back. Then I thought I need not leave there at all. I had found my heaven and Berren and the dreamlands would not miss me. I forgot all the things I had once thought important. Life became a carefree round of eating and sleeping, dreaming and dancing, in a long balmy summer.

Late one evening, I heard human cries coming from the path to the pass. I strolled down through the trees to see who was calling, as I had seen no-one since I had left the Tree.

Three wraith-like people were fighting their way up the path to the pass. They struck at nothing with their swords and sticks. They seemed to fight powerful foes, and something I could not see was matching their blows. Their unseen foe cried out in many pained voices.

The three wraiths came upon me, battering and slashing at me. I tried to ward them off, but that made them fight even harder. I fell to the ground, wounded and crying out in pain. They moved on, still fighting. I stumbled to a beck and

plunged into its bracing waters. My cries echoed through the wood and were answered by others, also unseen.

The hard fight put up by the three wraiths, reminded me of something in the past. I recalled how Astor had fought against the trees when the six of us had walked through that same wood long before.

Suddenly, I recalled my promise to save my lady Tamara. Guilt flooded through me. I had betrayed my quest, my faith and my life, idling in that land.

I threw myself out of the beck and ran headlong through the wood. On the far side, a steep valley took me through the mountains into the foothills. I ran on, resting only when the sun or the moon did not light my way. After the foothills, I ran through a lush plain of wheat and flowers. Many days later, I reached the edge of the black cliffs.

The sea mist rolled back from the beach, shaded in the rose colours of evening. In the bay floated the pale blue ferry boat which had brought us there. In the boat sat five people gazing across the ocean of cloud. The boat sailed out of the bay towards the sun.

'Stop!' I cried, but my pleas were useless.

I raised my wings to follow the boat. The wind forced me down onto the rocky beach. I tried to fly using the powers of my keys. They did not work, because I had been left behind through my own fault. I knelt at the edge of the high tide and prayed for pardon and help. Then I turned to find shelter for the night.

A ribbon of leaf-green material fluttered by a cushion of

sea grass. The ribbon had caught on a small silver-green flower. With trembling hands, I picked the zana and wrapped its short stalk in the torn cloth. A familiar warmth and strength flowed through me as I held it. I wept.

Zana wanted me to follow them. She had left me her sign, trusting that I would. With her amulet and the key of faith in my hands, I took to the sky and made headway against the wind. I left behind the enchanted Land at the Top of the World and followed the path of the cloud ferry.

Night fell with a fine rose sunset and left with a golden glow. I flew in a world with no up or down, no land or sea below and no sun or stars above. When my body felt tired, my flight changed into a glide. I fell into a welcome sleep. The air gently lifted me, and the breeze took me in a new direction.

I awoke, still gliding through the night, but another night. Below me lay a bleak country of moonlit mountains. They stood tooth-sharp bright against the sky's black cloak. It felt good to have land beneath me once more.

The new day started with a grim red sky barred with amber cloud. The orange sun shone on my flight that day with an unpleasant warmth. The air felt very close.

Towards dusk, the land became more gentle, with rounded fells marked by old dry-stone walls. Mauve smoke rolled across the evening sky. In the valleys, fields of ripe wheat rippled like water, glowing with an eerie brightness. Shutters covered the windows of remote farmhouses and haystacks had been rough-thatched. The land was preparing

for a storm.

The storm broke without warning. A gale-force wind blew up. The heavens split open in a flood of rain and hail. Lightning danced about me with spears that stabbed too close. I had to find shelter.

Weary and wet, I knocked at the door of a farmhouse. The chink of light between the shutters looked warm and inviting.

'Go away! You're not welcome!' said a gruff voice from behind the barred door.

It was the same everywhere. The only shelter I found was in the ruins of a barn.

The rain became more showery next day. I flew on over hills and fields and reached land I knew by late afternoon.

The sky darkened, the wind dropped, the rain stopped, and the air became sultry. The land trembled in a foreboding silence. The dust-filled clouds made the light a sickly yellow.

Ahead of me lay the long ridge of Doudern Fell. I fought against the strong wind to fly to the cairn. It battled me to a standstill in the air.

'Zoust!' I cried, naming my enemy.

Lightning flashed across my eyes. Blinded for a moment, I spiralled downwards. I grasped my keys in panic and again held up the fourth, for faith.

The air around me became a charmed circle of peace through the storm. A moonbeam lit the cairn on Doudern fell. The mountain shook beneath me when I landed there. Too tired to wonder, I sheltered by the cairn for the night.

15: The Red River

The wind woke me shortly before dawn, when night is darkest and all is silent.

'Eregendal, Eregendal,' it moaned. Its cry chilled me.

Down the valley, beyond Sluthe wood, I saw a large fire burning in the distance, a short way beyond Halsanger. My wings were too tired to take me there. Instead, I set off on foot down the fellside.

The path took me past the shepherds' hut. The hut had been wrecked. Its roof had been torn off, the shutters smashed, the door ripped from its hinges and the stack of firewood burnt to ashes.

Alarmed, I hurried on down the path and ran through Sluthe Wood to the Tarn of Mirrors.

Sluthe Wood was uneasy. The trees tried to warn me, but I cannot understand trees. A faint whisper of their message told me to hurry to the cave but not to Arzandel.

I reached the Tarn of Mirrors by early afternoon. The cave was empty and the fire circle had been destroyed. In the ashes lay Arzandel's green jade ring. When Arzandel turned the jade ring on his toe, the Green Lady rose out of the Tarn of Mirrors to take all travellers home. As the ring only worked for Arzandel and he had gone, I was now trapped in Berren with no way of leaving.

Near the cave lay a heap of baggage. They were the things the expedition had left on Doudern Fell for fate to look

after, so that I could carry my friends to the cloud ferry. The bags had not been touched.

I picked up the jade ring from the cinders and saw a symbol scored into the ash It was the three-point star breaking a circle: the sign of Zoust. In anger, I scratched out the loathed symbol with a stone. In its place I drew the plain circle of perfection, which Ashleigh had taught me about in my youth.

From there, I flew on to Halsanger. The town was silent but not deserted. Every door I knocked stayed shut. Every cry I made seemed unheard. I stood in the marketplace and prayed for a sign.

A silver-green flower beckoned to me from a wall. I picked it and wrapped it in the green ribbon Zana had left me. Then I pinned it to my robe.

Behind the wall, Tamara's white mare stood cropping the grass. She carried a saddle and a halter which trailed on the ground. I caught the halter and led the mare up the hill towards the castle. She stopped and nuzzled me as if she wanted to be ridden. I sat astride her. Before I had settled in the saddle, she raced off. She took me up the hill and across the drawbridge into the castle courtyard.

The portcullis clanged down behind us. A farm worker hurried out to lead the mare to her stable. He waved to me to enter the keep.

The great hall was deserted. A chill silence brooded in the empty place. I climbed the stone stairs to Ashleigh's turret room. When I opened the heavy wooden door, the air

crackled, as if lightning was about to spark.

By the window where I had once stood, was Maredudd the Wise, one of the Judges' Council. His amber robes were covered in dust and his handsome face looked haggard.

'You are Eregendal?' he asked, as if he trusted no-one at face value any more.

'Aye, though I have little proof.'

He looked me up and down. Then he touched the silver-green flower pinned to my robe with the leaf green ribbon.

'I need no more proof. I must apologise to you on behalf of the Council, Eregendal. We did not realise how important you quest was until it was too late.'

'Great Ashley taught me it's never too late.'

'Perhaps. But we have little time to talk before we are discovered. Halsanger is at war.'

Maredudd gazed at the view before he continued to speak. He picked his words with care.

'Four days ago, the day the expedition left, a foul cloud of smoke covered Berren. Then a great storm broke. Then the forces of the enemy attacked. When your comrades returned, we realised why. Ashleigh is dead, Tamara is their prisoner, Zana and you had gone away. Though Zana came back within the day, they were able to attack in power. When you did not return with her, we knew our fate was – uncertain.'

'What of Arzandel?'

'He is dead.'

Maredudd waved to a bier across the room. I looked at the only man who could free me.

'Nay, he is not dead. He only sleeps,' I said, and placed the jade ring on the largest toe of Arzandel's left foot. Though Maredudd shook his head, I knew I was right, because Ashleigh had told me Arzandel could never die.

'And the expedition?' I asked.

'Your friends came back three nights ago. They are hiding in a safe place. They spoke highly of you. They were sad they could not hold back the cloud ferry. Zana knew one day would make all the difference. She knew how much we need you, so she left you her sign, the amulet you wear now.'

'Need me? For what?'

'Arzandel told us before he er, slept, that you had vowed to rescue Tamara from the er, enemy. He said you would come back from the Land at the Top of the World to fight the er, leader of the enemy. When you did not return with the others…'

He stopped short, struggling against the enemy he could not name. His silence told me he doubted I would honour my pledge when the one witness able to hold me to it, could no longer do so.

I walked over to the window and looked across Halsanger to the raging fire beyond. A song poured from my lips like the songs of old in Berren.

> 'My lady upon the white mare,
> Robed in white yourself,
> With purple orchids in your flaxen hair,
> And in your hand a lover's ivy wreath.

'My lady, born inspiration,
In its High Castle,
When I returned and brought your father down,
You knew I heralded fair Berren's fall.

'My lady, kept in caves afar,
Held by jackdaws now,
I see your proud lands ravaged by this war,
For Zoust's great army fights us as our foe.

'My lady, trapped who should be free,
I too am fast chained,
Yet still I must fight on for what must be,
To bring you to your castle once again.'

Maredudd looked sternly at me. 'So you knew,' he said.
'Knew what?' I asked, turning back to face him.
He shrugged his shoulders and looked at Arzandel.
'Then we wait,' he said, as if he was no longer there.
'No!' I cried. I hit Ashleigh's desk with a clenched fist.
'To wait is to descend further. To wait is to give up flying against the wind and get blown backwards. Tell me to wait, and I shall go my own way.'
'And what way is that?'
'To save my Lady Tamara. To go to the stronghold of Zoust!'
The tapestries rattled. The turret room dimmed.

Maredudd turned away in a trance and walked out of the door. I followed him. The quicker I walked, the faster he strode.

We walked out of Halsanger to a stone bridge across the river that fed Doudern Lake. Maredudd strode down the steep bank into the water. I watched him from the bridge.

The smoky haze lent the eerie scene an enchanted air. Maredudd floated and drifted with the red water under the bridge towards the lake. As he sank, I realised the river flowing beneath me was red with blood.

16: The Battle

I followed the red river through the trees. As I walked between the hedgerows, jackdaws rustled in the branches nearby. Ahead sounded the harsh noises of battle. The cries came from the fields close to the fire.

Choking smoke and flying dust clouded the battlefield. Citizens of Halsanger, clad in chain mail and carrying weapons, fought valiantly against an undefeatable foe. The enemy, soldiers of Zoust, were better equipped in every way. When one fell, he rose again as if untouched. They mowed down the people of Berren without mercy. Yet more people stepped forward to take their places. Somehow, they saw hope in defending their beliefs to the last.

I knew I had to end the battle somehow. Surely, one of Ashleigh's books could tell me the way. He had kept his library of wisdom in the keep of the High Castle. I ran back to the bridge, intent on returning there.

The jackdaws gathered around me. With each step I took, they fluttered a step closer. When I came to the crossroads, they circled me and blocked my way. I opened my wings to escape them. They opened their powerful wings and crowed in glee. They had trapped me.

I had always thought that being alone was a strength, but here I was powerless. Alone, I had overcome lesser battles, but now the odds against me were too great.

'Astor!' I called, hoping the wind would carry my cry to him. 'Yammas? Arzandel! Tamara. Anya, Kohtel, Zana? Can anyone help me?'

The only replies were the mocking cries of the jackdaws and the terrible song of battle.

I took up the key for bravery and stepped onto the road to Halsanger. The jackdaws dived on me. They tore at my clothes and clawed at my limbs. Rough feathers, grey wings, sharp beaks and savage claws blocked my vision. I fell to my knees on the road.

Out of the bushes stepped a winged man holding a rusty sword. He drove off the surprised jackdaws. When they had fled, he sheathed his sword and helped me to stand.

'Let's go, Eregendal. There are things you must see in Halsanger,' he said. He opened his broad white wings.

'Thank you for helping me, sir. But I don't think I can fly. The jackdaws savaged me.'

'Then I will carry you, star of my life. Even though you once refused to carry me.'

He took me up in his arms and flew to Halsanger. We landed in the market square. After he had set me down, he raised his wings to fly off again.

'Thank you, sir, for saving my life. I'm sorry, I don't remember you,' I said.

'Don't feel ashamed. We only met once. You helped me take my first step to freedom. A lot has happened since then, and I have changed. See: my wings, which you untied, are now stronger than your own. But I must leave you for other battles.'

He flew up into the cloudy sky. I tried to follow but struggled to leave the ground.

'Winged Man, at least tell me your name,' I shouted after him.

'Arken, the fallen star,' he shouted back. 'Now go! And do what you must.'

I set off up the hill to the High Castle, thinking that was what he meant. Ashleigh had kept his library in the castle keep. I was sure one of his books would have the answer I needed.

As I drew closer, I saw that the castle had been sacked. The battlements had been torn down. Stones from the curtain walls filled the moat. In the courtyard lay the body of the farmhand. The white mare nuzzled his shoulder, trying to

rouse him to feed her.

I climbed over the ruined walls and ran to the keep. Ashleigh's study in the turret room had been destroyed. The bureau had been smashed, and the tapestries ripped. The books I needed had been pulled apart and their pages scattered over the floor. Their timeless wisdom had been trampled in the dust. Upon the ceiling, someone had painted the three-pointed star in orange. It broke the silver circle Ashleigh had taught me to respect so long before. His holy sanctum lay wrecked.

I fled down the stone spiral staircase and ran out into the courtyard. The white mare cantered away from me in contempt. I could find no food to give her. Instead, I raised the portcullis so that she could go out and graze on the hillside. Then I walked off down the road to Halsanger. The mare overtook me and vanished into the dusk.

Halsanger looked deserted. Odd hushed noises told me that fearful people hid behind the bolted doors and shuttered windows. I stood outside the boarded tavern in the marketplace and wondered what to do.

'Arken?' I called in hope.

My call echoed around the empty square. I called again.

A cry from above made me turn. Arken fell from the sky with a flaming arrow through his chest. He was covered in blood and dust. His blunted rusty sword was strapped to his belt, broken.

'I heard your call, and came,' he whispered.

I blew out the flames and knelt beside him on the

cobbles.

'Now I travel to true Heart's Ease at last,' he said with a peaceful smile. 'Why did you call me, Eregendal?'

'I want to help you all, but I am shunned. I don't know what to do.'

'Can't you see why you are shunned?'

I shook my head. He tried to explain, struggling to breathe as he spoke.

'You didn't tell the Judges who you were. The things you did caused the death of your teacher. You forgot your pledge. You drove Maredudd the wise to his death. You caused Berren to be sacked and Halsanger Castle to fall. And still you don't see why you are shunned?'

'I didn't realise. I didn't know that what I did would have such an effect.'

'Aye! Your eyes are open but you are blinkered. Even Arzandel fell, because of you. Now Berren has nothing to trust in.'

'Nothing? What of Za…'

'Hush! Say nothing more that may destroy. Your friends are safe, but only if you take care.'

'Then what should I do? I must know. I have to end the battle so that I can rescue my lady from the stronghold of…''

'Hush! When his name is said, there he is. Though you are strong enough to say it, others aren't. And because you didn't realise that, you have destroyed so much.'

Arken sighed and placed his hand on the arrow wound in his chest.

'This is the message I pay for with my life. The battle will not end until our lady returns from afar. So go! Fulfil your pledge quickly, before the battle is lost.'

The jackdaws descended upon him. I turned away in shame. I looked back after the last jackdaw had flown away. All that was left of the winged man were some feathers and a broken, rusty sword.

17: The Stronghold of Zoust

I raised my damaged wings skyward once more and launched into the air. A following wind lifted me up from the market square, helping me to fly. I headed west towards the distant Grey Mountains, the land of Zoust. Soon a train of jackdaws gathered about me in the air. They joyfully led me to their master's kingdom. They even hung back when I fell behind.

We soon passed the Berren border into Sulien. The bleak Grey Mountains stood like vicious teeth on the far side. This rugged country had once been the home of a great nation, the Elutha. They were famed throughout the world in myth and legend for their courage, their power and their love of peace. But that was before the jackdaws came. Now the Elutha had settled across the world, taking their message of hope with them. They spread their light to save other countries from the jackdaws' darkness which had taken their own.

Further and further led the jackdaws. Dusk had become

night. Night stretched towards dawn. Then suddenly the jackdaws vanished. I landed on the edge of the foothills between Sulien and the Grey Mountains, wondering which way to go.

In front of me drifted a dark grey cloud, stabbed by random shafts of flame. I headed into its darkness. The choking evil in the air told me I was going the right way.

The cloud led me into the heart of the mountains. It stopped in a steep-sided gorge. Along the bottom of the gorge, ran a turgid beck which oozed out of a cave in a cliff. Its stench was so awful that I knew it must be the place to start searching for Tamara.

I waded through the clinging waters of the stream into the cave. In that blackness, my belt and keys did not shine. I had entered a region where even God and virtue did not go.

The first face Hell showed me was not the pit of fiery brimstone I had been told about in my childhood. That bright picture held none of the evil menace I stumbled through in that unlit cave. It reminded me of my journey through the Labyrinth of Lethee on the expedition. That helped me keep going.

My path went through narrow submerged passages, deep chasms, and slimy cliffs with slug-like bats. It took me past demons who mocked and mobbed. Some of them hunted me like game and trapped me in spiderweb nets. They dropped me in a deep hole with walls too tall and smooth to climb. My wings were so ragged, I could no longer fly. There was only one way for me to end that journey. I

stood tall and raised my arms.

'Zoust, by the sign of the circle, I call you here!'

The ground trembled and tore apart beneath my feet. I fell down a long, deep hole into a vast cavern. The cavern was lit by the fiery glow of a sea of boiling magma.

'Lo! Here is the one who can fight Zoust himself!' a voice boomed. 'Aye, can fight us, but not a simple hole!'

The cavern filled with mocking laugher. It did not upset me. Though evil surrounded me, the sign of the circle protected me.

'I have come for my lady Tamara,' I said.

A cloud swirled out of the fiery sea and touched the grey rock. A shape inside the cloud became a tall, lean man with cruel eyes. He wore long flowing robes of orange and grey. They were the same fire orange and ash grey that Tuzos the tempter had worn when we had met at Halsanger carnival.

'Here is your lady,' he announced in a voice which had the power of thunder.

Towards me walked a lady dressed in black. She was the twin of Tamara, but not her.

'I seek the Lady Tamara, not Ydal Aramat.'

A child dressed in deep red robes appeared to my left. She looked like Zana.

'But she is the one you seek,' said the child.

'You must be Anaz. I did not travel to the Tree of Knowledge with you.'

'In the eyes of men, I am the youngest of the expedition,'

she replied. Her tone implied that I was much lower than men.

'Aye? Then what am I?' I asked.

'You are Arzandel's puppet. Your downfall came only when he fell asleep under my spell.'

'That was not your work. He sleeps because the land is at war. He will wake up when the war is over.'

'And to end the war, you need your lady. If you take me back with you, we will let your lady come with us.'

She winked at the lean man and smiled at Aramat. Her face had the look of an old man, not a young girl.

'Get behind me, demon. I won't be your passport for the destruction of the world! Become what you are, Anaz! I see through your mask, old man. Your promises are all lies.'

Anaz raised a defiant fist. Even as she shook it, her body changed in shape. She grew thinner, taller, more bent. Her hair became white and her face became lined. She glared at me, a bitter old man.

'You may have the eyes to see, but you don't have the advantage, butterfly!' Anaz said in a cracked voice. 'I will be born when your young goddess dies. Every day I grow younger while she grows older. The day will come when I am stronger than her.'

Anaz turned on his heel and walked off across the sea of magma, He disappeared like vapour in its fiery light. Aramat watched him leave. Then she turned a flattering face towards me.

'But I am thy lady. I have been disguised by our great…'

she began. Her lips curled slightly, like a vicious dog.

I remembered the first time we had met on Doudern Fell, before I had carried Zana to the cloud ferry.

'Get behind me, wretched wolf! You can't even say the name of Zoust without revering him. And you daren't speak my lady Tamara's name. She is the blessing, and you the curse. She inspires people forward to creativity; you hold them back to destruction.'

With an animal howl, Aramat threw off her black robes, unable to bear them over her rough fur. She writhed as her body changed shape and forced her to balance on all fours. In wolf-form, she threw herself at me, her jaws at my throat. I fell to the ground by the magma sea. The heat and fumes choked me.

Thunder rolled about the cavern and seemed to form words.

'We do not keep you here, for then you would take a path of virtue. Instead, we let you return to Halsanger having failed. Our power in the human kingdom of Berren will make you sing a different song, as surely as my name is Stuzo.'

The voice faded, the cavern shimmered, and its walls melted. The magma sank back into the earth and sedge sprouted where it had been. The hot, foul air blew away on an icy breeze. Hell had made way for Earth.

I sank to the ground, exhausted. Though I did not know where I was or the meaning of what I had gone through, I felt intensely happy to be free.

18: The Return to Halsanger

Stuzo had left me stranded in a vast bog in the foothills of the Grey Mountains, on the edge of Sulien. I sat on a tussock with peat water all around me. My wings had gone. Hell had ripped them from me. Stains and tears had ruined my beautiful robes. A heavy weight pressed down on my shoulders and bowed my back. No longer was I proud Eregendal, ready to face any foe to save a person in need. Now I was the one in need, but no-one was there to help me.

My first challenge was to cross the bog. I tried to jump from the tussock to a clump of reeds but misjudged the leap. To stop myself falling into the mire, I kept leaping from clump to clump. Then my foot slipped. My body landed across a gravel bank, but my legs lay in black water up to my knees. The evil-smelling mud sucked my feet down. When I struggled, I sank even faster.

Terrified the mud would swallow me up whole, I grasped a clump of sedge to stop me sinking. I held onto the sedge with my right hand so that I could reach my keys. When I clutched the third key for bravery, my fear fled. It freed my mind to think out a way to escape.

This time I inched forward, using my hands to drag my body across the firm gravel bank. My legs stayed still. After a while, my left foot pulled free. My other leg soon followed.

The mire flowed back unmarked. It left me coated in foul-smelling mud and worried about crossing the rest of the

bog. I planned my path and steadied myself before making each leap. With no further falls, I reached the edge of the mire by early afternoon. It felt so good to be safe, I cheered.

The sound of hoofbeats made me look east. Tamara's white mare galloped past. She had a broken halter around her neck. I wondered why she headed for the Grey Mountains without a rider and who had tried to hold her back.

The misty Sulien plain stretched towards the east beyond some foothills. In the far distance, I could see Doudern Fell. I set off on foot down a grassy track which led through the hills towards the plain.

The track took me to a small market town. I washed myself in a nearby river before daring to set foot in its neat cobbled streets. The tall thin houses stood very close together on the wide main street. They looked as if people had built them so that everybody could live overlooking the marketplace. Traders bustled around me, packing up their wares after a good day at the autumn fair.

'Sir, that stale bread you are about to throw away: could you spare a piece?' I begged: 'Kind lady, that bruised apple you couldn't sell: please could you give… Young child, that water you draw from the well: may I have a sip…?'

They threw me out of the town. I spent the night near where I had landed, in a dry roadside ditch below a tall dyke.

The sound of hoofbeats woke me next dawn. I stood up in the ditch to see who rode out so early. Coming towards me was the white mare. On her back rode my lovely lady, Tamara, clad in white.

I pulled some ivy from the dyke to shape into a rough wreath. Then I climbed up on to the road. Tamara saw me and halted her mare.

'Who art thou?' she asked. Her voice and face were kind.

I saw the purple orchids in her blonde hair. They made my crown of ivy look poor.

'My Lady Tamara, do you not know me now?'

'Nay!' she said. She gathered her reins to ride on.

'Wait, my Lady. Truly I went to Zoust to rescue you, but I failed. At least you are free, and Halsanger will live again. When you get back, Arzandel will wake up and the battle will end.'

I turned to walk away, sad in my defeat.

'Who art thou, traveller, to know so much?'

'I am the one who sung the song you inspired. Its curse lies heavily on my soul. So don this ivy crown: even beggars can honour you. And go! Go back to Berren and end the pointless war.'

Tamara took the ivy crown and looked at it. She turned back to me.

'I charge thee to tell me thy name. Then will I don thy crown without further word and ride back to Halsanger Castle.'

'I am the one you knew as the butterfly. Eregendal is no more. God speed your journey. I will follow after you.'

Tamara put on the ivy crown and made to speak, but her promise sealed her lips. She urged on her mare and

galloped off down the road.

I walked after her towards Berren. No-one passed to offer help or company, but I did not want for food. An old orchard gave me a lunch of fine apples.

An hour before sunset, a horse-drawn cart came into view on the road ahead. It halted beside me and a friendly Eluthan couple climbed out. They were tall and broad-shouldered. Their faces were round, and they had auburn hair. He wore an inn-keeper's apron over his tunic. She wore a leaf green shift gathered by a beaded belt.

'Eregendal?' they asked.

'Aye, that I was, though I have no wings now.'

'I am Finian, and this is my wife Beatha. Come with us to Dubrai, the next town. A room awaits you at our inn.'

'But I have no money.'

'All has been paid for by a lady on a white mare.'

They took me to their inn and treated me with great kindness. Beatha set out a large meal which we ate together. Then we sat beside the fire and talked.

'What happened to you in the Grey Mountains, Eregendal?' Beatha asked: 'I can tell from the way you stoop that it was very hard.'

I told them about my journey into Stuzo's lair. They listened with such attention that I talked far more than I meant to. They heard me without judgement and helped me understand it all.

'I failed in what I had set out to do,' I said. 'I dreamed of proudly leading Tamara on her white mare back into

Halsanger. That would save Berren and quash the death sentence over me. It turned out to be the nonsense everyone else knew it to be. I did not enter Hell. It was just an illusion created by the demons to torture me. I did not meet Zoust: I only saw his minions: Stuzo, Aramat and Anaz. And they did not return to their true shapes because I got the better of them. They only changed back because they didn't need to keep their guise. My only joy after all this is that Tamara is now free. She is on her way home to save Halsanger.'

Finian opened a goatskin and poured me a drink in a silver goblet. He fetched tankards of ale for Beatha and himself.

'Truly, Eregendal, we feel privileged to have you in our house. No matter the result: you acted in honour. We toast you for that.'

They raised their tankards to me. I sipped my warming drink and thanked them.

'What happened to Tamara? Was she able to tell you?'

'The jackdaws treated the White Lady very well, for them,' Finian said: 'They kept her in a cave that had no light, but for a white crystal in the room. During the day, this crystal was bright and at night, very dim. The crystal showed her all that went on in Berren. When you stood at the turret window and sang, she was the one who put the words in your heart.'

'So that was the tapestry she wove. Why did she not know me on the road?'

'The crystal looked out only on Berren, the land of men.

She could not see into the land of Zoust.'

I looked up, startled to hear someone else say the dread name.

'Fear not, Eregendal,' said Beatha: 'Zoust has our home, but never will he have our hearts and minds. We are exiles. We have no cause to fear him. He already has the one thing dear to us besides God – our homeland.'

'We armed Sulien against his coming,' Finian said: 'Because of Sulien, he could only trouble Berren at night when it was weak. Alas, Berren became too weak after the jackdaws took the White Lady and the expedition left. We can only wait and pray now for the time the White Lady gets back to her castle.'

'How did Tamara escape?'

'When Zana and the expedition got back to Berren, her cell could no longer hold her. Nothing can stop the White Lady when people support her cause. But she needed her horse to make the journey back. Sadly, the Judges kept the white mare for her return. They used it for silly errands. When you freed the mare, you caused great alarm in Halsanger. No-one knew the White Lady needed the mare to fetch her home.'

I sighed to hear the people of Berren still doubted me.

'What hope is there for me when I return?'

'None can say.'

Finian's firm voice told me he knew but would not say.

'Then it is only as I thought.'

I slept there the night and rose early next morning to set

out on my way. Beatha had washed and mended my torn robes while I slept. Finian saddled a horse for me and gave me some money for the journey.

Three days' later, I reached the river border between Sulien and Berren. The broad beck flowed into the river that fed the lake at the foot of Doudern Fell. On the far side of the beck lay the field where the battle had raged.

Now no trace of the battle could be seen. A woman drove a team of oxen to plough in the soil. On the edge of the field, a mason carved an inscription on an ancient standing stone to mark the battle.

I forded the beck and reined in my horse to speak to a woman working by the path. She wore sackcloth to dig the ditch. When I stopped her, she narrowed her eyes at me.

'Greetings. How goes it in Halsanger?' I asked.

'Fear no longer walks the streets, and the song of mourning is over. But you cannot plough the memory into the ground.'

'Where can I find the Lady Tamara?'

'At the grave of her father. She waits for the one they call Eregendal.'

I thanked her and rode off to the graveyard. There stood Tamara by the grave of her father. I stepped down from my horse and walked over to her.

'You have come back,' Tamara said.

'Aye, my lady. I must thank you for the help you gave to get me here.'

'Help only to see you dead the sooner. Come: there are

things to be done in Halsanger.'

We rode our horses through the fields to the town. In the market square sat the Judges' Council, now only of eight.

'We waited on your command, Lady Tamara,' said Micheldor.

The square filled with people. Fury filled their eyes.

'Honoured Council of Judges, here is Eregendal,' said Tamara: 'You know the facts of the case. Now let them speak for themselves.'

19: The Judgement

Judge Micheldor stood. His face and voice were grave.

'Eregendal, these are the crimes you are charged with. First: you tried to destroy Berren. Second: you caused the death of Lord Ashleigh. Third: you delayed the return of the Expedition to the Land at the Top of the World. This caused the deaths of thousands in battle. Fourth: you gave up your quest in the Land of Peace after reaching the Tree of Knowledge. Fifth: you caused the death of Judge Maredudd. Sixth: you caused the death of the wizard Arzandel. Seventh: you caused the sacking of Halsanger Castle. Eighth: you freed the white mare owned by Lady Tamara against the wishes of the Judges' Council. Ninth: you caused the death of Messenger Arken. Tenth: you failed in your pledge. You did not free our Lady Tamara from the stronghold of the enemy. How do you plead?'

'Sirs, I did take part in all those events. But I did not cause them all. I ask you to hear the charges one at a time. I ask for a fair hearing.'

The Judges discussed my requests and agreed to them.

'The first charge, that you tried to destroy Berren. How do you plead?' demanded Micheldor.

'During this stay here? I am not guilty by intent. Who has raised this charge against me?'

'Our two witnesses, Lord Ashleigh and the wizard Arzandel, are both dead by your deeds. The Council therefore finds you guilty of…'

'Stop!' ordered a woman in the crowd.

People turned to watch her as she came to the front. She wore a rough woollen cloak with the hood pulled low to hide her face.

'Let me give my evidence,' she said: 'I was…'

'Your name, Madam?' asked Hapis the bull.

'My name is not important. My words are. I met the accused the day after the carnival. We walked to the shepherds' hut on Doudern Fell. We knew each other from the time the accused studied here. The accused had stayed in the shepherds' hut six years ago. It was the talk of the town at the time. Ashleigh was a hard teacher at times, as we all knew. The accused could not cope with the lessons and hid. None of us helped that troubled youth. Eregendal came back that spring with a bitter heart we had not tried to ease. We ourselves destroyed our land when we did not help one with the power to destroy it. So we should answer this charge, not

the accused.'

'First charge dismissed,' said Micheldor with a yawn. 'The second charge: the accused caused the death of Lord Ashleigh.'

'I plead guilty. I have already offered myself as the black rose wreath. I regret that my deeds caused Ashleigh's death.'

'Poor thing to use as a mark of respect,' said cat-like Sekma with her nose in the air.

'Third charge: the accused delayed the return of the Expedition. This caused the death of thousands more in battle.'

'Why bother with this?' a man shouted from the crowd. 'Eregendal has admitted murdering Lord Ashleigh. The rogue is already as good as dead!'

'Aye,' agreed another: 'What's all this for? To give a bad dog a good name?'

'Murderer! Burn the traitor! Stop the hearing!' shouted the crowd, surging forward.

'Stop! Come to order!' Micheldor said in a voice all could hear. 'Respect your court or it will not respect you.'

The crowd halted. Some people drew back a step. I could hear them muttering.

'Let me stand as a witness for the third and fourth charges,' said the cloaked woman. 'Yes, it is true that Eregendal forgot the quest in the Land at the Top of the World. But so it charms all people. That is one of many tests we all had to face. It only delayed us in dream time: at the most, less than a second. And we had faced many trials we

could not have overcome without Eregendal's help. We would not even have left Doudern Fell.'

'Madam, if you claim to be a member of that expedition, please show yourself.'

'If I must.'

She drew back her hood, undid the pin and let her cloak fall to the ground. Anya stood there, proud and tall, dressed like a princess in azure blue. The crowd hid their faces from her radiance. Only Tamara and I could face her. Anya turned to me.

'Why I should come back from the Top of the World in ease and with great honour, but you should come back through your own efforts and face hatred, I do not know, dearest Eregendal. But after all you have done for me, I could not leave you to be hounded by this vicious pack, who have destroyed many as good as you before.'

'But I shall die anyway unless my lady Tamara chooses otherwise.'

'Aye, and she is as hard a master as her father was before her. But these? O Eregendal, after all you have seen and done, why do you seek a just verdict from this pit of vipers? Here you will find only closed minds, hardened hearts, greed and hatred. Come, let us away.'

'But we must close the case,' bleated Kanum the sheep.

'If you must,' Anya said. 'Your fifth charge: Judge Maredudd the Wise died trying to help Eregendal bring Tamara back here. Your sixth charge: we all know Arzandel never dies but only sleeps. Even now he awakens. The

seventh, the destruction of the High Castle. Tamara herself caused that when her thoughts led Zoust there to destroy it. We all heard the strange song that day, sung by Tamara through Eregendal. Eight, the white mare. Lady Tamara, you would not have got back here from the Grey Mountains had Eregendal not freed your mare. Nine: Arken chose to die out of his gratitude for Eregendal. He answered the call for help when no-one else would go. And finally, that Eregendal failed to free Lady Tamara? O hypocrites! Did you even think of trying to save our lady from the stronghold of Zoust? That Eregendal came back from there is miracle enough in itself!'

'How do we know the accused even went there?' asked Torpeth the Sage, his ear horn waving.

'Eregendal, kneel and bare your back so that the Judges can see your shoulders.'

I knelt and lifted my singlet over the painful stubs where once my proud wings had been. Anya's cool hand traced a burning circle and three-pointed star between my shoulders. It was where I felt I carried a heavy load.

'Tamara has the same mark, as did Ashleigh. So too did Petros the Martyr, an ancient prophet now forgotten by Berren. So, Judges, you make a mockery of your Council, seeking to destroy that which you could never aspire to yourselves.'

I straightened my clothes and stood.

'You were right, Anya, and I was wrong. Let us leave them to their judgements. I know I have been true to myself, my friends and my God as ever mortal creature can be. I can

go to my fate in peace.'

Anya and I pushed our way through the angry crowd and left the square to walk to the graveyard. The people waited a little before they followed, to give me time to make peace with God before I faced my fate. As we walked, the cobbled streets turned to a cart track and the houses gave way to fields of oats.

'Eregendal, why don't you go down to the Tarn of Mirrors and leave now?'

'I live in hope that Tamara will have compassion.'

'As much as her father.'

I walked three paces and said, 'Arzandel will not be there. I need his help to pass through the Tarn of Mirrors.'

'He is there.'

We walked further in silence.

'I cannot go against my word. This is the path I must take, no matter how hard it may be.'

I picked up my five keys in my hands.

'I have learnt so much in my short stay here. I now know that we can only learn some things the hard way. I need to accept that. I know that on the true path, I will face trouble. I must face that trouble bravely, as many have done before and others will do after me. I should accept help from others as well as give help to them. And through all, if I trust in God and do my best, I will do God's will. God alone can judge, and God does not judge us on our virtues or our deeds, but by our hearts and our repentance.'

'And the belt?'

'This showed me that if I live by the virtues of the keys: experience, patience, courage, fellowship and faith in God, I have not lived in vain. So it does not matter what others see me as, nor how my journey through the world has been.'

'But to face death?'

'Is to touch the handle of the door into the next room. And to die is to fall asleep on a winter night and waken to a spring morning. To die is to pass from a world of dreams into a world that is real. To die is to walk further along the circle that is life, to rise at length from its depths into peace.'

Birdsong filled the air as we reached the graveyard. The birds sang more brightly than they had ever greeted the day. Their songs ended when the people arrived from the town.

We walked to Ashleigh's grave. In front of the tomb stood a large funeral pyre. Tamara and Micheldor took places on either side. A crowd of people gathered around us. A weary man walked through the circle. His body looked shrunken inside his long purple robes. I ran to hug him.

'Arzandel, you are awake!'

'Aye, I am, and full sorry too. For I do not have the black rose wreath. Someone stole it from me when they stormed my cave. And those who stormed it were not the forces of Zoust. He would prefer us to burn the wreath than you, Eregendal.'

'Then why did he set me free?'

'Because he knew who does have the wreath, the one who fooled him with a mask of compassion. But Inspiration is never compassionate. It can only be as kind as its father,

Experience. Lo, see the woman who bears the wreath and will also bear your fate.'

I looked at Tamara and saw in her hand the black rose wreath. Before I could speak, Micheldor raised his arms and silenced the crowd.

'Citizens of Berren, the Judges Council has agreed this verdict with Lady Tamara. The condemned prisoner, Eregendal, will be burnt on the grave of the victim, the great Lord Ashleigh. But because we cannot use a criminal alone to show our mark of respect for the deceased, we will burn the black rose wreath too.'

The crowd cheered. People pushed me towards the pyre. Micheldor let them jostle me for a while before he raised his arms to stop them.

'People of Berren, if any of you want to speak your last words to the condemned, do so now.'

Many did. Most spat on me or cursed me. But one person shook my hand and thanked me for rescuing his coin from Epoh. A second placed my hand around the haft of his sword and said, 'Shartere is at your command.' I replied, 'Thank you, but I choose to go this way.' A third hugged me and recalled our flight with the useless books.

A fourth, shorter than the rest and hidden by a hood and cloak, gave me a small green flower in a green ribbon. She whispered, 'Take strength. This is the way it must be. Hold fast to the end, and you will see why.'

Anya spoke to me last. She hugged me, tears falling down her face. When the soldiers stepped up to bind me to

the pyre, she tried to order them off. They pushed her away.

Tamara placed the black rose wreath as a crown upon my head. She lit the sticks at the base of the pyre.

The flames curled up around my feet. It became hard to breathe. I held the zana flower close to me and felt its power flow through my veins. Though I felt the heat and the smoke, they did not hurt me. A feeling of great peace stilled my body and my thoughts ceased.

20: The Vision

I found myself looking down on a country scene. Songbirds sang around me. A crowd of people stood in a graveyard near a lake. A long fell cast a shadow over them. The people stared at a large bonfire. I settled on a branch to watch.

Something moved in the ashes of the fire. Two wings shook out some embers from their feathers. They were the wings of an eagle. At first it looked small and weak. It preened its feathers and gained in strength. People watched in awe as it grew up before their eyes.

The eagle stretched and stood proud. It had grown to six feet tall. Its outstretched wings spanned fifteen feet. Its feathers gleamed gold like the sun. Its talons, beak and eyes shone like silver. Its majesty awed the crowd. Some people ran away in fear.

'Ladnegere!' cried Tamara.

The eagle lifted its head to the sky. It gave a haunting cry. The ground shook. Lightning split the sky. The heavy stone door of the Castle Tomb slid aside.

A hand reached out of the tomb. Weak fingers gripped the doorpost. Ashley stepped out of his grave. He lifted his hands to the sky in thanks.

Three people helped him onto the path. Others brought water and food. Astor lifted him onto a cart and Yammas drove him back to Halsanger. The crowd streamed down the road behind them, amazed at the miracle.

Ladnegere flew to the river mouth on the lake. The eagle landed near Hearts Ease Island. Its haunting cry echoed across the fell slopes and out over the plain. The lake rolled back. Out of the mud rose the soldiers who had fallen in battle. They looked young and fit once more. They marched towards Halsanger in a column five abreast. The air rang with their songs of victory. After the last soldiers had gone, Ladnegere circled the lake. The waters came back together.

The eagle flew over to the ploughed battlefield. Its cry turned the new memorial back into the old standing stone. The bare ploughed field filled with wheat.

On the eagle flew to the bridge where I had watched Maredudd drown. At its call, the judge walked out as if he had never entered the river.

Ladnegere flew on up to the shepherds' hut. Its cry mended all the damage. Even the fuel store became full again.

The eagle flew on to the Tarn of Mirrors. Nothing changed there at its cry. The damage to Arzandel's cave had

not been caused by me or the work of Zoust and his forces.

Ladnegere flew to Halsanger Castle. It landed on the tallest turret still standing there. Its harsh cry raised the walls. The moat filled with water. The farm labourer awoke. The keep and Ashleigh's study returned to their former order.

The eagle flew down to the market square. It gave a soft cry which brought Arken back to life. The winged man praised the eagle and gave thanks to God.

Ladnegere landed on a column beside the Judges' tables. It balanced there with open wings, silhouetted against the setting sun.

Dusk brought more people onto the streets. They carried torches to light the square. Those who had not seen Ladnegere's power looked uneasy. They talked in whispers with their eyes fixed on the ground. Those healed by the eagle's voice looked up at it with adoring eyes. They pointed it out to grateful friends and families.

A trumpet blew to announce the Judges' Council. The nine Judges walked to their places and sat. Eight cloaked people stood behind them.

Micheldor rose. The eagle's shadow fell across him. The crowd hushed to hear him speak. He spoke of the great victory over the enemy and the miracles that had happened. He spoke as if he had led the land to that victory and he had caused those miracles.

Maredudd the Wise could listen no longer. He sprang up in rage and raised his arms to silence Micheldor. As he spoke, the moon came out.

'Hasty to condemn and murder! Hasty to give yourselves the victory! Hasty then will be those who judge you!' he accused.

Ladnegere raised its head to the heavens and gave a raucous call. A thunderbolt smashed down upon the centre table, splitting it in two. Eight jackdaws rose screaming from the stone benches. They flew off into the night towards the distant Grey Mountains. Only Maredudd remained. He stood, a prince among judges, wearing a crown of beech leaves. He turned to the crowd.

'How many of you came to this table to be turned away. To you is this land given. How few of you came to this table to receive a fair verdict that you obeyed. To you is this city given. How many of you came to this table and won your case unjustly. More dishonest than foxes! You acted like scavenging crows. You hid like snakes among the rocks when your land needed you. You feasted like rats on its rotten core. You bolted your doors against the luckless stranger in the night. You came out at dawn like wolves to take that which was not yours. As you have judged and acted, so be it judged and acted upon you!'

Ladnegere cried out. People screamed in the uproar that followed. Between the feet of the crowd fled foxes, snakes, rats and wolves. Fifty crows flew into the sky and headed west. Only a third of the people were left. Their rough tunics had become rich new robes. They clapped and cheered. Maredudd raised his arms to hush them.

'The night has just begun. The last battle is not yet over.

Your faith has saved us from the first attacks. Now we must watch and pray. God can work through our faith in God's power. We must trust as one that God will save our land.'

Maredudd paused to let the people grasp that.

'Messengers will have told Zoust by now that Berren is free. Soon, his forces will cross our border in a final bid to take us. Stay with me in this square. Unite your hope with mine. Pray for those who will fight to save you as they go into battle.'

He bowed to the eight cloaked people standing with him at the stone tables. They mounted eight horses and galloped off up the hill. The eagle soared above them. I followed them to the cairn on Doudern Fell. There, I tried to speak to them. They could not see or hear me.

Midnight deepened. A heavy cloud hid the face of the moon. Eight gathered in a circle to talk. The eagle watched.

A man stepped forward onto the patch of moorland that became the field of contest. His torch blazed through the cloud. The flame lit up nine strangers with cloaks of ash grey.

'Lethok, come forward!' cried Kohtel.

A crowned woman met him on the field. She carried a rod of darkening. They grappled for an hour in mental fight. Her tactics failed to defeat Kohtel. Maddened, she struck him with her rod. The torch flew from his grasp. She reached to pick it up with her left hand. It flared in her face. She screamed and flung it from her, turning away from its blinding light. Then she melted back into the dark cloud.

Kohtel lay still on the moor. A gentle breeze blew up

from Halsanger. It carried the prayers of the people in the town. Their hope and strength revived him. He struggled back to the cairn.

Astor leapt forward, wielding Shartere. A bronze-clad woman clashed with him. Her feigning tricks gave her the upper hand. He fought only to defend. As he parried each blow, his strength faded like the torch which lit the scene.

The breeze returned. Astor gave a mighty blow. Shartere disarmed the woman but broke below the hilt. Astor reached to take up her sword. It leapt from his hand and stabbed him through the chest. He turned and fell at the cairn. She melted back into the cloud.

Yammas walked onto the field, carrying just his coin. He faced a strange dark monster, the Sammay. Its claws and teeth glinted in the torchlight as it struck at him. Its sleek rounded body tried to smother him.

A gentle wind swept across the moor. The coin grew into a shield. Yammas parried the Sammay's attacks. The torch grew brighter in the wind. The Sammay screamed with anger and turned on itself. Yammas herded it with the shield until it got caught in its own jaws and fell.

The dark cloud became smaller and thicker. The torch blazed brighter.

Anya stepped onto the field to face an ancient man. He wore the fire-coloured robes of an enchanter. His spells created a maze through which no human could find a way. Anya formed the Mirror of the Hand to turn his spells upon himself. She raised her left palm towards him with her elbow

as high as the fingers shielding her face. Then she drew a circle with her right hand to hold him. Her counter-spell trapped him inside his own maze.

The dark cloud settled on the field and floated back. Anya stood alone like a stone statue on the moor. The circle drawn by her right hand haloed her face.

Zoust called out from the cloud that was him.

'But where is your next champion? The one who thought to fight Zoust alone?'

The night went very cold. One of the four still standing threw off her cloak. Tamara stepped forward.

'Eregendal is dead,' she said.

'Then who shall fight in Eregendal's place?'

Arzandel walked onto the field.

'It was Tamara who killed Eregendal. This fulfilled the old prophecy. "From the funeral pyre of one shall come forth two: one but reawakening, the other newborn of the martyr's ashes".'

Ashleigh walked forward, looking as if he had already fought his battle. He drew only scorn from Zoust.

'Why do you three face me when I have already done with you? Where is the newborn? Ah, but such a babe must be too young to fight!'

Ladnegere raised its wings and screamed a chilling cry. The torch flared up to reveal its opponent, a huge and terrible dragon four times the eagle's size.

The dragon was slate grey, with the sheen of polished stone. Its body was long and thin with spines along its back.

It had four thick legs armed with barbed claws and two leathery wings. Its neck was so long that it could coil it once and still face forward. Its long face had sharp ears, large eyes and flared nostrils. Its head turned towards Ladnegere. A strange bellow came from its fanged mouth. Fiery breath scorched the moorland grass.

The dragon lumbered up into the air. It tried its wings as if it had not flown before. Ladnegere gave chase and harried it. The dragon struggled to fight back while it learned how to use its limbs. It looked the more newly born of the two. But with each action, the dragon became more able and its weapons more deadly.

Berren stopped. Everyone watched the two fighters in the sky. Neither creature had the upper hand. The dragon's flames could not harm the child of fire. Weighty strength was matched by swift flight. Barbed claws and sharp fangs fought against hooked talons and curved beak. Two equally armoured bodies of stone and metal rebuffed attack.

As the night wore on, the dragon looked the better fighter of the two. Its parries and thrusts pushed Ladnegere towards the Grey Mountains. When the eagle clawed at the dragon's wings, the dragon's lunge forced the eagle back a yard. The closer they drew to the Grey Mountains, the more the dragon tasted victory. It teased the eagle as well as fought.

Far away on Doudern Fell, Zoust marched about. He wheeled the dark cloud like a cloak around his unseen body. The last of the eight cloaked riders ignored his show. His cloud moved onto the field.

'And where is the greatest of you who thinks to defeat the truly greatest?' Zoust challenged. He knew the eagle's strength came from the prayers of that cloaked rider. To win the battle, he had to stop the prayers.

'Do you doubt your dragon?' Arzandel replied. 'Even now when they fight at the edge of the Grey Mountains?'

Zoust ignored the wizard. He threw balls of lightning across his cloud to frighten the one who prayed. Still, Ladnegere held the exultant dragon on the mountain border.

The Halsanger clock rang in the fourth hour. The dragon slowed. Ladnegere looked stronger. Zoust gave an angry roar which shook the earth. The first light of dawn had touched the eastern horizon with a faint pink glow.

The battle in the dark west sky became more brutal. The winged fighters danced and darted in the air in fearsome combat. Now the dragon gave way more than the eagle.

The sun emerged from behind the mountains. It haloed the winged fighters in gold. The light was so blinding, every eye turned away. Zoust raged, but the rising sun sapped his thunder. Soon his grey cloud drifted in tattered shreds on the dawn breeze.

The sun rose fully into the sky and lit the deepest valleys in the fells. The brave eagle flew a feint around the dragon's eyes. The dragon's neck twisted and looped. Its head turned and darted. Its attack tied a knot in its own neck. It fell through the air with a strangled cry and landed lifeless on the sinking Grey Mountains.

Ladnegere glided back to Doudern Fell and slumped

with open wings across the shining cairn.

The last of the eight riders lifted her black hood. Her cloak fell to the ground and revealed Zana in radiant glory. To all who saw her, it seemed as if the sun itself stood on the top of Doudern Fell.

'Come down, Zoust!' she called in a voice I thought nothing could disobey. 'My champions fought yours in the depth of your night. Now it is your turn to fight, with me as your match, in the height of my day.'

Zoust took his shadows into himself and replied in a low rumbling voice.

'Nay, Zana. I must leave thee now. Or thy world will take me where I cannot face to go, the country of Ever Day.'

'Then I claim this forfeit of you as you will not fight. I claim back the people stolen by your servants and your jackdaws. I claim back all creatures imprisoned unjustly in your caves and jails. You will put them on the boats I send. Then I will return them to their rightful homes.'

'Aye,' Zoust agreed, willing to promise anything as he fled from the sun. He flew to the Grey Mountains as the last peaks slipped below the horizon.

Zana looked across the field of combat at her fallen warriors. She sent Tamara to fetch some water and knelt beside Kohtel. As she bathed his wounded hand, he awoke. He leapt to his feet to fight on but saw that all was over.

'Where can this be? Heaven?'

Then he saw Astor lying with the sword through his chest. He knelt at his side to weep for his friend.

'Aye, my trusty servant,' Zana said. 'Now, shed no tears, for Astor lives.'

She pulled the evil sword from the soldier's chest and bathed his wound with fresh water. Astor woke as from a deep sleep and stared at Zana's face.

'My Lord!' he cried and tried to kneel at her feet.

'Rest, my defender. Sheath your sword: it will be of further use.'

She took the two parts of Shartere and gave them back to the soldier, whole.

Zana blessed Yammas and brought him out of his trance. She hugged Anya and turned her back from stone to flesh. She washed Ladnegere's wounds and healed them. Then she turned to Tamara and Ashleigh. Her face was stern.

'Make good the damage done by your foolish followers. Then you may stay in the High Castle. The voices of experience and inspiration are still needed in the dreamlands. You will still be heard beyond the Tarn of Mirrors. Now go!'

Tamara and Ashleigh bowed their heads and mounted their horses. They cantered off down the fellside.

Zana turned to Arzandel. He spoke to her as her equal.

'Now is the time of the new heaven and the new earth.'

'Yes, Arzandel. It is good that you will stay by the Tarn of Mirrors, where you have always been. Keep guiding people on the last part of life's circle. The Green Lady and the sky ferries will still be there to help you. But before you go back to your fire, please go to Halsanger one last time. I need your help at noon.'

Arzandel nodded to show he would do as she asked. He mounted his horse and rode off.

Zana rode down from the fell soon after him. Her champions Anya, Kohtel, Yammas and Astor formed her guard of honour. Ladnegere flew above their heads, dancing in the air to please her. People came up from Halsanger to meet them. The men cheered the heroes. Women put garlands of flowers around their shoulders. Children scattered petals to carpet their path. Songs of wild beauty rang through the fells. Deer gambolled and birds sang.

A feast had been set out in Halsanger market square. Someone had wedged the broken Judges' table to level the top. Zana took the place of honour at its centre. To her right sat Astor, and to her left Anya. At the other tables sat Kohtel, Yammas, Maredudd the Prince-Judge and Arken the Winged Man. Over them watched Ladnegere. Before them stood Arzandel. Behind him stood a crowd of people from the town and beyond.

The last to arrive before the ceremony began were Ashleigh and Tamara. They looked chastened and tried to join the crowd. Zana invited them to take the two empty places at the stone tables instead. Ashleigh sat beside Yammas. His stern face became gentle in the light of Zana's smile. Tamara sat beside Arken. Her beauty looked like a poor copy of Zana's pure beauty. I saw them together, and realised that all my life, I had worshipped a lesser god.

Arzandel recited an old prophetic poem to welcome Zana. It told how she had chosen to live among humans as a

child, even though she was the source of all creation. Arzandel asked her to accept the people's crown and become their queen. She stood and thanked them all for the honour they gave her, quoting the same poem.

'Your home is mine: I come to stay with you, and will for ever in this happy land,' she promised.

The people cheered. Ashleigh handed Arzandel a crown. It was a fine circlet of white gold.

The wizard held up the crown to frame the sun as he gave the blessing of fate. Then he placed the crown on Zana's silver-blonde hair. A boy sang a song of welcome in the old tongue. Then Arzandel raised his hands again.

'People, not all the guests have got here yet.'

He pointed to the far side of the square. In rode a column of people from Sulien: the broad-faced Elutha and their friends. Then he pointed upwards to Doudern Fell. Ten pale blue sky boats sailed down on silver clouds. Zana stood up to greet the latecomers.

'Here are those who lived in exile for me, who faced prison for me and who died for me,' she said.

Her smile healed all their pain and sorrow. The lines left their faces and they became young again. The people of Berren welcomed them.

Zana held one last ceremony before the feast began. She called for her champions to come forward. First, she spoke to Kohtel. He handed her his torch.

'Kohtel, you brought light to the traveller. You led the way. Let this torch burn always. It will honour the people you

stand for: the spiritual leaders in the dreamworlds.'

She placed the burning torch on a pillar. Then she turned to Astor and took his sword, Shartere.

'Astor, you defended the traveller with your sword. You fought only to protect. Let Shartere grow into a beech tree, our symbol of peace. It will honour the people you stand for: defenders of the faiths in the dreamworlds.'

She placed the tip of Shartere's blade in the soil behind her seat. It grew into a huge beech tree with silver branches and copper leaves. Then she turned to Anya. She took her five diaries.

'Anya, you wrote about your own journey. You used your writings to guide others. Let your diaries become pillars for my new temple. They will honour the people you stand for: the prophets in the dreamworlds.'

Zana placed the five diaries on the ground beside the beech tree. They grew into tall marble pillars. Behind them, a marble temple grew out of a great mist. Then Zana turned to Yammas. She took from him the cauldron and the coin.

'Twice blest Yammas, you were the good shepherd. You knew when to try chance and when to use foresight. Let this cauldron become a window to look out on the flocks in the dreamworlds. And let this coin become a statue at its head. They will honour the people you stand for: the faithful shepherds in the dreamworlds.'

She placed the cauldron in front of the centre table on the square. It changed into a marble-edged pool of clear water. At the foot of the pool, she placed the coin. It grew and

changed into a life-sized statue of the lamb pictured upon it.

Finally, Zana gazed into the pool. I looked with her through its misty waters. There I saw myself sleeping beside a tarn in a wooded clearing.

'Eregendal, you were the willing servant who faced hell and death to do what you thought was right. You do not yet live with us in Berren. But the child born of your ashes, Ladnegere, is what you have become in our land. Your belt and keys are now a part of our temple. Each key has opened a chapel. Each chapel is linked by the belt that now supports the dome. Here in my house, all will remember the people you stand for: the believers in the dreamworlds.'

My gaze moved from the pool's view of my sleeping self to the inside the great temple. Five chapels led off a vast domed hall. Their wrought silver gates stood open. Each chapel honoured the virtue of one of the five keys. The posts of each gate fitted into a crown of stone which supported the great dome. A gold-cloth tapestry of faces covered the stone crown. Some of the faces were famous, most were not. My last view was of a small tortoiseshell butterfly, embroidered where the dawn sun would first touch.

21: Arzandel's Farewell

The misty dawn made Sluthe Wood look grey. My horse stood nearby, cropping at some grass. I knew I was back in the dreamworld and felt sad. Others had been allowed to stay

with Zana, but I had not. I looked into the misty waters of the Tarn of Mirrors in hope, but only saw my reflection.

That day, I rode back along the grassy lane to the village where I had last stayed. I yearned for my friends, the Four who followed after me, to be there. They would help me make sense of my adventures in Berren. But they were not there.

With winter on the way, I rented a cottage. I spent the next few months writing down all that had happened, so that I would never forget. Writing helped me understand it more. I saw how my old naïve butterfly self had had to die for me to become the brave eagle. I saw how my new self was able to make good the damage done by my old self. And I saw how cruel my false god creativity could be without God's love to control her.

Though the winter was long and hard, I barely noticed it. The day I penned the last word and set down my quill, I went for a walk to celebrate.

The sun shone and the air felt warm. The beck was an angry torrent with meltwater from the snowy fell pastures. The fields were a fresh emerald green and the bare branches of the trees and hedgerows had sprouted new leaf buds. Spring had come at last. It was time to continue my journey.

I went looking for The Four, but never found them. As Arzandel had said when the Song of Time danced around us at the Tarn of Mirrors: they were people who had never come, were not coming, and never would come this way. Zoust had not used their images to tempt me out of that charmed circle:

he could only use their voices.

I gave up my search and settled for a while in a market town. My room looked out over the main square. I visited the market one morning and bought an old silver locket from a stall. The locket reminded me of Arzandel. It had no picture inside, just a highly polished silver back. It looked like a mirror, but all I could see was my face.

That evening, I looked out from my high garret window. The night-lit streets were alive with glittering coaches carrying veiled ladies to the theatre. Around the half-domed theatre's entrance, a throng of people jostled. In the crowd of faces, one glanced up at my darkened window. He stood still for a moment and stared at me. The people milled around him. I gazed into his eyes and felt cold.

There below me stood one of the Four. His clothes were still the same, but oh, how he had changed. He looked bored, aloof and proud. There stood the reason why Zoust had not used his image to tempt me. I had lost my friend to the changes caused by experience.

Saddened, I sat down at my table and opened the locket. No longer did the polished silver reflect my face. I cupped the locket in my hands and gazed through the mirror into darkness.

Reeds waved by the banks of the Tarn of Mirrors. The cold moon shone down. Three people walked up to the water's edge. The Green Lady rose to guide them through the circle. She took their hands and led them each in turn down through the water. They came out safely to the shore where

the Song of Time weaves endlessly on. Arzandel stood by his roaring fire. He invited them to rest a while.

The first traveller was fat and bullish, with a sour look on his flabby face. He did not want to wait. He hurried off along the first path Arzandel showed him, towards where Halsanger had once stood. Only Doudern Lake lay there now, I found as I followed him. On a smoky cloud above the dark waters, floated a fiery orange boat weighed down by invisible passengers. They had been arguing about seats and greeted the traveller with curses. After he had climbed aboard, the boat lurched, throwing everyone onto the seats. The boat drifted across the lake, heading towards the Grey Mountains. I turned and flew back to the Tarn of Mirrors.

The second traveller also looked well fed, but his face showed all the past kindnesses he had done. He listened to Arzandel and chose the steep path which climbed Doudern Fell. By the cairn at the top, floated one of Zana's pale blue cloud ferries, on the mists of a spring dawn. I tried to climb aboard after him, but the boat glided out of my reach. It sailed away across the sky to the place where I could not yet go.

I returned to the tarn. There Arzandel sat with the third traveller beside his fire. A thin hand lifted the frayed hood from the traveller's face. I looked and saw me: the gaunt, dark frame that held my soul.

'Others I would send to the Tree of Knowledge, but you have already been. I can only guide you back to your dreamland home.'

'This guiding, is this your eternal work?'

'Not just this. I shape the paths of those in the dreamlands.'

'Then can you call me here? Make it happen?'

'That was arranged long ago, my child. Your visits here were all written in the Book of Days. You did not choose to come here then. But your choices while you were here: they were yours and yours alone.'

'What of me now? What will my future bring?'

'That you must find out for yourself. Else, life may seem too hard or too plain for you to live on to the end.'

A shout from the edge of the clearing made us look up. A young woman strode out of the trees. She wore a rough wool tunic and leggings. Her olive face was framed by straight black hair. She sat down beside Arzandel at the fire.

'I understand now. I am at peace,' she said in great joy.

'You have seen the Tree of Knowledge?' I asked. 'How was it?'

'I can't remember. And it doesn't matter. The only thing that matters is that I now know what I need to do.'

I sighed and drained my cup.

'I cannot go back to the Tree of Knowledge, even though my friend Anya once did. I pray that Zana will show me the right path to take. And then, one day, I will find my true friends again and come back to the land I love.'

Arzandel smiled and turned the green jade ring he wore on the largest toe of his left foot. The tarn rippled. The Green Lady rose out of the water.

'Come, my friends,' she said: 'It is time for you to return

to the land of your birth. Your work here is done, and you have seen what needs to be seen. Come back with me, to those who await you near the end of the road.'

The young woman and I took the Green Lady's outstretched hands. Arzandel followed to the water's edge and took out a handful of stars from his pocket. As we descended, he sprinkled the stars on the water. They glinted brightly, but all too soon faded and died.

'Farewell, my butterfly. Life still holds three stars for you.'

I saw his lined face in the locket mirror still, as I became aware of my room again. Then I blinked, and he had gone. His words reminded me of the past. I looked out of my window at the crowd flocking to the theatre below.

A woman cut through the people milling there. She stood for a moment, staring up at me. I had seen her olive-skinned face before. She was the young woman who had travelled back through the Tarn of Mirrors with me. Though she looked ten years older, she had hardly changed at all.

'Time gave me three stars, which I held in this hand,' I said.

I looked again. Her face had gone. Hope just raised, fell again just as fast. My shoulders sagged. I sat downcast on my windowsill.

'The stars reached out and destroyed the rising sun,' I whispered to her memory.

'Leaving you in present darkness?' she asked.

She came into my room like a sister who, though rarely

seen, is always welcome.

Our eyes met. I knew at once that Arzandel had sent her in answer to my prayer. I drew out a chair for her.

'Sit, eat,' I invited.

She sat at my table and handed me a present. The small parcel held a length of ribbon and five uncut keys.

'I have sought you many years, Eregendal, though you did not know of me,' she said. 'My name is Selene, Daughter of the Moon. A long time ago, I had a dream. I found the Tree of Knowledge and slept in its gnarled roots. A young child came to me as I looked down on the world. She wore a dress of green and silver. "Take this gift to my servant Eregendal," she told me. I obeyed. No matter that the gift is worthless, no matter that you might not be real: I obeyed. Strange that such a dream, and such a child, should so change my life.'

'No: it is more strange that others don't heed her voice. For we all hear it. But human beings have the right to choose.'

I held the ribbon to my cheek and looked up at a drawing I had once sketched. It showed Zana as I liked to remember her, holding out the fragile green flower which is her symbol. A faint whisper moved the air.

'Well done, thou good and faithful servant. Now go out into all the world in the name of God. Seek justice for the poor, defend the abused, and set the captive free.'

THE END